For Burt

Thanks for your service

COUNTERCLOCKWISE

ROGER L. CONLEE

Here's a little different take on WW II.

Ryan Conlee

Pale Horse Books

Library of Congress Control Number: 2006934552
ISBN-13: 978-0-9710362-8-4
ISBN-10: 0-9710362-8-4

Cover design: Mark A. Clements
Map: ArtSmartMedia (artsmartmedia@yahoo.com)
Author photo: David Friend Productions

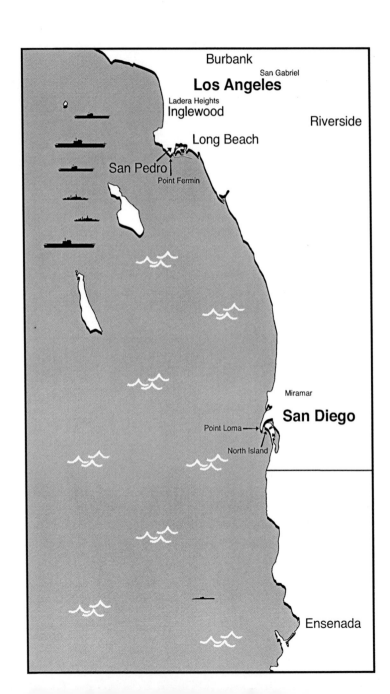

"The distinction between past, present and future is only a stubbornly persistent illusion."

— **Albert Einstein**

PART ONE

CLOCKS AND BOOKS

A spring day, 1988, Los Angeles.

That damn song kept running through his head as he strolled through downtown Los Angeles. "*From the great Atlantic Ocean to the wide Pacific shore . . .*"

On the flight down from Sacramento, he'd tuned his headset to a country classics channel and "The Wabash Cannonball" was the first song he'd heard.

Tom Cavanaugh had come to L.A. with Cass to visit her parents. He'd decided to pass the day downtown while his fiancée and her folks went to the Huntington Art Gallery in San Marino.

Tom looked around. He knew Los Angeles was half-circled by mountains. He couldn't see them—the Santa Monicas, the San Gabriels, the San Bernardinos—surrounded as he was by tall buildings and murky bronze smog. He pondered the mountains' Spanish names and wondered what the Indians had called them. A little more than two hundred years ago, a band of Shoshone Indians had lived in this basin. Maybe a couple thousand of them, tops. They'd had this whole valley to themselves. Then the Spaniards came and wiped out even their place names, whatever they'd been.

Tom had been told many times that being a history buff was an odd passion for a narcotics detective. Most cops were into sports or fishing on their days off.

". . . *From the green ol' Smoky Mountains to the Southlands by the shore . . .*"

As he walked along in front of a shoe store, he came upon two well-dressed Asian men sitting on a bench. One had hair the color of steel, the other no hair at all. Suddenly one of them hopped to his feet, spry for an old man, and held out a camera.

"Sir, would you mind taking our picture?" Straight California English. Not a trace of accent.

"Sure, glad to." Tom took the camera. A nice one. Nikon.

"Are you gentlemen related?"

"We are cousins," the bald man said, also getting up. "We have known one another for fifty years but we have very few pictures. Here is the shutter release," he said, pointing.

The men stood side by side as Tom put his eye to the camera. As he played with the focus, they suddenly became young men, the bald one in khaki pants, worn leather jacket, old-fashioned leather flying cap on his head and a white scarf thrown rakishly around his neck. The other's hair had flashed from silver to jet black. His suit-coat was now a blue windbreaker. What the hell? Was this a trick viewfinder?

Tom twisted the lens and refocused. The illusion was gone. Two old men stood before him again. Had it been the light, some freak chimera caused by the angle of the morning sun? Had he inadvertently focused on someone else? No, there were no other men nearby.

"Stand closer, Mori," the bald man said. Tom snapped the picture, then took another to be sure, and handed the camera back.

"Thank you very much," the man with gray hair said with a slight head bob. Tom smiled feebly and walked off, still trying to sort out what he had or hadn't just seen.

". . . *Listen to the jingle, the rumble and the roar, as she glides along the woodland . . .*" That damn song again.

He walked on, checking the sights. He thought about the two spring-training home runs Carney Lansford hit for Oakland yesterday. Maybe '88 would be a good year for the A's. On Olive, Tom passed Pershing Square and the old Biltmore Hotel. Soon he was back on Grand, just off Wilshire, for the second time in the last half-hour.

He looked around, then stopped, surprised to see a tiny clock shop sandwiched between a Kinko's and a bank at the street level of two glass and steel high-rises.

I swear to God that was a shoe store a while ago. I was right in front of it when I took pictures of those old men. It was part of his job to be observant.

He shook his head and tried to think about something else. Cass's parents, for instance. They had said they'd only been able to procure three tickets to the Huntington, which Tom had found unlikely. He'd always suspected that Cass's father, a wealthy retired banker, thought a mere cop wasn't good enough for his clever daughter. Tom was actually a bit relieved that he wouldn't have to try making small talk all day in the Huntington with Cass's folks. Whatever—they would all meet up later for dinner.

On the glass door of the clock shop in front of him, old-fashioned gold-leaf letters read A TIME AND A PLACE. The window displayed all sorts of clocks: electric, pendulum, grandfather, carriage, cuckoo, even an ornate gilded job with a huge windup key and a tiny bronze statue of George Washington beside the clockface.

Funny—not funny, weird—that he hadn't seen the shop before. Now it beckoned, and he couldn't resist. He opened the door, entered to the tinkling of a bell, and found himself immersed in ticking sounds. Timepieces everywhere, an orgy of chronometry. They occupied tables, ledges, sconces, plinths, and sideboards. Elaborate grandfathers standing upright, other clocks—Waterbury, Ansonia, Seth Thomas—hanging from the walls, pendulums in motion, weights and pulleys balancing and pulling. The place smelled of mustiness and old wood, but there was something else. A trace of incense?

A thin woman, gray of hair and face, and wearing an honest-to-God black cape, appeared from a rear room. A cape. The only time Tom could recall eyeing a real cape was when he and Cass saw *Phantom,* that great new musical.

"Welcome," the old woman said in a scraggly voice, extending elegant, pale hands, palms outward, to punctuate the greeting. Rings adorned her long, slender fingers.

"Thank you," he said uncertainly. "Quite a place you have here."

"I have been waiting for you."

"Business been slow, has it?"

"No. I have been waiting for *you.* I knew you would come."

This lady is starting to spook me. "You knew *I* would come?"

"That was impertinent of me. I apologize. But please look around. There is much here that will interest you."

"Well, maybe I will browse a little. You do have some terrific clocks."

"Yes, and some wonderful old books and periodicals in the back. Do make yourself at home."

After Tom had looked around for several minutes, he heard the woman's soft footfalls as she came up to him again. What now? he wondered.

"The clock," she said," is just a device invented eons ago when man first became aware of the lengthening of shadows, the passing of days, and felt compelled to make some artificial measure of these changes." Her diction was perfect, but with a touch of accent. Eastern European? "I have always been enthralled by the subject of time," she said, a slight severity to her consonants.

"Obviously." Tom spread his arms, gesturing at the clocks. "Einstein called it the fourth dimension."

"Yes, time is no less real than matter and energy. Some physicists hypothesize that under certain conditions time can actually flow backward." She fondled a large purple ceramic knob of a button that secured the cape at her neck. "Einstein believed that."

"He did?" *Physics* now? While this woman was weird, she was interesting.

"In his curved space-time theory, Einstein showed mathematically that just as a particle can reverse its direction in space if it loses enough momentum, so can it reverse its direction in time if it loses enough energy."

Tom's brow pinched. "Particles can reverse direction in time? Go backward in time?"

"Theoretically. Some later scientists confirmed his mathematical calculations and endorsed the theory."

"Who, for instance?"

"Scholars at the Lebedev Institute of Physics in Moscow, three or four of them."

"Time flowing backward." Tom whistled. "How do you know all this?"

She shrugged and offered a thin little smile. "My late husband, Sergei Kadinsky, was one of those scientists in Moscow. He was a disciple of Einstein and Minkowski." She stepped back. "Do make yourself at home, Mr. Cavan-augh, and let me know if I can be of help."

"Mr. Cavanaugh? How the devil do you know my name?" He didn't like surprises like that. It felt exactly like being burned on undercover. "And what was that about knowing I would come here?"

"Later. We will go into that later." The woman turned and went into the rear room with a graceful, almost Asian, gait.

Tom shook his head as if to clear it. He'd run into a

psychic—or a nut case. Puzzled and curious, he continued to explore the room.

Tom wandered from clock to clock. Some were simple windup alarm clocks, but many were magnificent and complex. Although a few were of recent vintage, most were old, some very old. A Roxbury grandfather clock caught his eye, its elegant rosewood brightly varnished. The Roman numerals were Gothic black.

Then he spotted a porcelain Japanese doll on a shelf, the exquisite face alabaster white, the hair held in an elegant swirl by a large ornamental comb. The figurine was about eighteen inches tall and quite lovely, but decidedly out of place among all these clocks.

The old woman came up again. "If you've seen enough timepieces for the moment," she said, gesturing, "you must see some of the wonderful old periodicals and calendars in the next room."

"Good," Tom said. "I love old books."

Gathering the cape around her, the woman led the way into a room filled with bookshelves, wooden filing cabinets, a carved credenza and a cedar reading table. A wall calendar dated 1955 featured a girl in a Peter Pan collar, circle skirt, saddle shoes and ankle socks. Another from 1936 pictured Dizzy Dean smoking a Camel. Funny, he remembered his father telling how Dizzy Dean loved "The Wabash Cannonball," used to sing snatches of it when doing play-by-play on TV. The same darn song had been running through his head this morning.

The woman was saying something about old magazines when Tom's attention was caught by the front page of a newspaper, framed under glass, displayed on a small oak table. The giant black headline shouted:

JAPS BOMB L.A.

Tom squinted. He hurried to the table for a closer look. The masthead said *Los Angeles Herald-Express* and was dated April 3, 1942. Beneath the fantastic headline were photos of a fire raging at an oil refinery and smashed B-24 bombers scattered beneath torn, scorched camouflage netting.

"This is one of those gag newspapers you can get printed up," Tom said. "It's one of the best I've seen."

"No, it's quite genuine."

"Genuine? Don't give me that. The Japanese never bombed Los Angeles."

Tom studied the newspaper. The rest of the page bellowed:

SNEAK ATTACK!
GOOD FRIDAY RAID KILLS HUNDREDS
AIR CORPS, COAST GUNNERS STRIKE BACK

"Where's the camera? I'm on 'Candid Camera,' right? This is good, ma'am, real good."

"I seldom watch television," she said. "It's mostly trash."

Tom read the byline on the lead story.

By JAKE WEAVER
Herald-Express Military Writer

And shuddered. Jake Weaver was his great uncle. He'd been struck and killed by a car in the Sixties. Tom's mother had been Jake's niece. Weaver had been a newspaperman, all right, and had published a couple of books after the war.

Cass! Tom's fiancée must be behind this. A top aide to California's governor, Cass Nesbit was a great kidder—although she hadn't been kidding this morning when she'd griped about his snoring last night. She'd really topped herself this time. Getting back at him like this was by far her greatest gag.

"Cass was in here, wasn't she? How long did it take you two to cook this up?"

The woman's brow tightened. "I'm afraid I don't know anyone named Cass."

"There wasn't a woman here, tall, with short auburn hair, telling you about Jake Weaver, the guy who wrote this story?"

"No, no one like that. But yes, Jake Weaver was your uncle, I believe."

"Great uncle, actually. He was the military writer of the old *Herald-Express* before it folded. Wrote a lot of great stuff during World War II . . . Wait a minute. What did you say? You *knew* he was my uncle?"

"Yes I did, and how splendid that you're here now."

"But how—"

She held up a hand to stop him. "I have two copies of his first book here someplace. It's very important that you see it." She took mincing steps to one of the bookshelves, looked about for a moment, then pulled out a bound volume. She blew off some dust, brushed more away with her hand, and gave it to Tom.

The book was not large, maybe six by nine, bound in wine-colored leather. The spine read:

THE DAY THEY BOMBED L.A.
JAKE WEAVER

Tom flipped to the back to see how long it was. Two hundred and sixty pages. Then he turned to the flyleaf. Published by the University of California Press, copyright 1965.

"I'd like to believe this," Tom said. "It's a fascinating notion. The Japanese lofted some incendiary balloons into the jet stream and a few reached America. They didn't do much damage. Their submarines sank a couple of ships off the coast. One sub even fired some shells at an oil refinery near Santa Barbara—and missed. But that was the extent of their attacks on California. They never bombed L.A."

"Didn't they?" Her mouth formed a wisp of a smile.

"Please have a seat," she said. "Browse through it. This is why you've come."

"Why I've come? To see this book?"

"Yes, Mr. Cavanaugh, that is why you have come. Would you like a cup of tea?"

A stiff shot of brandy would be more like it. He was way down the rabbit hole now.

Out in front the bell jangled. "Excuse me a moment," the woman said, and disappeared in a swish of black linen.

Tom had to admit Cass couldn't have pulled this off. How could she have known he'd even come into this shop? So far this morning he'd seen two old men turn young before his very eyes, got a physics lecture on particles moving backwards in time, now this.

He suddenly saw another calendar. A picture showed a huge dome bubble structure on what could be the surface of Mars. A dish antenna beside it looked like a radar receiver or a radiotelescope. It was a photograph, not a drawing. The date on the calendar read 2052.

Tom let out a large breath. I'm in the fourth dimension, he thought, or losing my mind. Any minute now, Clarence, that funny old angel from "It's a Wonderful Life," will pop in here. Well, he thought, I'm a fast reader and I've got some time on my hands. Might as well see how far I can get in this thing. He plopped himself down at the table and opened the book to page one.

THE DAY THEY BOMBED L.A.

CHAPTER 1

At last we had something to write about, Pearl Harbor had seen to that, but I had no idea I was about to brush up against the biggest story of my career.

My life had been missing two important elements, job satisfaction and—I hate to admit it—a woman. Two months earlier, Japanese warplanes attacking Oahu from six aircraft carriers solved one of my problems. That sucker punch on a Sunday morning had thrown the country into World War II up to its eyeballs.

Bad as it sounds now, that put some real meaning into my role as the military writer of William Randolph Hearst's *Los Angeles Herald-Express*. Europe, the hotbed of journalism for the past two years, no longer had a monopoly on the war.

The Japanese followed up with their big attack on Southern California on Good Friday in 1942, and that led to the writing of this book. I was there when they bombed Los Angeles and I covered it for the *Herald-Express*. I'm a typewriter jockey, not an author, but I hope you'll find this chronological account of that shocking event accurate and enlightening.

I write in the first person when describing what I personally saw and experienced. The rest is reconstructed from interviews and other research. Occurrences I didn't actually witness have been dramatized and written in the third person. These made-up scenes and dialogue are based on the historical record and what survivors have told me. The gist of them is accurate, I assure you.

The story really begins in February 1942. The Japanese warriors had given my job new importance. My woman problem, well, I kept attacking that in all the wrong ways. And places.

Friday, February 13, 1942, Long Beach.

I racked my pool cue, paid my debt and headed for the bar. How could I have missed that six-ball, side-pocket shot and given that guy his opening? Well, it's Friday the 13th, maybe that's it.

I didn't like to lose, but I was gracious when I did. Ask anybody. I normally didn't hang out in this Long Beach bar, called the Bomb Shelter, just down from the new Douglas plant, but I knew it well enough. My regular haunts were the chili joints on Trenton Street up in L.A.

I found a stool and ordered an Eastside beer. The jukebox was playing "The Dipsy Doodle." Kay Kaiser's orchestra, I thought.

Outside, Lakewood Boulevard, a new four-lane strip of concrete, droned with working-class Chevrolets, Studebakers, Plymouths and Indian motorcycles.

The man next to me—big shoulders, thin dark hair, probably late forties—stared straight ahead. If he'd noticed me at his left elbow he didn't acknowledge it.

The Java Sea.

Thousands of miles to the west, Lieutenant Kazuo Okada, a pilot with the Japanese First Air Fleet, guided his dive bomber on its base leg approach to the aircraft carrier *Akagi*. He studied the flagman and the pitch and roll of the flight deck, which often seemed to bounce like a cork, even in calm seas. It always looked frighteningly small.

His Aichi D3A dive bomber was banking in from the left, standard approach doctrine. The ordnance rack beneath his plane was empty, his bomb having been dropped an hour before on a Dutch airfield on the island of Sumatra. The flagman dropped both arms, which meant, "Keep coming, complete your landing."

The ugly ship—an old battle-cruiser hull with a rectangular slab of heavy timbers clamped on top—now filled most of Okada's vision. He cut power just before reaching the deck and the plane sank, thumping down on the rough planking. The first arresting cable devoured his tailhook and the plane jerked to an unwilling halt at mid-deck. Despite his sturdy leather harness, the abrupt stop always hit like a judo-chop. Carrier landings were simply controlled crashes, and Okada had just completed another of these dangerous maneuvers. As always, relief and pleasure swept over him. Another mission completed for the Emperor.

Twenty minutes later, seated before a desk answering the questions of de-briefing officers, Okada recounted his mission. Describing his bomb run, he made liberal use of his hands and arms. The opposition he encountered, only ground fire, had been light. The film shot by his rear-seat gunner and observer, Kai Iguchi, was already in a shipboard lab for processing.

Long Beach.

The door swung open and a tall, middle-aged, slightly graying Mexican walked in, decked out in a brown suit and tie. I noticed because few people in the Bomb Shelter were that well-dressed. This was a blue-collar saloon. Also, you didn't see many Mexicans in Long Beach. Not in those days.

I thought his bushy, silver-gray moustache was dignified. He claimed the unoccupied stool on the other side of the large, quiet man. With no trace of an accent, he ordered an Eastside beer, then casually asked the big man if he'd ever played baseball.

"Yeah, when I was a kid. Second base."

That's rich, I thought. This oaf is built more like Mickey Cochrane than Charlie Gehringer. A catcher maybe, but not a second baseman.

The Mexican didn't follow up on the brief exchange, although their eyes met again. After about a minute of silence he got up and slid into a booth across the room. Several minutes later Big Shoulders followed.

Now, that was odd. These guys seem to be strangers, they don't get into a conversation exactly, just that little bit about baseball, then go off to a booth by themselves. But I dismissed it from my mind. Almost. To be honest, I seldom forgot anything completely.

I pulled some folded paper from the breast pocket of my jacket. Notes from an interview that afternoon at the Long Beach Naval Station. I re-read them, scribbled something else I'd just remembered, a possible story item, and slipped the paper back into my pocket.

I was a good reporter. No, really. I had intuition, curiosity, and I wrote fast and well. Ask anybody. Ask my city editor, Gus Dobson. Well, maybe not Gus. But, whenever something import-ant took place in L.A. military circles, I usually had it before the other reporters. In the weeks since Pearl Harbor I'd steadily dug up better stories than my rivals on the *Times*, *Mirror* and *Examiner*. That Gus Dobson *will* confirm.

I wasn't the cat's pajamas in the looks department, with a ruddy complexion, red-brown hair and a medium build. Dixie Freitas used to say my face had more angles than Huey Long. But I was gifted with natural charm and could make things happen with my smile. Just ask Dixie Freitas. Well, maybe not Dixie.

My folks, immigrants from Germany, are Louisiana land-holders who also own sugar plantations in the Caribbean. They're prominent in Baton Rouge society. Agriculture bored the hell out of me, though, and I always had a craving to see the world. So I took off at the age of seventeen and became the family renegade.

Dixie used to say the appeal of my smile came as much from my eyes—they're light brown—as my boyish, lopsided grin. Honest, those were her very words. She also said my hands, which are kind of coarse, looked more like a sailor's than the hands of somebody who made his living with a typewriter. She was right.

My full name is Raleigh Ashford Weaver, but I got the nickname Jake when I ran off to sea. Working on freighters, whenever we had problems, like cargo sliding around during a storm, I'd usually say, "Everything will be jake." Optimistic old me. I must have said it too often—pretty soon that was my name.

After hitches in the merchant marine and the Navy, I worked on a small paper in Longview, Texas, before deciding to try on L.A. for size.

I had a brief marriage in Longview to a cocktail waitress. You guessed it: Dixie Freitas. This was truly the mistake of an immature man. She was not a bad girl at all, very nice in fact, but her bulb was only a twenty-watter.

After joining the *Herald-Express* in 1935, I moonlighted at MGM in publicity for a few months. One night I was exploring one of those giant sound stages when I came across a famous actress getting bonked behind some scenery by a grip, or maybe a gaffer. I won't mention her name, but you'd know it. She was in a lot of big pictures, even "Gone With the Wind." No, not Vivien Leigh, the other one. She saw me, smiled a little, and kept right on giving herself to this hearty studhorse. Is it any wonder I'm cynical?

The *Express* was L.A.'s biggest paper in those days. We actually had a few more readers than the *Times*. Our masthead trumpeted that we had the greatest circulation of any paper west of the Mississippi. Which wasn't that big a deal—if you sold the most papers in L.A., you sold the most papers west of the Mississippi.

Within six months, I got the military beat. I was thirty-five when the Japs threw that low blow. By 1942, I'd been single for seven years. I lived by myself in a small white bungalow in Compton, halfway between the *Herald-Express* and the bases in Long Beach and San Pedro, where I did a lot of my work. I took occasional pleasure with girls like Dixie, but made them no promises.

To be honest, I was always looking for two things, the right woman and a good news story. I had better luck with the stories. Gorgeous but insincere women were my weakness. Collected them like matchbooks. I wanted brains and substance, too, but those kind were harder to find. The town was full of would-be actresses and models, and I liked the feeling it gave me to have a knockout on my arm at a party or the fights. But, oh, I had a talent for finding the artificial one, the woman who would use me for whatever she could get for herself—an introduction to a rich businessman or a contact that could boost her career—and give little or nothing in return. I had a saying: "If there's a bad woman out there, I'll find her."

Oddly enough, some of my married friends were envious of me, with my long list of phone numbers. But I would've gladly traded my little black book for someone nice to settle down with.

Tom Cavanaugh found a paper napkin, brittle with age, pressed between pages like a bookmark. A note, printed in pencil, read, "TCav. Hicks. Ft.Mac." Must have been written by Uncle Jake himself. Hmm. What did it mean? TCav could be shorthand for Tom's own name, but no doubt something like Third Cavalry. Ft.Mac might be Fort MacArthur, the old Army post down by the harbor. He had no idea who or what Hicks was. TCav? Yeah, probably Third Cavalry, or Tenth, or Twentieth. He replaced the napkin in the book and read on.

Inglewood.

Ten miles to the north, at North American Aviation, Valerie Jean Riskin made an erasure on the sheet of vellum flattened out on her uptilted drawing table, picked up a hard-lead pencil, swung the arm of her drafting machine into position, and drew in a small correction. She had silky black hair, cheekbones a model would kill for, and large blue eyes that seemed to expose some inner grief. The thirty-one-year-old widow was the only woman in Tool Design at the aircraft factory. It had caused a minor sensation when North American hired her to a white-collar job. Women were secretaries and assembly-line workers. That's the way things were in 1942.

Long Beach.

Back at the Bomb Shelter, I tossed down some of my beer

and asked the bartender, "Walt, you ever seen that big guy before? The one who was sitting here?"

"Yeah. He's ex-Navy."

"Ex-Navy, huh?" That got my attention. "Wonder what he's doing out here, next to an Air Corps base." Daugherty Field was practically across the street.

I continued to jaw with the bartender for three or four more minutes. I was still thinking about those two guys and the strange stuff they'd said. A lot of my stories started in joints like this. I drained my glass, threw down two bits for the beer and a couple of dimes for Walt, and got to my feet.

I left and hopped in my 1940 Chevy Ridemaster sports coupe. Driving north on Lakewood, heading for the *Express*, I rehashed it. A former Navy man tells an apparent stranger that he's an ex-second baseman, even though he's slightly smaller than Mount Baldy. In the agility league, he's more of the Boris Karloff school than the Fred Astaire. Then he and the stranger go off to a booth. What was going on?

CHAPTER 2

TOM CAVANAUGH looked up and glanced around the clock shop's back room. My Great Uncle Jake, he thought, was a hell of a character in those days. Tom remembered his mother's stories of the sugar plantation and her uncle running off to sea. He wished he had a cup of coffee, then remembered that the woman in the cape had offered him tea. As he turned his head to call to her, she was already at his side, saying, "Would you like tea, then?"

"Um, yes, that'd be nice. Thanks." Who *was* this woman—the cape, the mind reading—a witch? And why had she said this book was the reason he'd come here?

He still didn't believe a word of this tale, but it was entertaining. Uncle Jake was a pretty good writer of historical fantasy. Tom wondered how well the book had sold.

Say, he remembered, my father was in L.A. in early '42, being inducted into the Army. If the Japanese had attacked, he might have been in danger. But of course the Japanese hadn't attacked.

Tom's father had become a cop after the war. Although he was busy working his way up the ladder in the San Francisco PD, he still found time to watch most of the Little League games in which Tom and his older brother played. Now Tom was following in his father's police footsteps, although not intentionally.

Long before he'd met Cass, Tom had endured a seven-year marriage that hadn't worked out. Good thing they hadn't had a child. Tom knew that bickering with Sharon over custody, child support, visitation and all the rest would have been painful for him and damaging to the kid. Sharon—pushy, contentious, and now *dead*—shot by a hoodlum after getting mixed up with some bad people in her eternal quest for the big bucks.

Tom didn't want to think about Sharon. He shifted his thoughts back to his father, who would have been twenty-two at Fort MacArthur in the early part of 1942. An innocent young man about to become a soldier in a war that would kill about half a million American kids a lot like him before it was over.

Tom sipped his tea and looked at his watch. Still plenty of time. Cass and her folks would be at the Huntington for hours yet. Might as well read on and see what Uncle Jake says next.

Thursday, February 19, 1942, Inglewood.

I would learn about Valerie Jean Riskin in a few weeks. She was a widow and a thoroughbred. She was not just the only woman tool designer at North American Aviation, but one of the few in the United States. She knew it and was proud of it.

Her apartment in Inglewood was one of several low, stucco bungalows with tile roofs, arranged in a U-shape around a small courtyard, some builder's idea of Spanish style. A large wrought-iron archway framed the courtyard and the apartments, facing a concrete street lined with cement lampposts ridged vertically to simulate Ionic columns. Frosted glass ovals had been illuminated atop these posts until the war brought the blackout to L.A.

That night, Valerie Jean was pouring the last of the chenin blanc for Corky Held, a parts inspector at the plant.

After the dinner she'd prepared—baked chicken, mashed potatoes, creamed corn and salad—they listened to the radio; then, over their wine, they retired to the sofa and talked awhile. She put some 78's on the record-player. Duke Ellington and Tommy Dorsey, contrasting styles, but Valerie had a broad range in musical tastes. "Dorsey's vocalist, Jo Stafford, is great," she said. "There's a smoky quality to her voice that I like."

She turned the lights down and a George Bellows print on the wall was lost in shadow.

Since her husband's sudden death, Valerie had been trying

desperately to re-invent herself and put new meaning in her life. Moving to the West Coast had been Step One. Corky Held was a pleasing diversion, but he wasn't Step Two. She hadn't found Step Two yet.

Soon they strolled arm in arm into the bedroom. She stepped out of her skirt and was peeling off her nylons when Corky said, "Widow lady, you are so gorgeous . . . Does it bother you that I'm younger?"

"Four years? Phooey."

Corky nibbled on her ear. Valerie let out a sigh and stroked his back.

"You don't feel funny about it?"

"No reason to," she murmured between wet kisses, pushing herself against him.

Corky pulled off his boxer shorts, put an arm around her back and laid her on the bed.

Her blue eyes closed, Valerie pictured her late husband Jim and fantasized that he was the one making her nerve endings quiver.

"I've got a nice warm place for you," she used to tell Jim during the preliminaries.

Soon she and Corky were thrusting against each other in passionate heat. He got there first, as usual.

"Slower . . . slower, lover," Valerie said. "This isn't a race."

She began to moan, nearing her peak.

The crest broke and it was over too soon for Valerie, the fulfillment transitory. With Corky Held, it often was. Darned kid.

She lay with her head against his strong young chest, riding the rhythms of his breathing. Her hand idly stroked his face, her thoughts roaming.

It had taken her awhile to relax and enjoy this fling. Her dictionary defined adultery as sex between a married person and someone other than the spouse, but her minister back home said it was any sex out of wedlock. Unmarried people sleeping together were sinners. Six months ago, Valerie might have agreed with him, but not now. She'd concluded that, okay, she'd lost something precious, but to start living again, she had to let go. Like this.

Sometimes Corky talked of marriage, but Valerie wasn't interested. Besides, he'd be in the service before long. He'd already received notice for his pre-induction physical. He'd have no trouble passing that, she thought devilishly.

She planted a quick kiss on his cheek and smiled playfully. She'd soon send Corky on his way. It wouldn't do for them to be seen leaving the apartment together in the morning. Not with my landlady, she thought.

"Why don't we just get married?" he asked.

"Well, Mr. Held, that makes four—or is it five?—proposals now. You'd better write me off as a lost cause."

She knew Corky didn't consider himself the marrying kind. He was a playboy in fact, but she apparently affected him in a way no other woman had. She liked that.

"Sweetheart, what would I do with a husband like you? You'll leave me, go off to the war, and . . ." Her voice trailed off. She didn't want to mention the possibility of death.

Corky spoke of finishing college some day, when the world situation was clearer, but Valerie wasn't buying that. The war was just an excuse. No, Corky was definitely not Step Two. She wished she knew who or what was.

Well, she thought, these are crazy times. Nobody is performing rationally. I'm certainly not.

"I'll bet I know what you're thinking." Corky punctured her musings. "You're thinking it would be swell if I didn't have to go."

"What? Oh yes, you're right," she fibbed. "Maybe one of these days my landlady will go away for the weekend." She pushed her index finger against the tip of his nose. "I adore you, Mr. Held. You and Gary Cooper."

Twenty minutes later he was dressed and Valerie sent him on his way with a pat on the butt.

Tomorrow morning she would walk the few blocks to the North American plant and start her shift in Tool Design. She would get the usual looks of resentment from the secretaries and messenger girls as she took her place among the men at the drafting tables under long rows of fluorescent lights. So they're jealous. Too bad. Let them make something of themselves, too.

* * *

Tom often said that he had two minds, the romantic history buff and the ever-curious detective. This Valerie Jean triggered something in the detective mind, but Tom couldn't put his finger on it.

Did she remind him of that teacher he'd had long ago in the fourth grade? Was that it? What was her name? Mrs. Something or Other. Intelligent and proper, yet somehow sexy in an unconscious way. He'd liked the way her skirt swished when she walked, and he'd liked her ankles, especially when she wore those shiny black high heels.

Years later, Tom recognized that Mrs. Something or Other had awakened in him the first prepubescent stirrings of his young libido. And suddenly it struck him—with a twinge of guilt—that Uncle Jake's descriptions of this Valerie Jean had produced similar stirrings. Hmm.

Monday, February 23, 1942, Compton.

I could sympathize with Corky Held. I had woman problems of my own. I found a used-up lipstick of Stella's today. (Behind the toilet. I really *should* clean more often.) God, it made me blue.

Stella! A model I'd met long after my divorce, in a fancy bar on the West Side, not far from RKO. Reddish hair, 5 feet 8, taller than me when she wore heels, a truly striking woman. We'd had a wild seven-month affair and I'd kidded myself into thinking it was the real thing.

I loved being with Stella, being seen with her. Our personalities seemed to mesh. We always had plenty to talk about, joked about the same things, and the sex, well, we were truly compatible there.

Stella's claim to fame had been a Camels ad that had run in *Life* and *Collier's*. That national ad was the highlight of her portfolio, which she loved showing me. There were other gorgeous photos, too. Lately, though, she hadn't gotten any more work from that ad agency.

In the back of my mind I knew this fling wouldn't last, but in the *front* of my mind, I couldn't admit that. I wanted to believe that Stella was the girl of my dreams. One day at a party I introduced her to a minor producer from Republic Pictures. Or maybe he was a director. Or director's assistant. Everyone in the movie business bullshits so much. I hadn't even known the guy well, just somebody I'd bumped into a few times in this gin joint or that. Stella's eyebrows shot up like startled birds. She took the man's arm and asked what projects he was working on. They talked for a good twenty minutes, with me being a definite outsider in the conversation.

Stella didn't say much when I drove her home that night and then wouldn't let me come in, claiming extreme fatigue. She broke a movie date with me the next night, saying she had to meet a girlfriend who was having a family problem. I called several more times, sent flowers, but always got nowhere.

Stella had shown me the door. I finally got that through my thick head.

Frailty, thy name is woman. You thought I didn't know my Shakespeare? They had me read plenty of it at Catholic High in Baton Rouge. *I wasted time and now doth time waste me.* Once in awhile old Will knew what he was talking about.

Oh, I had lots of other phone numbers and what seemed to my married friends like a cornucopia of dazzling dates. Most of that catting around, though, if you really want to know, was overrated.

I was plopped on the sofa, thinking all of this, my head on an armrest. An open bottle of beer on the floor was getting warm.

Suddenly I slammed my right fist into my left palm with a loud smack.

"Thank God for the war," I said out loud. I'd been talking to myself a lot since Stella. Thank God for war? What a weird thing to say. But the war was saving my life.

CHAPTER 3

TOM REFLECTED on the fact that his father had been in Los Angeles in early '42. Desmond Cavanaugh had been mustered into the Army at Fort MacArthur in San Pedro as a twenty-two-old. He'd have been there at the time Jake Weaver was writing about. If the Japanese had really attacked L.A., Fort MacArthur might have been one of their targets. For dive bombers coming in from carriers, it would have been easy pickings, right out there by the coast. His father would've been right smack in harm's way. Was that why the woman said it was important for Tom to see this book?

But Desmond Cavanaugh, who later fought in Germany and then served as an MP at the Nuremburg Trials, had never mentioned even the notion of a Japanese attack on L.A. It was common knowledge that it hadn't happened. Yet the idea disturbed Tom. He looked forward to discussing it with Cass that night at the hotel.

Meantime, he'd read some more. But why was a shiver trickling down his spine?

Thursday, March 5, 1942, San Diego.

From his seat at the end of the bar, Commander Reed McBride watched Chet Sickles pull out his Zippo lighter. The Brass Rail at Sixth and B was busy, servicemen and office workers lining the noisy bar, topping off a long lunch. On the jukebox, Ernest Tubb drawled, "Walkin' the Floor Over You."

Sickles flicked the lighter and fired up McBride's Old Gold cigarette. Smoke snaked upward, blending into the blue-gray haze shrouding a cut-glass chandelier that seemed to be slumming.

McBride, wearing his winter blues, was having an old fashioned. Sickles worked on a gin on the rocks, his second. They leaned on a well-worn mahogany bar that had kept company over the years with a multitude of elbows, glasses and coins.

McBride didn't want to be here. He didn't feel right around Sickles any more, not since the court-martial, but what could he do? Sickles had saved his life after that explosion on the cruiser *Omaha* back in '35, and they'd been friends for years even before that.

"This town's really jumpin', Mac," Sickles said. "Navy everywhere, aircraft workers pouring in. Damned hard to get a room."

McBride, a staff officer at DesPac, the destroyer base, smiled at his old shipmate. "Yeah, major wartime port. If you think San Diego's bulging at the seams now, wait'll the *Benson*-class destroyers start coming in. It'll be a zoo around here in a few months."

Sickles said, "That a joke?"

McBride overheard two Navy men debating whether Paris could have been saved and Dunkirk prevented. "The French and Brits could have done it if they'd immediately counterattacked the day the Germans broke through on the Meuse."

"Bullshit. The Panzers would've still had 'em for lunch."

Sickles was an ex-Navy officer himself. The guy they used to call Sick, now a civilian in a blue canvas zip-up jacket and gabardine slacks. McBride thought the picture was all wrong. The mahogany eyes, large shoulders and thinning brown hair— looking like it was slicked back with Wildroot—should have been framed by a uniform.

They'd been talking about old times in Norfolk and San Francisco. And about the war and how strapped the Navy was, trying to protect against German U-boats in the Atlantic and hold out against Japan in the Pacific at the same time.

Sickles' heavy dark eyebrows lifted slightly. "What do you think about the new ack-ack gun, Mac? The forty-millimeter."

"The Bofors gun. Swedish design. It's a honey. Gets off 140 rounds a minute. The big problem in destroyers—the subs too—

is our torpedo. Reliability and range problems. The magnetic ex-ploders are a piece of shit. Hard to believe, Sick, but the Japs have a better fish, long legs and accurate as hell."

"Tell me more about the Bofors," Sickles said. "They on the *Sims*-class boats?"

Sickles leered at a statuesque young woman who'd just captured the Brass Rail simply by coming through the door. A tight skirt showed off a slender waist, and her white ruffled blouse was a size too small. She scanned the room, then slid onto a stool next to a sailor.

"Jesus, Mac, look at the hermans on that little number," Sickles said.

"Glad to see your libido's still kicking, oldtimer."

"She can't be a minute over twenty."

"But her eyes look forty, Chet. Like I said, it's a wartime port and it's full of young broads looking for a good time and a sailor's paycheck."

"This one's a cut above most of the B-girls in this town, Mac. It'd be fun moving in on that little item."

"Think you still could?"

Sickles laughed unconvincingly.

"Got a French skipper staying at the house for a couple of days," McBride said. "Name of Fournier. Nice guy, for a Frog. With the merchant marine till the war broke out. Helped the Limeys bail out of Dunkirk. Hates Petain's Vichy guts. Fournier's working for us now, running supplies to Australia. He's got some great stories, Chet. Poor guy's damned homesick, though."

"He may never get back to France, way this war is going." Sickles took a gulp of gin. "I've never seen this place so jumpy, Mac. Southern California's scared to death, just about shit when the Japs sank the *Montebello* and *Emidio* right off the coast. Even moved the Rose Bowl game to North Carolina. Ever think you'd see something like that happen?"

McBride sipped his old fashioned. "It was that Jap sub shooting at Santa Barbara that really did it. That and the 'Battle of L.A.'"

"Yeah, the night the ack-ack boys panicked and threw up a

hell of a fireworks show."

"That's it, Chet. The Battle of L.A. they're calling it."

"Hell, Mac, I saw it. Had a ringside seat at my place in Ladera Heights. All hell breakin' loose. What's the scuttlebutt?" The Artie Shaw Orchestra's "Begin the Beguine" drifted from the jukebox.

"The Navy's clean," McBride said. "It was damned Army gunners who went crazy. They still claim there were unidentified planes over L.A. that night. It was weather balloons, probably. Roosevelt had to step in and tell both services to clam up."

"The paper said there was a Jap plane down at 185th and Vermont," Sickles said. "What crap. Only injuries were air raid wardens and such, dickin' around in the blackout. Traffic accidents, too."

McBride knew the war news was disaster after disaster. The Nazis had driven deep into Russia and were beating the pants off the Brits in North Africa, while the astounding little Japanese were overrunning the whole South Pacific.

"Here's one you'll be hearing about pretty soon, Chet. The Army's going to round up all the Japs along the coast and ship 'em to camps in the boondocks."

"No shit? That'd be a huge operation, Mac."

"It's true. Some Congressman actually told FDR California couldn't be defended, that we should pull back our lines of defense to the Rocky Mountains. It's mass hysteria." McBride shifted in his seat and fiddled with his glass. "The coast watchers are jittery as hell, and no wonder. We're gettin' beat everywhere. Don't quote me, but there's no way we can relieve the Philippines. MacArthur's army'll be behind fences before long, eating fish-heads with chopsticks."

A couple of stools down, a short, thin-haired, streetwise little man in a plaid shirt nursed a glass of Apache beer. His chin bore the stubble of a couple of days without a shave. He could have been a cabby or a racetrack tout.

Sickles' face seemed to sag. "You've heard of Mozart, right?" he asked. "And George Gershwin?"

"What? Sure."

"Oh nothing. Just thinking. Did you know Mozart was only thirty-five when he bought it, and Gershwin was thirty-eight? I'll be fifty next time around and still haven't made any mark—the world doesn't know I exist."

McBride puffed on his cigarette and studied his old friend. I've never seen his eyes so flat, he thought, so empty. He's more down than I realized.

"I know it's been tough," he said, putting a hand on Sickles' shoulder. "But you've got a good job now. Things'll get better. Hell, I'll probably get my ass shot off by the Japs while you're high and dry over here making money." McBride let out a sigh. "I've been in this man's Navy going on twenty-four years now. Finally gonna see some shooting."

"When you gonna get that fourth stripe?"

"Got passed over last time, but that was before Pearl. Promotions come fast in wartime."

"God knows you deserve it, Mac. 'Surely there is a reward for the righteous; surely there is a God who judges on earth.'"

"Huh?" said McBride.

"Oh, something from Psalms. Applies to you, I think."

McBride knew Sickles was the son of a Presbyterian minister. He took out another Old Gold and tapped it on the bar to firm up the tobacco. Sickles leaned over and lit it for him.

Into the small talk, Sickles spliced questions about the number of pursuit planes at North Island, the shipping of ammunition from the Fallbrook arsenal through San Diego, and those new anti-aircraft guns. McBride thought he still trusted Sickles but, holy smoke, these were delicate subjects in wartime.

"Mac, there any battleships or cruisers here?"

"Hell no," McBride said, looking around to be sure he wasn't overheard. "Maybe an old battle wagon in Long Beach, like the *Idaho*. Nothing here but subs and a few destroyers. Anything that can shoot is either at Pearl or pulling convoy duty. Jap navy's got us spread damn thin."

Sickles moved his glass in small slow circles and watched the ice rotate.

Two stools down, the little man in the plaid shirt clutched his beer and shot a silent glance at Sickles.

"How many fighter planes we have around here, Mac? Ones that could really fight if they had to?"

"Asking a lot of questions, pal. You writing a book or something?" McBride laughed at his little joke, then glanced around and lowered his voice. "I shouldn't be talking about this, but, well, fighters? Not many. Just some replacement F4F's that'll be going out to the carriers." He scanned the room again. "The Marines have a few more Wildcats up at Miramar, and the Army keeps a P-38 squadron at North Island. That's it. Twenty-five, maybe thirty planes altogether." He laughed softly. "The war's way the hell out in WestPac. We couldn't put up much of a fight here, but keep that under your hat."

Sickles seemed unusually somber, but McBride dismissed it. He knew he'd had a rough time since his separation from the Navy. Anybody who'd been through what he had was entitled to a bad day.

Sickles had held the rank of commander and was the skipper of the supply depot in Norfolk in 1939 when he was court-martialed for stealing supplies. The scuttlebutt was that he'd been lifting explosives and selling them to building contractors. Also peddling M1 rifles, binoculars, engine parts and tires to racke-teers. A chief petty officer and two other enlisted men were indicted with him. They were all found guilty and kicked out of the service.

McBride knew most of this. The Navy had a hell of a grapevine.

Sickles' wife Marjorie had divorced him. His two daughters, grown and married, seldom contacted him. He was a bitter, disillusioned man.

The year he was sacked, he'd moved to Los Angeles and gone into machinery sales. McBride knew that, too. It was what he *didn't* know that troubled him: What else was Sickles up to?

CHAPTER 4

AT THE HUNTINGTON Art Gallery, Cass Nesbit was browsing her way through one of the large rooms, admiring this painting and that, and thinking it was too bad that Tom wasn't there. She hoped he was having an interesting day, doing whatever it was he was doing.

She remembered the day, about two years ago, that she made up her mind about Tom. They'd met for lunch to discuss the death of a mutual friend. It took her ten seconds to see that Tom had a good soul, and ten minutes to know that she would marry him some day. There was something magnetic and appealing about that rangy narcotics cop who'd rather be teaching history.

She smiled at the recollection.

Then a painting caught her eye. She thrust her chin forward and took a closer look. It looked a little like a Norman Rockwell, only a bit more Impressionistic.

An American soldier in a World War II-style uniform, light brown, was climbing onto a train, a duffel bag slung over his shoulder, his cap tilted back at a jaunty angle. He was looking back wistfully, as if he'd just said goodbye to someone special and was trying for a last look at him. Or her.

The resemblance to Tom's father struck her. "Look, Mom," Cass called to her mother. "This guy here looks like Tom's father. Tom has a studio portrait of his dad taken during World War II and the faces look a lot alike."

An elderly couple overheard, and the woman smiled pleasantly.

Tom's father, Desmond Cavanaugh, was a retired San

Francisco police captain. The Peace Officers Association had thrown a testimonial dinner for him last year that had brought out all the relatives.

Cass gazed back at the painting. The soldier seemed to stare right into her eyes. A chill crept up her spine.

Cass's mother said, "Well, the young man in the painting is quite handsome in a forlorn sort of way."

"Yes. Forlorn is the just the right word." That queer feeling still gripped Cass.

Friday, March 6, 1942, Mariana Islands.

Kazuo Okada was one of the more intriguing figures I came across during my research. On this day, Lieutenant Okada was trying to hold his nerves in check while Commander Minoru Genda sipped herb tea. Maps and charts sprawled before them on a table in a small wardroom aboard the aircraft carrier *Akagi*. Genda was the operations officer who'd planned the glorious raid on Pearl Harbor.

"I have developed a strong liking for you over the past four months," Genda said, "an intense period of final training and combat. You have proved yourself to be one of the finest dive bomber pilots in the division . . . Your uncle, I believe, lives in Los Angeles."

Kaz Okada squirmed inwardly. "Yes, my Uncle Eichi Kawahara emigrated to America in 1917 and lives in the suburb of San Gabriel with his son Mori." Okada was fond of his *Nisei* cousin Mori.

"And you lived with them while taking your education?"

"Yes, commander, at the University of Southern California. My degree is in aeronautical engineering. I learned to fly there on weekends."

"Show me."

On a Los Angeles map spread before them, Okada pointed to a spot along Rosemead Boulevard. "Here, at Fletcher Airport. That was in 1937. I was nineteen."

*   *   *

Tom suddenly remembered the two old men whose picture he'd taken. They'd turned into young men for an instant, one of them in an old-fashioned flier's uniform. "Stand closer, Mori," one of them had said. Had he actually seen this young pilot his great uncle was writing about? Impossible. Wasn't it?

"Tell me about the neighborhood they call Little Tokyo," Genda said.

Okada pointed out Little Tokyo and described it, his emotions wildly mixed. He loved California and was fond of the robust, good-natured Americans who'd become his friends.

"And what do you think of America in general?"

How should he answer that? Was Genda laying a trap?

"I respect the United States," he said, picking his words carefully, "but overriding that is a deep love for my own nation and my Emperor. Mine is an old family. My ancestors were *Samurai*. I will gladly do battle with the Americans if it is the will of my people."

"Despite your love for your uncle?"

"I do revere my uncle, yes, and my cousin, but duty to Japan is paramount."

Genda poured tea for Okada, a signal. Apparently the answer had satisfied.

"Having flown all over the Los Angeles basin, you are of great value to our commander, Admiral Yamaguchi, and to me."

Okada sipped his tea and felt his muscles relax. His loyalty didn't seem to be in question.

Genda lit a Kinshi cigarette. "We will go over maps of the target area in detail."

"I am at your service, commander."

Genda, who had never been to the United States, asked question after question about specific locations and landmarks.

Then he said, "These are fast, resplendent times for the Imperial Navy, Okada, but the Americans need one more convincing lesson. This new operation is a brave undertaking. It may end the war." Genda drew on his cigarette, put it down, and sipped a little of his tea.

"The arrogant Americans think they control the destiny of our part of the world. But the South China Sea is not the Mississippi. When they took the Philippines and Guam from Spain, it was merely a cheap expropriation from a bankrupt old empire. The American flag in Manila stood between us and the Indies, a fishbone caught in our throats. As the Emperor says, we must create an Asia for the Asians, and put an end to the humiliation of Western exploitation."

"Could this have been achieved, sir, without war against America?"

"No, Okada, war was inevitable from the moment last year that Roosevelt seized our assets in his country and cut off our oil. Before then, most of our oil and steel came from America. Without it, we had to give in to Roosevelt's demands to abandon China and most of our other possessions—or fight. He put an economic noose around our necks. We had no choice." Genda was getting shrill. "Our oil reserves were sufficient to operate the Combined Fleet for only six months. We attacked in *five* months. After you and your comrades shot up the Pacific Fleet at Pearl Harbor, we destroyed their air power in the Philippines, and eradicated their proud old Asiatic Fleet in the Battle of the Java Sea. Now we must consolidate our new holdings, but their weakened fleet is still being troublesome. The Yankee dog needs to be sent home with its tail between its legs."

Genda's hands were fists. "Now we will cripple the enemy in his home waters and crush his aircraft factories." Genda's eyes blazed. "With the success of this operation, he will give up his Pacific war and concentrate on Germany. Our empire will be secure, masters of the Western Pacific. You will see to that very soon, Okada-san, you and your brave associates. Remember, our nation has not been defeated in 3,000 years."

Genda clasped his hands in front of him. He searched Okada's eyes for a moment, then turned his gaze back to the maps.

The force of four aircraft carriers and nineteen other ships, anchored off the island of Saipan, would sail in a few days.

Tom pictured them, not in grainy black and white as in old newsreels, but in full color under a bright Pacific sun . . . red battle flags streaming in the breeze . . . fast, deadly Zeros pouring off the decks to fly combat air patrol . . . bombs and torpedoes, fused and ready, stacked below decks . . . the ships sailing in perfect formation toward California, toward Fort MacArthur and his father. It was a beautiful sight, and he hated it.

Compton.

I thought about calling a script girl from 20th Century-Fox. I saw her two weeks ago and that had turned out to be a lively evening. I was driving south on Atlantic toward Long Beach Navy headquarters and an appointment with a friend and source, the public information officer, Lieutenant Commander Deke Rickey. Deke's uncle was the general manager of the St. Louis Cardinals.

On second thought, I didn't feel like a date that night. The script girl was fun, but nobody to get serious about.

Stella was on my mind again, damn it. Her memory always popped up to ruin my romantic moods. I also was thinking of Rifty LaPlante. The squirrelly little San Diego grifter was onto something. He had described a man who sounded a hell of a lot like the big guy I myself had seen three weeks ago at the Bomb Shelter in Long Beach, talking with a middle-aged Mexican. They had said something goofy.

"You ever play baseball?"

"Yes, second base."

If that hulk was ever a second baseman, I'm Errol Flynn. They went to a booth together, acting like they'd just met. Could that be the same guy Rifty saw? Hell, anything's possible, especially in wartime.

*   *   *

Tom pulled himself away from the strange tale, smiled, and glanced around the shop's back room, amused. What's next? A Tin Woodman creaking through the doorway? Too bad he'd never known his Uncle Jake. On the one hand, this was a good book—he was hooked. It was what they called alternative history, a story about something that might have happened but never did. But in his mind's eye he could still see all those ships, laden with warplanes and bombs, surging across the sea toward the United States.

San Diego.

After Chet Sickles said his goodbyes to McBride, he walked over to Broadway, passed the Walker-Scott store, and headed west toward the Palace Buffet on Second Street.

Striding through the afternoon throngs, bright sun reflecting off the windows of the Land Title Building, Sickles thought about how he got into all this.

A year ago, he'd been quietly contacted by a Mexican government official about doing some consulting work. The Mexican was a polite, well-dressed man named Arturo Rivera. The pay was good, he said, and the work would be performed for a third party, not Mexico. Rivera would be the go-between.

Of course Sickles was interested in good money. The Depression wasn't entirely over. And why not money from a foreign government? His own had treated him like shit.

Provide information on ship movements in the San Diego and Los Angeles harbors? Why not? The Japs would get it anyway, from someone.

Later in the year, after President Roosevelt froze their assets in the U.S. and cut off their oil, the Japanese had increased their demands. They wanted up-to-date maps and more details on weapons, bases, dry docks, and the construction of ships and planes. Three months before Pearl Harbor, Sickles' retainer was raised to five hundred dollars a month.

Sometimes he paid for information, but he usually got it for the price of a few drinks from casual acquaintances like Commander McBride.

He never met a Japanese official face to face. At first, the handoff system was to meet someone from the Mexican consulate in a coffee shop on Spring Street in downtown Los Angeles. Pearl Harbor changed all that. Rivera himself became the contact. He said meeting in L.A. was now too risky; the payoffs would be made in more remote spots. They met in Santa Ana or San Clemente, and sometimes even in Baja California.

In front of Hamilton's Coffee Shop, a streetcar clanged its bell while sparks flew from its overhead wires. Sickles jumped, and realized he'd almost reached his destination.

Half a block behind, a small man in a plaid shirt kept his eye on him. He'd been following Sickles since he left the Brass Rail.

Inside the Palace Buffet, Sickles settled onto a barstool, pulled out his pack of Wings cigarettes and lit one. In the ornate mirror that faced him, he saw himself place one elbow on the bar. Scores of eight by ten glossies populated the walls, taken over the years by photographers from the *Union* and the *Tribune-Sun*. They included a very young Ted Williams, a prizefighter named Elmer "Violet" Ray, a football player called Crazylegs, and strippers from the Hollywood Burlesque. On the jukebox, Guy Lombardo and his Royal Canadians were playing "Boo Hoo."

Arturo Rivera, smartly done out in a gray three-piece suit, entered and took a seat beside him. Rivera looked to be about twenty-seven or -eight. Nodding as if they were strangers, he said, "Nice day. Have you ever played baseball, *señor*?"

"Sure. First base," Sickles replied. "But that was quite awhile back. How about you?"

"I have played in Ensenada," Rivera said quietly with a slight accent. "There will be a big game there tomorrow. If you like good baseball, you should go and see it. Do you like to watch baseball?"

"Sure. I follow the Angels up in L.A.—Coast League."

"Tomorrow afternoon," Rivera repeated. "Be there by two o'clock if you wish to see the game."

"Important game, huh?"

"Yes, *señor*, very."

Saturday, March 7, 1942, Los Angeles.

About this time I learned that Jimmy Doolittle was training a squadron of B-25 crews at a secret base in Florida for something special. The Army Air Corps had inducted the famous L.A. airplane racer and made him a colonel. I put this and that together and figured maybe Doolittle was going to lead our first air raid on Japan. This posed quite a problem for me. On the one hand it would be great story, but on the other, reporting it could jeopardize the mission.

Strict censorship had been clamped on correspondents out in the war zones. It hadn't begun on the home front yet, but I'd be damned if I'd run my copy by some military censor, and I knew my editors would back me on that.

Nevertheless, driving back to the paper, I decided to keep hands off the Doolittle thing so as not to endanger those men. We were like that in 1942.

My thoughts turned to something else where I wouldn't keep hands off. Tonight I would favor the most stunning blonde west of the Mississippi—okay, so I exaggerate some—with dinner. Afterward . . . .

CHAPTER 5

THE ROOM WAS QUIET, the book now very real, a part of his great uncle's life unfolding before Tom's eyes. Supposedly, at a family reunion picnic in Golden Gate Park, Jake Weaver had bounced four-year-old Tom on his knee and carried him on his shoulders, playing "horsey ride." Tom thought he had a vague memory of that, holding tight to a big man's head as he bounced along.

That picnic had been in the summer of '55, shortly after the Salk polio vaccine had been introduced. Jake's wife, Great Aunt Vee, had been at the reunion and taken a great liking to little Tom. He'd heard that story from his mother, who was Jake's niece. Although the big picnic was in July, it hadn't been warm. A bone-chilling San Francisco fog had stolen in from the ocean, his mother had said. Tom thought he remembered that, too, a pretty woman wrapping a sweater around him and hugging him, Aunt Vee probably. It was one of his earliest childhood memories, if indeed it was a memory at all. Maybe it was an image he'd created when he was older, after hearing his mother's recollections.

Whatever. He knew he felt a strange attachment to Jake Weaver and that this book, though mostly fiction, provided an intriguing window into his life and times.

One of the clocks in the other room chimed. Tom looked at his watch. 12:15. He'd been reading for nearly an hour. He had a strong urge to talk with his fiancée. Cass would still be at the Huntington with her parents.

The chief assistant to the California governor, she had made his life a much sunnier place the last two years.

Before meeting her, he had endured a few bleak years after his divorce, the bleakness not helped by the moral muck he wallowed in every day as a narcotics cop.

Cass had it all: brains, a feisty sense of humor, looks, and inner toughness. Whenever she thought he was wrong about something, she didn't hesitate to let him know it, and that was all right. They had traveled together to Washington, D.C., and to Europe. Six months ago, on the best day of his life, she'd agreed to marry him.

He pictured her sharp hazel-green eyes inspecting works of art at the Huntington, one leg poised in front of the other, the way she did, balancing on a heel. She'd have a hand at her chin as she contemplated the object.

He was warmed by the thought that he'd be with her tonight in their hotel room. Not yet married, they lived together, but getting away from the familiar surroundings of their home always seemed to add some extra zest to their sex life. He couldn't wait to see her; needed a long talk with her about all this.

Tom glanced at the wall. Dizzy Dean, still claiming he'd "Walk a Mile for a Camel," looked down on him from the 1936 calendar. His eyes had a devilish, inside-joke look to them.

". . . *No changes can be taken on the Wabash Cannonball.*" That crazy song!

Tuesday, March 10, 1942, San Gabriel.

Mori Kawahara squirted some Oxydol into the hot water in the kitchen sink and thought about his cousin, who was now a pilot for the Japanese navy. The *enemy* navy. Mori recalled not wanting cousin Kazuo—he called him Kaz—to take flying lessons when he'd been a student here. For some reason, Mori'd had a bad feeling about that.

Mori's girlfriend Sumiko Uyeji had been over for dinner. She'd left twenty minutes before and now Mori was washing the dishes with his father.

A harsh banging suddenly rattled the door. Mori dried his hands and dropped the dishtowel on the counter. He knew this was trouble. The Terasaki family had been confronted last night, the Yamadas on Friday.

A thin, lanky man said, "FBI," showed his ID and bulled right on in without asking. A second, much heavier man, followed, carrying a briefcase. Both wore gray, double-breasted suits.

Mori's father bowed slightly. Mori did not. This rude intrusion insulted their home. He was glad Sumiko had left. They come at night, like cowards, he thought.

"We're searching the place," the thin one said. Mori didn't ask to see a warrant. He didn't know he had that right.

Mori and his father watched in sullen silence while Thick and Thin began their search. The burly one, Thick, who hadn't shown his ID, soon had collected an armload of Japanese-language papers and books.

"Those are personal letters and school books," Mori protested as Thick began chucking them into his briefcase. "That"— he pointed—"is nothing more than the ABC's and this one deals with irrigation in various soil types. Real dangerous," he sneered.

"Wise ass, huh," snapped Thick. "There's subversive material all over these neighborhoods, propaganda for the Jap system. Democracy is the American way and you're living in America. This is a democracy, damn it!"

"I had thought so," Mori said.

"Shut your—"

Thin silenced him with a raised hand. "We can't be too careful," he said in a softer voice. "I'm sorry, but we've got orders. Where's the woman of the house?"

"There is no woman of the house."

"Oh?"

"She passed away many years ago. There is only my father and me."

As Thick and Thin continued to search, Mori was thinking, It means nothing to them that father has been a farmer here, a steady taxpayer and a model citizen for twenty-two years.

Mori reached out a hand as if to say "Wait!" when Thin went

into the rear den and strode across traditional Japanese matting to a small Buddhist shrine in the corner. Never before had shoes been worn in this room. Indignation flared across Mori's face as, one by one, Thin examined items from the little altar—candles, a silver tray, a statuette of Buddha himself—turning them over in his hands and looking closely.

Finally, it was Thick who glared at Eichi Kawahara, the father, and said, "Gather your things. You have to come with us, now, tonight."

"You can't do that," Mori cried.

"Guess again, sonny boy. Executive Order 9066," he said, stabbing a hostile finger at Mori. "Are you over twenty-one?"

Mori looked at the man as if he'd been dropped from the rear of a passing horse. "Yes."

"Born in the U.S.?"

"Sure."

"Okay then, you're *Nisei*. You have exactly thirty days to dispose of all your property and report to the evacuation center."

"Dispose of our property?"

"Right. As of now, you people aren't allowed to own property in the coastal war zone. And you are not permitted to travel more than twenty miles from this point. Understand what I'm saying?"

Thin brought out some papers, federal orders spelling out the restrictions being imposed on Mori. Thin signed them on the line marked "signature of server." He told Mori to sign and pointed to a line labeled "signature of person acknowledging receipt of order."

"Not until I read them." Mori read the papers very slowly, then read them again, while Thick drummed his fingers on the radio console. Finally, exchanging a look of sad resignation with his father, he signed with an angry flourish.

The father knew this day would come, had known for weeks. "I must dress suitably," he said. "Excuse me, please." He bowed somewhat and went to his bedroom.

"Where are you—"

"Let him be," said Thin.

Several minutes later, wearing his best dark suit and lugging a suitcase, Eichi Kawahara walked to the front door. He turned and took a look around the room, his eyes resting on the two-foot-high glass cases containing delicate statuettes of Japanese women in traditional kimonos. Long black hair was swept gracefully high above their exquisite alabaster faces, the arrangements held in place by *kanzashi* combs.

Tom looked up from the book, remembering the figurine he'd seen on a shelf in the other room. It matched exactly the description he'd just read. He covered his eyes with his hands, kneaded his forehead with his fingers, then turned back to the book.

The elder Kawahara had spent many happy hours in this room during the past two decades. He had been through so much, the emigration to America and the hard early years getting established. The death of his wife. The four years here with his nephew, Kaz. And now he was being wrenched away from his son.

He and Mori embraced. Tears moistened their cheeks.

Then, walking with erect dignity, he allowed the men to lead him outside.

Mori watched from the window as the car drove away. The taillights disappeared down the street. He hammered his fist into the sofa and sobbed.

"Those poor people." Tom had always felt a bit ashamed about the World War II internment of Japanese-Americans, but this personal account really drove it home. He knew it was easy to judge in hindsight, and hard to comprehend the temper of the times, the anger and hysteria that swept the country after the treachery at Pearl Harbor. Still, he firmly believed President Roosevelt had made a big mistake.

Two full minutes passed before he got up and stretched. He scanned the room to be sure he was alone, then did a dozen squats. It felt good. He'd been sitting too long. He walked around, inspected the calendars, the books, the old newspapers. He made a steeple of his hands and pressed outward, cracking his knuckles. Then he sank into the chair, sucked in a deep breath, and read some more.

CHAPTER 6

Wednesday, March 11, 1942, San Diego.

Chet Sickles' coffee was black and so was his mood. He'd been sitting in a booth in Haynes' Streamliner for ten minutes, his three-button corduroy jacket tossed casually on the table. Outside the steakhouse, cars buzzed by on El Cajon Boulevard.

Sickles nursed the strong coffee and fiddled with the menu. He knew he was in over his head. Since Pearl Harbor had plunged America into the war, he'd begun to recognize his limitations. He was close to some real trouble. He was scared.

The headwaiter's voice made him jump. "Is that your gentleman?"

Sickles looked up, saw Arturo Rivera approaching, carrying a thin leather valise. Rivera looked around briefly, walked nonchalantly to the booth, made a "May I join you?" gesture with eyes and hands, then seated himself on the cracked leatherette opposite Sickles.

"Nice weather we are having," he said. "How is the coffee here?"

"Not bad." Sickles hunched his large shoulders forward and put an elbow on the hard resin tabletop. He wanted a taste of gin. Real bad.

Rivera ordered coffee. The Mexican consular official was much smaller than Sickles. He wore a dark blue, double-breasted suit and a monogrammed shirt with matching pearl tie pin and cufflinks. His black hair was neatly cut and trimmed, but longer than the American fashion. His light bronze face bore a thin moustache on the upper lip. His air was confident and snobbish. Sickles had never liked him.

When the waiter left, Rivera glanced about. Sickles' jacket

still lay on the table. Rivera slid a large manila envelope from beneath it, and slipped it into his valise with a quick, easy motion.

After a few moments of polite conversation, Rivera said the menu didn't look very interesting and passed it across the tabletop to Sickles. In that same motion he'd slipped an envelope, concealed beneath the menu, under Sickles' jacket.

A bit later, an untidy little man in a plaid shirt watched them leave—two minutes apart. They'd had only coffee.

The little man went to the pay phone in the back and dropped in a nickel.

"Long distance, please. Person to person. Jake Weaver, *L.A. Herald-Express.* Richmond Four-One-Four-One . . . Yeah, Weaver. Make it collect."

And of course the phone on my desk soon jangled. I'd been thinking about a hatcheck girl from The Trocadero I'd seen the night before. The phone erased that pleasant thought.

"Weaver," I said.

"This is long distance in San Diego. Will you accept a collect call from a Mr. LaPlante, Cypress One-Three-Seven-Nine?

"LaPlante? Sure, operator, I'll take a call from that nosy little weasel . . . Rifty? Lucky you caught me in. Been down at Terminal Island. 'Bout ready to knock off. Whatcha got, keed?"

"Something good, I think," said Rifty LaPlante's voice, small and metallic over the line from San Diego.

Nine minutes and two pages of notes later, I hung up the phone. I'd received a similar call from a different source, Peg Darroch, just the day before. Their descriptions of the large man and what he was up to were remarkably similar. I read over the notes I'd just taken from LaPlante.

Then it hit me. First base. He'd said *first* base, not second.

My heart started pounding. I was a step closer to smoking out a spy, an American selling information to the Japs. This guy was a spy, I was sure of it. As sure as French mustard goes great on Wisconsin bratwurst. Proving it—the spy, not the bratwurst—and breaking the story would assure me of a place among the greats of journalism. Okay, so I exaggerate. I smiled and inhaled a breath of high hopes.

I hadn't thought about Stella for hours. Good for me.

Inglewood.

At North American Aviation, several miles to the west of the *Herald-Express*, tool designer Valerie Jean Riskin and her friend Corky Held were making plans to take in a picture show that night in Santa Monica. "Meet John Doe," with Gary Cooper.

"My friend Gary," Valerie kidded. "Now *that's* a good-looking man. Just my type." She knew Corky thought he was God's gift, and didn't like hearing from women about Gary Cooper or Tyrone Power. So sometimes Valerie couldn't help herself—she just had to give him the rib.

"Pick you up at 6:30," he said, sounding hurt.

Valerie poured on a little salt. "No, I'll meet you there. 6:45." She loved to push Corky's button.

"Gee whiz," Corky grumbled.

Still in love with a dead man, Valerie thought about the life she'd once had. She'd been deeply shaken when Jim Riskin was killed. They'd met and fallen in love in their senior year at Bradley University.

Jim's death after five good years had been a cruel shock. His car had gone out of control one night at an icy railroad crossing and smashed into a tree. Valerie couldn't comprehend the suddenness of it. I was just getting to know him, she told herself. One day he was there, the next he was gone.

The week after the funeral was the toughest. Night after night she cried herself to sleep.

When she pulled herself together, she decided that a whole new environment was needed. With her drafting skills, she'd have no trouble finding work in an aircraft factory on the West Coast. They were all hiring.

Her mother back in Illinois didn't like the idea and longed for her to come home, especially now that America was in the war. Almost every letter made the same nagging appeal. Come home.

Mom would never understand about Corky. Boy, would she not understand! Valerie had written about him only once, a casual reference to going with him to a company picnic. She'd been testing the water. She laughed when the next letter from home was full of questions. What kind of a man was he? How old? A churchgoer? What kind of job did he hold at the plant? How much did he earn? Valerie didn't answer the questions, and the topic fizzled out as an item in their correspondence.

"Are you enjoying the book?"

Tom jumped. He hadn't heard the cape woman come in.

"Yeah, it's quite a tale."

"Yes, and entirely true."

"Some of it, maybe, but not the Japanese bombing Los Angeles."

"But they did."

"Not to be disagreeable, ma'am, but it's well known that they didn't."

"The word ma'am is so impersonal. My name is Alexa Kadinsky. Please call me Alexa."

"All right, and I'm Tom Cavanaugh, but you knew that." She extended a ring-laden hand and Tom took it.

"I assure you your great uncle did not concoct a hoax," she said, seating herself in a chair opposite him. "You look like an intelligent and open-minded man. I think now I must tell you something that might change your mind about what Jake Weaver describes in his book, something very few would understand."

Tom leaned forward, his elbows on the table. "Okay, try me."

"In the time track you and I occupy at this moment, you are right, the Japanese did not attack Los Angeles. But in another time track, they did. Your Great Uncle Jake lived in that other one and he forthrightly recorded this major, shocking event that indeed occurred there."

"A different time track?" Tom put a hand to his chin and stared. "You've got to be kidding."

"Tom, the earth's time path split in 1924 and from that point on there have been two parallel time tracks."

Tom's eyes widened. "You're serious, aren't you?"

"Yes, quite. It was an immense solar storm that caused this fracture in the space-time continuum. My late husband was an eminent Russian physicist. He believed the phenomenon to be more common in other solar systems, though not unheard of in ours."

"Two separate time paths? You're right, I'm open-minded, and I've even had an experience or two that were hard to explain. But *this*?"

Alexa's cutting eyes, blue-gray, looked much younger than the rest of her. "Is this so really hard to believe?"

"I'm a cop, ma'am, er, Alexa. I have my skeptical side."

"And your skeptical side is telling you not to believe in the earth's parallel time spheres?"

"Bingo."

"Well, you mustn't worry, the two are beginning to merge again."

"Then there'll just be one, like before 1924?"

"Yes." Alexa's cryptic smile would have done the Mona Lisa proud.

This was turning out to be one of the strangest days in Tom's thirty-seven years. He'd have quite a tale for Cass tonight at the hotel.

CHAPTER 7

Friday, March 20, 1942, San Diego.

Pearl Harbor had turned everything upside down, but the bomb that fell on Eddie Santos hadn't been dropped by the Japanese.

Just before dawn was Eddie's favorite time on San Diego Bay. His little tuna boat, the *Loma Queen*, swayed almost imperceptibly at its moorings. A few seabirds looped lazily beneath an overcast sky that looked like wet cement. Below them, the water was a mirror. He liked this time best of all.

Eddie had come down to the G Street Mole early to think and to work on the old CW radio, which had been acting up. He tossed down a Phillips screwdriver and grasped a mug of coffee that had been cooling at his elbow.

He took a sip, then ran a hand through his thick black hair. What if he had to take the boat out next time with no radio? Well, men have fished for centuries without radios. He could, too, although with a war on, he sure as hell didn't want to.

Eddie had owned the *Loma Queen* since 1932. He and his father had bought the boat from a family friend who'd gone belly up in the Depression. The *Queen* was a typical pole-and-line boat of that period. On top of her small cabin sat the wheelhouse and chartroom. The wheelhouse contained the helm, the ornery radio, and a sounding machine for determining the ocean's depth.

Now the *Queen* was creaking with age and Eddie was angry with himself for not having replaced her. After all, 1941 had been a good year, the catch was up and there was some money, in spite of the troubles.

Eddie needed the morning quiet to soothe his soul. Far worse than the radio was the separation from his wife, Shirley, a separation that had been her idea. He missed her, and the kids, too. He saw them often, but it wasn't the same as living with them under the same roof. Not having a family that was whole tore at his gut. He had expected the woman he married to be loyal to him for life, and for almost thirteen years he'd suspected no other possibility.

He also felt guilty that he wasn't a part of the Inshore Patrol, tuna boats conscripted by the Navy, crews and all. True, the *Queen*, a 75-footer, was too small for the Navy patrol, but he wanted to do something in the war, do his part against the Japs. He was thirty-five, too old for the draft. Would they take him if he enlisted? With his experience, he thought he'd make a great PT boat skipper.

The first wartime Christmas, with the boats tied up at G Street and the fuel docks south of the ferry landing, had been less festive than usual. Eddie had spent too much on gifts for the kids, but he loved them and he knew they were hurt and confused over the marital split.

After Christmas, when the Navy had rejected his boat as too small for the "Yippee Fleet," he'd been cleared to resume fishing. Now Eddie was nervous whenever leaving port. There were Jap subs out there, but if somebody shot his ass out of the water, it'd probably be those skittish Army gunners whose batteries honeycombed the Point.

When he went out, he always shouted greetings to friends on tuna boats with their new coats of Navy gray.

Eddie had been fussing with the radio for nearly an hour. It was not a voice set. The CW (continuous wave) radio sent impulses from an old-style Morse Code key. The condenser was shot. Even if the radio had been working, the Navy had ordered him to use it only in an emergency. Unnecessary radio signals off the California coast could become inadvertent direction finders, confusing young military pilots.

Frowning, he swung himself out of the chartroom, descended the companionway, and paused at the rail to gaze over the bay. A weak sun cleared the horizon like a dull yellow ball, turning the morning haze from pewter to ivory. The water developed a slight chop and the boat rocked gently.

He stepped into the galley, lit the burner beneath the coffee-pot, and went over the whole thing in his mind for the hundredth time.

Life would be good, he thought, if only . . . The trial separation—Shirley's term—was now four months old.

She had griped that he wasn't as thoughtful and attentive as he used to be. But damn it, he had a business to run, an engine that needed parts, crews to find and pay, a radio to fix.

He hadn't seen it coming. He'd just returned from a four-week trip to Mexican waters when she went and blew that hole in his hull. It just wasn't working any more, she said. He'd have to move out. She would take a job, of all things, and let her mother look after the two young kids each day. Things might work out eventually, but right now what she needed was to get away, some time to think, and a chance to achieve some things on her own.

"Poor guy," Tom thought, "married with two kids, getting dumped like that." He looked up from the book and pushed his chair back. "Happens all the time—now. Not so much in 1942, though."

He closed his eyes and massaged the lids lightly with his fingertips. His thoughts roamed from the tuna boat captain to his father. His father, who was here at Fort MacArthur in early '42. Why did that trouble him? Tom didn't believe that Fort MacArthur or any other place around here came under attack in 1942—in *any* time sphere.

He stood up, braced his hands against the edge of the sturdy table and stretched, alternately bending one leg close, extending the other rearward. The stretches relaxed his mind as well as his body. He tried to forget about his father. He took his seat, winked at Dizzy Dean, then returned to the book.

It felt like Eddie's heart was weighed down by an anchor

chain. His mind was stripping gears trying to make sense of it all. A job? Wives fed you, washed your clothes, ironed your shirts, raised the kids. *That* was their job. And they were damn glad they had a good man to support them.

He should have married a Portuguese. Shirley was pure Anglo-Saxon, from another part of town inland from the Point Loma fishing community. After their wedding, they'd settled into the routine of the fishing families on the Point. It was a passionate relationship for awhile. Then the children came. The marriage slowly turned threadbare and empty for Shirley.

She wanted more than a job and a vacation from him. He knew what was stirring in her loins, had sensed it, but wouldn't admit it to himself. There must be other men in the world who could make her feel better and at thirty-one she wanted to find out, before it was too late.

He went to the coffeepot, flicked off the burner and refilled his mug.

His family and friends had been shocked when he'd moved out and taken an apartment. What were his poker buddies saying behind his back? Did they assume he'd been cuckolded? In truth, he probably had. Pain stabbed his stomach every time he thought about it.

Eddie climbed out of the galley to the little deck. He saw Uncle Charlie Silva ambling down the pier in his rolling, wobbly gait, listing slightly to starboard. Behind him the sun had pierced the haze and was glinting off the cupola atop San Diego Trust & Savings, the tallest building in town.

Years at sea had shaped the way Uncle Charlie moved, even on land. Charlie had been working with Eddie for the past nine years and was solid as the keel of a battleship. The tattered old fisherman could fix anything on the old pole-and-line boat. Except that radio.

The North Pacific.

At that very moment, on the other side of the International Date Line, a Japanese task force of twenty-three ships, including four aircraft carriers, was taking on its last dockside fuel at

Minami Toreshima, which the Americans called Marcus Island. Aboard one of the carriers was Lieutenant Kaz Okada of the First Air Fleet.

The force, which had assembled earlier at Saipan, would now sail northeast to the 40th Latitude, then east on the great circle route to their attack point: one hundred sixty miles off the California coast. The ships would reach that spot in thirteen days.

So would Eddie Santos.

Tom looked at his watch. Four o'clock. He was hungry, hadn't eaten since breakfast. Cass would be back at their hotel soon. He'd better go. He couldn't wait to tell her about his bizarre day, about this strange woman who'd known his name and said she'd been expecting him. He needed to hear Cass's musical laughter, to feel the warmth in her eyes.

He'd been reading his uncle's book for nearly five hours. Besides Alexa in her black cape, bringing tea and a wild theory about parallel time paths, only two people had been in the room. They'd been browsing and hadn't stayed long.

Tom got up and stretched, then walked around. He saw a desk in an alcove with an odd device on top that looked a little like a portable microwave oven. Curious, he looked closer and touched the end of a cable dangling from the machine. It gave him a mild shock. *Hmm, the current's on.* He walked back to where the book lay open on the table, hating not to finish it. It was pure baloney. But he had to admit, fascinating baloney.

"Take it with you, sir." Tom jumped. Alexa was at his side again, having appeared soundlessly. "It is important that you read it all. You can bring it back tomorrow."

This is one spooky broad, he thought. *Reads your mind and moves like a ghost. Sacramento PD could use her.*

"I'd rather not borrow it, I'd like to *have* it," Tom said.

"I hope you'll let me buy it."

"Oh . . . yes, of course. I have the two copies. Yes, Mr. Weaver's great nephew should certainly own one of them."

"Good. I'd really like to show it to my fiancée. And for her to see your shop here."

"Yes, do bring her."

"I will. We'll be back tomorrow. How much do I owe you for the book?"

"Ten dollars."

"Ten? Oh no, it's worth much more."

"Nonsense. For you, the author's kin, ten is all I will accept."

Tom handed over a ten-dollar bill and said, "We'll be back tomorrow." He left and walked briskly back toward the hotel, thinking about his flamboyant Uncle Jake. His mother's uncle, actually. This book—never mind the mumbo jumbo of two time tracks—gave a fascinating look into the man's personality and his world of almost half a century ago.

Tom felt dizzy for a moment and put a hand against the wall of a building. The sensation passed and he walked on, deep in thought.

His love of history and his corny sense of humor—Cass called it the Cavanaugh Curse—were his escapes from the pressures he faced daily as a narcotics detective. Cass had become an even better tonic. He was eager to see her. They'd have maybe an hour or two alone before meeting her parents for dinner, time enough to show her the book and tell her about his strange day. He wanted to see what she'd make of it all.

He grew aware of something odd about his surroundings. All the cars looked old. There was a cool-looking Corvette, '64 or '65.

He turned left at the next corner, where the Downtown Suites Hotel would come into view a block ahead. And stopped dead.

"What the . . . ." A weathered, four-story brick building

occupied what should have been the hotel.

He looked closer at the parked cars. They were all from the Sixties. No Nissans, no Hyundais. Then he noticed the license plates were black. California had switched from black to blue plates and then later to white. He knelt close to an Olds Cutlass. It bore a 1968 license plate. 1968!

What the hell was going on? Had he made a wrong turn? Walked onto a movie set? Had there been something in the tea the old woman had given him?

This was freakier than those two old men turning young for an instant while he took their picture. This was totally, goddamned frightening. Whatever this mental delusion was, he wanted it to stop. Right now . . . *please*.

But it didn't. He remembered the shock he'd got when he touched that odd machine a moment ago.

To his left stood a newsstand he hadn't seen that morning. The headline on the *L.A. Times* read: NIXON WIDENS LEAD OVER HUMPHREY IN POLLS. The *Sporting News* proclaimed: LOLICH AND TIGERS SINK CARDS IN GAME SEVEN. Tom yanked the paper from its rack and looked at the date: October 11, 1968.

Feeling sick, he put the paper back. He sank onto a concrete bench and watched a woman walk past in a red polyester coatdress, years out of style.

He closed his eyes and covered them with the fingers of his left hand. Time travel was impossible. This was some kind of hallucination, something from that tea he'd had. Or a crazy nightmare. He felt another odd pang of dizziness, almost a mild shock. His butt suddenly hit the sidewalk, hard. With both palms flat on the sidewalk he began to push himself up, when he saw that the bench was gone. Vanished. No bench at all. So what the hell had he been sitting on?

At the curb sat one of those new Miatas, metallic blue. Pulling himself to his feet and peering around the sporty little car, Tom saw the Downtown Suites Hotel up the street, standing in peaceful afternoon sunshine.

He looked to the left. The newsstand was gone, replaced by a Denny's. A couple seated at a window booth gave him the kind of half-pitying, half-charitable look they'd use on a homeless person. Tom imparted an innocent, embarrassed shrug, opened his palms at them, then turned and shambled toward the hotel as bewildered as he'd ever been.

CHAPTER 8

CASS WASN'T BACK yet. Tom tossed the book on the bed, went to the bathroom and looked at himself in the mirror. He saw frown lines on his brow, worry in his blue eyes. Nixon and Humphrey? 1968 license plates and newspapers? Parallel time tracks? Had he sideslipped into the other one for awhile? He shook his head and splashed some cold water on his face.

He knew one thing for sure. He was a detective, for crying out loud. He would find out about the woman who owned that shop. His first step would be to call Pam Wells, the *Sacramento Bee*'s police reporter, see if she could get a line on the Russian scientist Sergei Kadinsky, maybe confirm that part of the old woman's story.

He knew Pam's number, one of twenty or thirty catalogued in his mind. He hadn't liked Pam at first. She was always butting in, trying to get a story before a case was closed. Gradually, though, he'd come to respect her dogged thoroughness, not unlike Jake Weaver's, come to think of it.

She answered. Good, she was in.

"Pam, it's Tom Cavanaugh . . . Fine, thanks, and you? . . . Look, I need a favor. Maybe you could ask the science writer to look this up for me. Was there a Russian scientist named Sergei Kadinsky? If so, if that's confirmed, did he leave a wife? . . . Yeah, been dead awhile . . . What? Yeah, his obituary should have it. Survived by, and so on . . . K-A-D-I-N-S-K-Y, I think . . . No, it's not a police thing . . . No, nothing like that. I'll explain later, when I can. Look, I'm in L.A., at the Downtown Suites Hotel. The number is, ah. . ." Tom read it off the phone to her. "Thanks . . . Yeah,

I know, I owe you one."

He disconnected for a second, then called another number he didn't need to look up: the LAPD. He knew a detective there; they'd shared information on cases over the years. "Vinnie? Tom Cavanaugh, S*acramento* . . . I'm good, thanks, and you? . . . Great. Yeah, I do need a favor, don't I always? Could you run a woman named Alexa Kadinsky, see if she has any kind of record? Even a traffic violation? K-A-D-I-N-S-K-Y, I think. She owns a clock shop on Grand called A TIME AND A PLACE . . . No, Grand here in L.A., downtown." Tom explained that he was in town and left the hotel's number. He thanked Vinnie and hung up.

He started reading again.

Monday, March 23, 1942, Los Angeles.

At my dilapidated desk, I went over the whole thing again, trying to fit some pieces together.

I smelled a bombshell story, one old man Hearst would love, but I didn't quite have it. I had seen this big palooka twice, so had Peg Darroch, and Rifty LaPlante had seen him three times! On three of those seven sightings this guy was with a Mexican consular official, twice with Navy officers, once with a civil defense guy, and once with an older Mexican I hadn't identified.

I doodled on copy paper.

"That's more than circumstantial. Statistically, that's over-powering." I was talking to myself. Out loud. "His name is Chet Sickles and he was court-martialed from the Navy—that's motive. Now 'first base' is always San Diego, 'second base' is Long Beach, 'third base' is L.A. and Burbank. Simple code. So simple it's dumb."

I'd just about convinced myself that a member of the Mexican government was the middleman between an American spy and the Japanese, but I had to prove it.

"Wonder where the girls from the Mexican consulate go for lunch. Shouldn't be hard to find out."

*   *   *

The traffic jam at Century and La Cienega was one of the worst Valerie Jean Riskin had ever seen. She was giving Pauline Hyatt a lift home from work in her 1940 Plymouth Mayfair. Valerie had kicked off her shoes. In city traffic, she handled the clutch better in her stocking feet.

She spotted steam billowing from the hood of the Chevrolet in front. "Oh God, he's stalled," she carped. "I'm due at the hospital. I'm going to be late."

When she started at North American, Valerie had been named Tool Design's first-aid person. Though annoyed—Why me? Because I'm a woman?—she had agreed, and now was taking a basic first-aid class one day a week at Inglewood Hospital. She slapped the steering wheel with the heel of her hand. "Damned traffic."

Pauline blushed. Valerie guessed the young inventory clerk rarely heard women swear.

The stalled Chevy up ahead was boiling over. The traffic snarl wouldn't clear up any time soon. On the car radio, the Andrews Sisters finished something or other and a commercial came on. "Rinso White, Rinso White, happy little washday song . . ."

Valerie turned it off. "How's that boyfriend treating you?" she asked.

"He's going to pop the question." Pauline giggled. "I'm sure he is. Women can tell about these things."

Valerie laughed internally at this eighteen-year-old calling herself a woman. "Is that what you want? Will you be happy?"

"Oh, gosh yes. Robby's the tops. We've known each other for two years now. I'm sure he'll try real hard to be a good husband. You want to get married again, don't you, Valerie?"

"I suppose, eventually. My Jim was a great guy, a good friend, you know. If I could find someone half as good . . ." Her voice was swallowed up by a B-25 Mitchell bomber droning low overhead, on final approach to Mines Field. "Marriage isn't my main goal, kiddo. I'm going to make something of myself, maybe design jet airplanes."

"Jet airplanes? No propellers?" Pauline looked awestruck. "You really think so?"

"Sure. Caproni flew one in Italy last year or the year before. Bell Aircraft has a jet fighter in the early design stages right now, but keep that under your hat. Still very hush-hush."

"I will, Valerie. Mum's the word . . . But what about Corky?" she persisted. "You love him, don't you?"

The driver of the Chevy had a couple of volunteers and they were pushing his car to the side. "Look!" Valerie said. "There's hope for getting through the intersection before nightfall. What were you saying? Oh, right, do I love Corky? No . . . and I'm not sure I even know what love is any more."

"Gee whillikers, I thought you were gone for him."

Valerie laughed. "Oh, I'm fond of Corky, but it's nothing like what I had with Jim. We had a great physical relationship. . ." Pauline's cheeks reddened again.

" . . . But it was much more than that. We had real respect, and we were great pals, too."

Traffic began to move and Valerie finally cleared the inter-section, turning east on Century.

"Sometimes on a Saturday," she continued, "we would goof around all day like little kids." A tear formed as she swung left onto La Brea. She couldn't brush it away till she'd gone through the gears. She worked the stick, mounted on the steering column, with her right hand.

"I hope Robby and I will be like that," Pauline said. "I have a lot to learn."

"You really think you're ready for marriage? It's a huge step. Have you thought it all the way through?"

"Sure I have. I love him. It's going to be a dreamy wedding. I know he's going to ask me."

"He's likely to be drafted and God knows how long you'd be apart. Thought about that?"

"I'll be proud to have him serve. I'll be here for him, waiting, no matter how long it takes." She paused. "This terrible war. Mom thinks we're in danger right here, says this is a war zone. But the Japanese wouldn't dare try and sneak all the way over here,"

Pauline said as Valerie turned onto Queen Street.

"Come on now, Val, I want to know. What would you do if Corky asked you to marry him?"

"He already has, and I said no."

"Golly, I guess we see things kind of differently."

"I think Corky's fooling around on me, Pauline."

"Fooling around?"

"Cheating. Making time with somebody behind my back."

"Jeepers!" Pauline's face more than blushed; it turned a deep red. "How do you know?"

"I don't, for sure. It's just a feeling. As you said, women can *tell* about things." Valerie shook her head sluggishly. "There are all kinds of men in the world, kiddo. Jim was one of the good ones."

"You said you and he had a great physical relationship." Pauline shyly bit her lip. "What's *it* like? Is it wonderful, you know, going all the way?" Clearly, Pauline had been saving herself for her wedding night.

"That," Valerie said, laughing, "is a subject for another day." She pulled to the curb and stopped in front of a two-story clapboard house. Pauline gazed at her parents' whitewashed porch. "What say we have a soda or something next week?" Valerie glanced at her watch and reached across in front of Pauline to turn the door handle.

"Okay. And you'll tell me all about *it*. Promise?"

"We'll see, we'll see. Now, I've got to get to the hospital and learn how to roll bandages."

Pauline jumped out and hiked up the brick walk.

What good will all this first-aid ever do me? Valerie wondered as she drove off.

CHAPTER 9

THE DOOR OPENED and Cass swept in, casually elegant in a pants suit of deep green. Tom jumped up and gave her his top volume hug.

"The Huntington was great. Let me tell you about . . . Hey, what's going on? You look all worked up."

"I've had a pretty bizarre day." Tom told her about the weird 1968 experience and the two old men who seemed to turn young for an instant when he took their picture. He gestured at the book lying on the bed. "And I've been reading a book by my Great Uncle Jake, a book I never knew existed. It's supposed to be a true account of some big Japanese air raid on Southern California, which of course never happened. But get this, the woman I bought this from says it did happen, in another dimension."

"Oh, geez, I leave you alone for one day and you find a bunch of L.A. cops to get drunk with."

"Haven't had a drop, babe. Been reading this so-called true historical account all day."

"By your great uncle?"

Tom nodded.

"That's tremendous. Did you know he wrote a book?"

"Yeah. But this is about—"

"Did you ever meet him?"

"No, he died years ago. But this book is about something that's supposed to have happened in some parallel universe."

"*That* stuff," Cass said, "you'll have to explain."

And Tom tried, covering the mysterious clock shop, the spooky conversations with its owner, the widow of a Russian physicist who had his own slant on Einstein's space-time continuum, and of course the book.

Cass made a whistling shape with her lips, expelled some air, and picked up the book. "Your great uncle. This is a terrific find." She gazed at the title. "'The Day They Bombed L.A.' Is this about the Watts Riots?"

"No, the Japanese, I told you. World War II."

She flipped through some pages, stopped at random, and read a little. "Your Uncle Jake had an interesting style, real informal."

"Inconsistent, but fascinating as hell."

"I think somehow," she said, "this intriguing book made a psychic connection with your subconscious—you've always had a vivid imagination—and *voila*, you saw a World War II plane and some pilots. This other stuff, though, the woman in the cape, Alexa, was it? This business about our time track getting split in two. Hmm. Quantum theory stuff."

Tom nodded. "She gave me a little lecture on how particles can flow backward in time." Last year Tom thought he'd been plunked down in the middle of a Civil War battle. It had all seemed incredibly real.

"Einstein theorized that, I think."

"Right. She said that, too."

"Did you have a headset on?" Cass called over her shoulder, walking into the bathroom. "This sounds like one of those new virtual reality things."

"Nope, nothing like that."

"Maybe you slipped through for a moment into that other time dimension . . . or maybe the woman's a witch." Cass was back with two glasses. She pulled a tiny airlines bottle of vodka from her purse. "Russia has a lot of witchcraft folklore."

"I don't know about that, but she's psychic or something. Whenever I got a little thirsty, she showed up with a cup of tea. Something else, too. She said she knew that Jake was my great uncle. Actually said she'd been expecting me."

Cass poured and handed a glass to Tom. "We both could use this."

"Russian witches. Vodka. Perfect," Tom said, clinking glasses.

Cass said, "Cheers," took a sip and went on. "There's still so much we don't know. The limits of our understanding will look pretty feeble a hundred years from now. Imagine Lincoln or Napoleon trying to make sense of computers or spy satellites. 'What's your PIN number, Abe?' Blow their minds."

"You're saying nothing's impossible? That we'll discover how to move around in time?"

Cass shrugged.

"And maybe in some dimension parallel to this one, the Japanese pulled a Pearl Harbor on L.A.?"

Cass took another sip of vodka and shrugged again.

Tom smiled weakly. "Why me? I didn't ask to be in the Battle of Antietam, and I wasn't looking to meet that funny little Russian woman today."

"You're a handful in any century," Cass said, flashing a coy smile. She reopened the book. "Whatever's going on, I'm hooked. Let's read some. We've got awhile before we meet Mom and Dad. Where'd you leave off?"

Tom showed her the page.

"I'll read aloud," she said. "Put your feet up."

Tom sank into a chair and took a hefty drink of vodka. A shaft of heat rushed down his throat.

Tuesday, March 24, 1942, Los Angeles.

Gus Dobson was a perfect city editor, had great news sense and knew L.A. like he knew his cue stick. He'd put eight versions of the *Herald-Express* to bed that day—three true editions and five replates.

He rubbed his tired gray eyes with the pads of his fingers. It was 4 o'clock, time to go across the street for some pool and beer, but Dobson always had time for a little chat with his military writer.

He called me his Southern screwball, said I spoke in a drawl. Imagine, calling my fine Louisiana enunciation a drawl. He said I talked like Pappy Yokum, but that was an act, that I did Alan Ladd when I got serious. If only I *looked* like Alan Ladd.

Dobson's newspaper years had made him a cynic, but he still had a great sense of humor. He was forty-eight, but looked older. Too much paunch, too little hair, drank and smoked too much, slept too little. But look who's talking. I didn't exactly take care of myself either.

Holding my notebook, I sat on the edge of his old cedar desk, one leg dangling over. Cigarette burns scarred the desk. Gray copy paper, a glass pot of glue, and yellow pencils with teeth marks were scattered here and there.

"The wife and I met some people in Pasadena last night for dinner," Dobson said, moving some paper around. "Drove up that new Arroyo Parkway. Been on that yet, Jake?"

"Yeah. Smooth ride. No traffic lights. Really somethin'."

"Transportation Department calls it a freeway. Say they'll build more after the war. Wonder if it'll catch on."

"I dunno. There's no place to turn around on the darn thing."

Dobson leaned back in his swivel chair and cupped his hands behind his head. "Anything good on your beat today?"

"Nah," I stalled. "Shipbuilding's starting to roll in Long Beach. This guy Henry Kaiser in 'Frisco claims he'll turn out eight transports a month soon's he gets tooled up. Gonna call them liberty ships. Not a story now, though."

"Hell, we need a hero in the Philippines, some local boy, or a naval battle we can win. Any chance?"

"Ain't gonna be any good news in the Philippines," I said. "You know the Philippines are lost when Roosevelt orders MacArthur to haul ass down to Australia. How about that guy, though? Breakin' outta Corregidor in a danged PT-boat with his wife and kid, Jap destroyers thick as flies on a bayou hog. Been safer in a sub but, oh no, he's gotta charge off on a white horse. 'I came through and I shall return!' That old boy's sure full of himself."

"He's full of something. Follow MacArthur around, you need

a shovel." Dobson lit a Wings cigarette and offered me one, but I waved him off. Somehow, I'd never taken up smoking. Aggie Underwood ambled past. She was our police beat reporter, the only female in L.A. covering the cop shop.

"Hi, Ag," Dobson called out.

"Now there's a pair to draw to," she answered, winking at us.

I had a case to make and it was time to make it. "Gus, I'm onto something. I may have dug up a spy, an honest-to-God espionage deal."

Dobson's eyebrows arched. "Yeah?"

"A guy who got thrown outta the Navy a few years back for stealing supplies. He's been meeting Navy officers, buying drinks, pumping these guys for all kinds of sensitive dope. He hangs around the bases, San Diego, Long Beach, Alamitos, and the aircraft plants, Douglas, North American, all of them."

"That's thin, Jake, pretty thin." I could tell that a game of eight-ball and a beer was on his mind. "You got an ex-Navy type who likes to have a drink, and he has it with his old service buddies, big deal. Prohibition's been over nine years, Jake, you don't need to mess with that rotgut any more."

"There's more to it, Gus, lots more. If he just drank for the hell of it, why would he do it all over this half of the state? Wouldn't he stick to one or two favorite spots? He's been seen from Tijuana to Santa Monica. Hangs around with aircraft workers, too—Navy brass and factory people. He goes off and makes notes afterward, like there's something he's got to put down before he forgets. Also been meeting guys from the Mexican consulate. On the sly, never in the same place twice."

Dobson stubbed out his cigarette and stared at me. "Maybe he's a pimp, Jake, and these Mexican guys got the supply."

A tiny Negro woman clutching a square white envelope walked past, heading for Society. She took small, meager steps and looked around timidly. Society was real close to Dobson's desk. We heard the whole thing. At Society's bullpen, she told Gracie Pike she had a picture of her daughter, who was about to get married. Would they run a bridal announcement?

"Fill out this form," Gracie said, shoving the woman a

mimeographed questionnaire.

When the particulars were filled in, Gracie—who was white—glanced at the photo and the form, squinting through smoke drifting up from the Lucky Strike on her lip. "My, she's lovely. We'll see what we can do."

After the mother mumbled her thanks and left, Gracie said, "That'll be the day, when the *Express* runs a spook bride." The Society bullpen erupted in laughter and Gracie flipped the photo and wedding form in a wastebasket.

I shook my head and exchanged a rueful look with Dobson. Meanwhile, I was still trying to sell him.

"This sounds like that crazy notion of yours about the Nazis trying to kidnap Walt Disney," he said.

"There's still something to that," I insisted—and there was—"but no, this is altogether different."

"You've been watching too many serials at the movies, Alan Ladd."

"Wait, listen." I was worried. Needed Dobson's backing. "I've seen him myself in the Bomb Shelter on Lakewood, just down from the new Douglas plant." I opened my notebook. "Here we are. February 13. Then last Wednesday I saw him in Santa Monica, over by Clover Field."

"You're sure about all this?"

"Well, natch."

"You got his name? Know where he lives? Besides yourself, who are your sources?"

"Well, there's Rifty—"

"Rifty La Plante? Ah, Jake, the cops ran that little con outta L.A. two, three years ago. Don't be wasting W.R.'s money—"

"Rifty's never given me bad dope. That nosy son of a bitch has a memory like an iron safe. He saw this guy March 6 in San Diego with a Navy officer. Later, same day, Mexican consulate guy tells him, 'Go to Ensenada.' Then four days later he meets the Mexican again on El Cajon Boulevard. If this guy's really a spy, I want to fry his ass from here to Havana. When he gets out of Alcatraz, his butthole will be reamed wider'n Santa Monica Boulevard."

"If you're right about this guy, he won't go to Alcatraz. He'll get the gas chamber."

"Know what else I think? The Japs are gonna attack. That's why they got this guy running all over collecting new dope."

Dobson gave me a major league frown.

"W.R. would love it," I insisted, referring to old man Hearst.

"So would I, *when* we really have something to hang our hat on. But attack here? The Japs?"

"I feel it in my bones."

"Well I don't." He sounded just like an umpire yelling, "Strike three."

"Tell you what, though," he said, "keep after it if you want. *Do not* make this a crusade. Don't let it interfere with your regular rounds. But if you get something hard, more names, stuff that adds up better than this, let me know. A spy scoop would do this old rag some good. And yeah, Hearst *would* love it."

One thing I had going for me with Gus Dobson: in his reporter days, he worked the way I did. The things I'd dug up on my spy were just the kind of items he would have been going after.

"Come on, Jake," he said, clapping me on the back. "Let's go over to the Continental for a bowl of chili, after which I'm gonna whip your ass in a game of pool. Two bits a ball." We got up and left the city room, Dobson grabbing his rumpled jacket and felt hat from a coat rack without missing a step.

"If I were the city editor, I'd turn him loose," said Cass. She took a small sip of vodka. "Back him all the way."

"You would, eh?"

"Sure. There's a war on and here's this guy sneaking around in places where he shouldn't be, asking the wrong kind of questions. Plus, Jake's got good instincts. This has spy written all over it."

"Maybe you should get out of government and become a reporter, babe. Want me to ask Pam Wells if the *Bee* has any openings?"

"Not just yet, thanks." Cass looked at her watch.

"How long till dinner?"

"We've got awhile yet. Mom always needs a nap after a big day like we had at the Huntington. Ready to hear some more?"

I wanted to warn the military. I thought about calling my friend Deke Rickey at the Naval Station, but if I didn't have enough proof for my own city editor, I sure didn't have enough for the War Department. To them I'd just be another crackpot seeing Japanese periscopes in every piece of driftwood floating offshore. I'd just have to keep digging. By the way, Gus didn't beat me at pool.

The North Pacific.

The carrier *Akagi* was strictly blacked out. Kaz Okada closed the hatch behind him and carefully stepped out onto the dark flight deck. He often came out here at night when he wanted time alone. Raw wind clawed his body, sent his hair flying. It pierced his frame and chilled him in spite of his heavy flight jacket.

The sea looked jet black against the charcoal sky. He made out the dim outline of a destroyer on the horizon, perhaps two miles off, rising and falling on the swells.

He gazed to the east, knowing that the United States drew nearer with each hour. Soon he would lead his squadron of Aichi dive bombers in that direction.

He thought about his uncle and cousin Mori in San Gabriel. Mori was fifteen months younger and the two had become close friends in the years he'd lived with them while getting his college degree.

Disturbing rumors had reached Japan that Japanese-Americans in California were being evicted from their homes and put in internment camps. He didn't believe it. Such a fate hadn't befallen his beloved uncle. His uncle had conducted himself honorably in America and was a model of U.S. citizenship.

Okada thrust his hands deeper into his coat pockets,

hunched his shoulders, and strolled to the catwalk that rimmed the ship. He stepped down onto the steel mesh, found a protected spot in the lee of a gun mount and leaned against a railing. Below, white water boiled away from the ship as its bow sliced the black ocean.

Without a word, he clapped his hand on the back of a half-frozen lookout, an enlisted man, as if to say, "Hello, comrade." Then Okada stepped through a hatch into an interior passage.

As always on war patrol, the ship's white lights were out. He strode down a passageway illuminated by the dim reds, beneath a jungle of pipes, ducts and vents, passing clusters of gauges and valves. He climbed down three companionways, then walked through another warren of passageways to reach his room, which slept six junior officers in steel bunks stacked three high.

Okada slipped out of his uniform. Instead of opening his steel locker—that might disturb his sleeping shipmates—he hung the clothes on a hook.

He crawled into bed. *Cousin Mori*, he thought. *You hadn't wanted me to take flying lessons.*

CHAPTER 10

Friday, March 27, 1942, Huntington Beach.

A truck stop on U.S. 101 south of Los Angeles. Chet Sickles got there late and slid into a booth where Arturo Rivera sat waiting. The place smelled of grease and frying hamburger. Beyond the window, a forest of oil derricks. Count Basie on the jukebox. "One O'clock Jump."

"How are you, my friend?" Rivera said. No code words, no countersigns.

Rivera has become a hell of a lot cockier since Pearl Harbor, Sickles was thinking. And less careful. Sure, they'd never been in this roadhouse before and it was a cinch no one here knew them, but it was still the first time Rivera hadn't used any of his stupid code words.

Across the table, above the napkin holder and the push-button selector for the jukebox, there was something odd about Rivera's grin.

Sickles despised the slick-dressing little Latin he was doing business with. He decided to let it show.

"What do you want, Rivera?"

"Please, my friend, keep your voice down. I have your money here, but only half." Rivera spoke just above a whisper. "My expenses have increased a great deal lately. In the future I will require half your fee."

"You get half? Half of mine? The hell you talkin' about? We got a deal. When do I get the rest?"

"As I said," Rivera's voice still calm, "this will be your full payment."

"Like hell it will." Sickles realized how loud that came out. His head throbbed hot with anger. He reached across the table and vise-gripped Rivera's forearm. Made an effort to lower his decibels. Wasn't easy. "Our deal is with the Japs. Stick to your part of it, little *amigo*, or I'll knock you on your *asiento*."

"I am your agent with the Japanese, your conduit." The words were clipped, condescending. Rivera wasn't hiding his dislike, either. "As I said, my expenses have increased a great deal. My decision is not negotiable. I'm quite sorry."

"Think you can squeeze me like that, sport, you got a few screws loose."

"What are you going to do, my friend, file a complaint? Go to the courts, the police, maybe the FBI? Those would be good ideas, you think? Yes, *señor*, I think I can get away with this." Rivera jerked his arm free from the grasp.

"You see, I have good connections with your FBI. Since your unfortunate war with Japan broke out, the FBI has been quite willing to part with considerable Yankee dollars for information."

Sickles' mouth dropped open. "A double agent. A fucking double agent? Workin' for the Japs and the FBI at the same time, and now you're blackmailin' *me*?" His eyes became narrow slits. "You're filth, Rivera."

Rivera leaned forward, their faces now close. His voice rose slightly. "My dear friend, I am not being disloyal to *my* country. My nation is neutral and—"

"We'll see how long your damn country stays neutral when the Germans get their U-boats into the Gulf and start putting your oil tankers on the bottom."

Rivera ignored the interruption. "My nation is neutral," he repeated. "It is your country that is at war with Japan. And not doing well, I might add. Yet you are selling information to the Japanese, the enemy of your people. Mexico is not at war with either party. As a neutral, why should I not consult with both of them? I, *señor*, am not committing treason against *my* homeland." Rivera spat out the words. "You are the traitor. Let us see now who is filth."

The jukebox was playing Glenn Miller's "String of Pearls."

Rivera slipped an envelope across the table to Sickles. Then he stood, adjusted his shirt cuffs, smiled like an arrogant matador, and left.

Ladera Heights.

That night, when he got back to his apartment in the hills of western Los Angeles, Sickles went to his closet and rummaged through a stack of sweaters, underwear and neckties. At last his hand felt something cold and hard. He pulled out a gunmetal blue Colt .45 semiautomatic pistol, Navy issue. He looked at it for a moment, examined the clip, then placed it on top of a dresser.

Los Angeles.

Me, I was having a much better night than Sickles. I'd just had dinner downtown with a beautiful young Mexican named Rosalinda and was driving her home to her apartment in East L.A. Rosalinda worked for the Mexican consulate. She didn't own a car; usually commuted by bus.

I'd met her the week before in a malt shop, of all places, a block from the consulate. I hadn't picked up a girl at a soda fountain in—what, fifteen years?—but a reporter close to a major scoop has got to do what he's got to do.

Of course, it hadn't been a chance meeting, although she had thought so. I'd bought a round of sodas for Rosa and two girl-friends and, drawing on my considerable charm and some faked innocence, I managed to sweet-talk myself into the group and become the fourth in their booth.

It was unique and exciting, if I do say so, for these young Mexicans—I learned later that Rosa was the only one over twenty-one—to be visiting after work with this gringo newspaperman.

One of them doubted my claim of being a reporter, so I flashed my press pass issued by the L.A. Police. I told them I was the one who coined the term "stop the presses."

Rosa laughed and said, well, her grandfather had invented the *tilde*, the squiggle above the "ń" in the Spanish alphabet. "How do you like that?" I liked that a lot.

Half an hour later, one of them said they'd better leave to

catch the 6 o'clock bus, the last one for an hour. That was when I convinced Rosa to stay and have a burger with me, letting the others go on ahead. I would drive her home.

My Southern charm and lovely smile had never been in better form. Alan Ladd all the way. I can do sincere, trust me.

Rosa was a beautiful young woman. I knew she'd agreed to stay against inner misgivings and all her upbringing. I played the perfect gentleman that night and won her trust.

Two nights later, though, we did the horizontal tango. (The things we do for our country.) Afterward, Rosa sobbed and clung to me tightly for an hour.

Tonight at dinner I scored in another way. I felt like a gambler on a roll. She promised me something other than her graceful young body, something Jake Weaver the journalist needed from the consulate.

As we drove toward her apartment, she slid over real close and rested her head on my shoulder. I felt sort of like a heel.

That dirty old reprobate," Cass said. "And to think his blood is flowing in your veins."

"I thought you said he was a good reporter with great instincts."

"Doesn't give him the right to be an asshole."

"He had a story to track down," Tom said with a grin.

"By deflowering an innocent young girl?"

"Hey, the lady was willing."

"Men!" Cass thrust her fists against her hips. "You'd better not seduce any cute young druggies just to make a big bust."

"If you mean seduce cute young druggies *with* big busts, certainly not before reading 'em their rights."

"Shut up, you bastard." But she smiled as she said it.

Tom put a hand gently on her neck. "You have the right to remain silent. Anything you say . . ."

Her smile deepened. It was forty minutes before they resumed reading.

Long Beach.

Millie Simpson was a nice kid, sweet, lonely and confused. She and her husband Jason came to Southern California a few months after getting married in their hometown of Ada, Oklahoma. He'd joined the Marines and was stationed at Seal Beach. They found an apartment on Second Street in Long Beach and were having a great time—until Pearl Harbor. They hadn't counted on Pearl Harbor. Jason was shipped to Hawaii and Millie wasn't allowed to go with him.

At twenty, she was alone for the first time in her life. She debated whether to go back home and live with her parents while the war was on. Meanwhile, she tried a couple of churches, but couldn't seem to make friends. She took long, solitary walks, surveying the town. Gazed enviously in the windows of the fancy shops along Ocean Boulevard. Sometimes she'd buy a pint of ice cream (twenty-one cents) at the Egyptian Pharmacy at Belmont Shore, or watch the double roller coaster at the Pike.

Millie was a decent girl and never went to bars without Jason, and not very often with him. She didn't drink much anyway. But loneliness got the best of her one night and she ventured forth. Wearing one of her best dresses and her hair waved the way Jason liked it, she stepped into a bar a few blocks from the apartment.

There she met a guy, who guessed she was a schoolteacher. Millie said, "Oh no, but I'm certainly flattered."

This guy was slicker than any man she'd ever met. And she was lonely. And she'd consumed more bourbon than ever before. One word at a time, the guy got to her. Later that night he made love to her in her little apartment.

Millie was hung over the next day and honestly couldn't remember all that had happened. But she knew she'd gone further with that guy than she'd ever intended.

He came by that evening, bringing flowers. She was still confused, but his calm manner reassured her. He was so nice and understanding.

They made love again. Afterward, still holding him tightly, Millie's anguished mind said, "This is wrong, wrong." But it was the first time in months that she hadn't felt lonely or afraid. She tried to shut out thoughts of her husband.

In an hour, they had an encore. Later, while still clinging to this man, Millie's mind turned to her husband. She still knew this wasn't right.

Even so, she knew she would see more of Corky Held.

And she did. After their next time, lying in bed still a-tingle, Millie found herself thinking, "I love him, I love him. He makes me feel so good. Oh, Jason, I hate to do this to you, but I've found someone else."

Corky Held was thinking, "She's one gullible little woman, but a great lay. So Gary Cooper sends Valerie Jean, does he? Well, we know who sends this little cupcake."

"Men!" Cass snorted, chucking the book down. "And don't read me my rights." She didn't smile as she said it.

CHAPTER 11

Saturday, March 28, 1942, the North Pacific.

Kaz Okada was back out on *Akagi's* flight deck, buffeted by wind that pinned his pants tight against his legs. He breathed deeply of the cold salt air. He'd just finished another extraordinary briefing with Commander Genda and had been made privy to the whole plan.

This operation had been planned by the great Isoroku Yamamoto, who was almost as revered as the Emperor. Admiral Yamamoto was supreme commander of the Combined Fleet, as big a hero in Japan as MacArthur was in America.

His plan was so daring, the gamble so great, that Japan's newest and largest aircraft carriers, the modern *Shokaku* and *Zuikaku*, would not be risked. The strike force was small and fast, capable of vanishing quickly from the California coast. The mission was code-named Operation *Seifuu*, which meant West Wind.

"Using four older carriers and no battleships," Genda had said, "we have assembled a force that can do great damage, but whose loss could be endured. If worse came to worst, we would lose a third of our carrier strength but still have eight carriers in the Pacific to the Americans' four."

"It still risks too much," the young pilot blurted rudely. "We need all our carriers."

"It was Yamamoto's decision," Genda said conclusively.

Okada felt sheepish and guilty. Questioning Yamamoto was like questioning Buddha.

The force would maintain strict radio silence for the entire voyage, relying on flag and blinker signals for more than two weeks. As an extra precaution, some of the carriers would be mentioned in faked radio reports as operating in the Indian Ocean.

Last-minute intelligence, gathered from agents in California and Mexico, was received before they sailed from Saipan.

A Kawanishi seaplane had touched down near the flagship *Soryu*. Kaz Okada had seen it himself but hadn't known it carried a top-secret pouch containing maps of San Diego, Los Angeles and Long Beach. They pinpointed the locations of the Douglas, North American, Lockheed and Consolidated aircraft plants, and the oil refineries in El Segundo and Wilmington. The packet also carried information on anti-aircraft batteries, combat air bases, camouflage at the targets, and the location—as of six days before—of ships in Long Beach and San Diego harbors.

On March 22, Chet Sickles had brought the packet to a cantina in Ensenada, a dusty town sixty miles south of San Diego on the Baja coast. A fishing skiff took it out of the harbor that afternoon. Just after sundown, three miles out, the Japanese submarine I-17 surfaced for ninety seconds and took it aboard. Four days later, the sub made rendezvous with the seaplane at a spot halfway between Baja and Hawaii. The plane carried the pouch to Saipan, where it was one of the very last items taken aboard before sailing.

After the briefing, Okada had spent half an hour on *Akagi's* hangar deck, sitting in the cockpit of his Aichi D3A dive bomber, fiddling with the controls.

Now he was up on the dark flight deck. As the wind flailed at his face, he thought back to the day they'd left Saipan. Final good wishes and toasts had been exchanged with shore officers. That first evening at sea, the sailors were treated to an exquisite rosy-orange sunset. Okada watched many of them bow in the twilight and ask the Sun Goddess for good fortune. The Sun Goddess was of the *Shinto* faith. Okada was a Christian, more or less. He didn't believe in the Sun Goddess.

One of his friends was aboard the carrier *Soryu* a few miles away. Commander Tatsu Matsumoto had begun to think the war was all wrong, that his *Dai Nippon* was making a tragic mistake.

He was writing to his wife in Niigata, on the island of Honshu. Matsumoto, a fighter pilot, had a son of five, and a four-month-old daughter he'd never seen. He had mailed his wife a letter from Saipan. This one could not be sent till after the attack. He might even see her before it could arrive. Still, he wrote.

"I think back to the distant days we spent together before this great war came. I often think how cozy it will be to return to the family circle I was so accustomed to. I miss you and my fine son whom you have raised so well.

My soul aches that I was not at your side when our daughter was born in December. I am certain she will be a fine woman like her mother. I yearn to see her.

We have come into stormy weather. That is good. The Americans will have difficulty discovering us.

In my mind, I can see your face clearly. The vision of you is a comfort. I always wear the little scarf you gave me. It makes me feel close to you. Your spirit is my companion.

My sadness becomes pain when I wonder if I will ever see you again.

Be sure to raise our children to love peace and the wonders of nature. They must respect all of mankind. In that kind of attitude is the world's only hope.

Arigato. For everything."

He put down his pen and brush, gave the orange scarf a tender touch, and closed his eyes.

Over on the carrier *Akagi*, Kaz Okada's eyes also were shut. He lay on his back, pondering the incredible task just ahead. He wondered if any of his friends would be working in the aircraft factories that would be bombed. Or flying the fighter planes he would face.

Okada would lead his squadron of dive bombers to Mines Field in Inglewood to attack North American Aviation and the B-25 Mitchell bombers it was building. After smashing North American they would strafe the nearby Standard Oil refinery at El Segundo.

Planes from the light carrier *Junyo* would attack the Lockheed plant in Burbank. *Soryu* would hit the Douglas plant at Long Beach, the nearby naval bases and the Texaco refinery. *Kaga*, whose name meant "increased joy," would attack the Navy bases and the Consolidated plant in San Diego.

Okada knew from his meetings with Genda that the four carriers held 209 combat planes, plus eighteen spares to fly combat air patrol while the attack was underway. It was a small force, just over half the 360 planes that had raided Pearl Harbor four months earlier.

He continued to lie awake, listening to the throbbing song of the steam turbine engines. Heard water and fuel swirl through pipes over his head, a murmuring sound, as if the pipes were whispering to each other. He liked the motion and the smells of the ship at night. At moments like this, while silent mess hands peeled vegetables for the next day's meals, and sailors changing watch moved stealthily, careful not to step on sleeping comrades, Okada thought of the ship as a slumbering colossus, sliding ever forward on a dark sea.

Cupping his hands behind his head, he remembered a picnic he and friends from USC had taken in Griffith Park one spring day five years ago. He had served cucumbers encased in rice rolls wrapped with *nori* (seaweed), as well as raw tuna on rice balls with a hot dash of *wasabi*. He'd packed the meals in traditional boxes called *obento*.

His American friends enjoyed it, although some complained they could never like raw fish. At least there was plenty of beer to wash it down. They'd laughed and talked together into the evening. That splendid day was now one of Okada's cherished memories. He wondered what his friends were doing and what they would think of him now.

He rolled over in his bunk and fell asleep.

Inglewood.

Valerie Jean Riskin hadn't been able to do that yet. She'd been lying awake thinking for an hour since kissing Corky Held goodnight and sending him on his way. His recent presence still lingered in her bed. She could smell his musk in the sheets and pillowcases. Her body was still flushed with the afterglow of love-making, a warm tingling that usually accompanied her into sleep. So why wasn't she content? Something was amiss. She couldn't put her finger on it.

Monday, March 30, 1942, Los Angeles.

Staring at my typewriter, I reached a decision. I'd done some pretty goofy things in my life, but nothing like this. I'd do it tomorrow night. There had to be some evidence in there, evidence I needed.

I was going to break into Chet Sickles' house.

CHAPTER 12

Tuesday, March 31, 1942, the North Pacific.

Aboard his flagship, the task force commander, Admiral Tamon Yamaguchi, bent over his charts, frowning. His strike force was nearing its destination. It was now down to fourteen ships, the tankers and two destroyers having been left behind after the last refueling. The rest were making twenty knots on a southeasterly course. In two more days they would be in striking distance.

Yamaguchi would have to send all his planes in at once, except for the few left behind to fly combat air patrol over the ships. There would be no second wave as at Pearl Harbor. He simply didn't have enough planes. His pilots would have to speed directly to their targets and do as much damage as possible in their first and only strike. When their bombs and torpedoes were expended, they would strafe with their guns. Every bomb and every machine-gun burst would have to count.

Coming from the west, they wouldn't have the advantage of attacking out of the sun, which was standard doctrine. If they circled around their targets and struck out of the morning sun in the east, they would fly over populated areas, giving up the element of surprise. They would also burn too much fuel. Attack in late afternoon? That was out of the question. The planes would get back to the carriers in the black of night.

If only he could make the sun rise in the west for one day.

Ladera Heights.

I'd parked five doors down and was watching the wood frame triplex like a cop on surveillance. If I could prove Chet Sickles was a spy I'd have my story of the year. Hell, of my career. I waited a full half-hour in the dark before approaching Sickles' apartment. Even then, I walked past the place twice, slowly.

No lights on. I glanced at my wristwatch. 8:43. I was trying to get my nerve up as well as convince myself that Sickles wasn't there. I was finally satisfied that no one was home in two of the three apartments, including Sickles'.

"I don't think I like Uncle Jake," Cass said, looking up from the book. "Seducing innocent young girls, breaking into homes."

Tom suddenly felt defensive for his distant kin. "He's got to prove this guy's a spy. Needs evidence for his story."

"He's a con artist."

"Good reporters need to have some con artist in them."

"Hmmph." Her forehead twisted into wavy lines.

"Cut him some slack, babe." Tom looked at his watch. "How's our time? When are we meeting your folks for dinner?"

"Oh, I forgot. That call I took when you were in the bathroom? Mom's pretty wiped out from walking all over the Huntington. Just wanted to go home and put her feet up. Dinner'll be tomorrow night instead."

Tom hoped his lack of disappointment didn't show. "Okay, we can grab a bite around here somewhere."

"Sure, but not yet. Let's get back into this, see if your morally upstanding uncle breaks in." Cass found an old paper napkin flattened between pages. She read the note printed on it. "TCav. Hicks. Ft.Mac."

"I saw that earlier," Tom said. "Uncle Jake must've written that."

"You're probably right. What a great find. Wonder what 'TCav' means. Looks like an abbreviation of your name."

"Yeah, but I wouldn't be around for another nine years. My guess is, something like Third Cavalry."

The phone rang and Tom answered it. "Oh, hi Vinnie."

"Tom, we got nothing at all on Alexa Kadinsky. Clean as a whistle. But guess what, one of my guys knows her. Bought a clock there for his wife. Says she's a sweet lady, straight as they come. But how come the interest, and what are you doing in L.A.?"

"We're visiting my fiancée's folks. Ms. Kadinsky told me something kind of funny today, so I thought I'd follow up on a hunch. Glad to hear that my infallible instincts can sometimes be fallible after all. This is a quick trip, but I'll buy you a cold one next time I'm in town."

"You'd better, pal."

After Tom hung up, he and Cass went back to the book.

I'd borrowed four skeleton keys of different styles and shapes from a cop friend who'd assured me that one of them should open Sickles' apartment.

"But why?" he'd demanded.

"Never mind," I told him. "You owed me one. In a couple of days I'll give you the dope."

The second key did the job. I pushed the front door open and closed it gently behind me, slipping the keys in a pocket and turning on a flashlight. My heart racing, I got my bearings, found a wall switch and flipped it on. The ceiling fixture was so dusty it gave off only a dim amber light. Stuffing the flashlight in a pants pocket, I tried to breathe quietly. Found myself walking on tiptoes. Breaking and entering wasn't my stock in trade. My skin was all goosebumps.

If I found some real evidence in here, Gus Dobson would be convinced. It would not only mean kudos for me for breaking a big spy story, it could save some lives. Forewarned, our defenses could be on full alert when the Japs attacked.

I gave the place a quick once-over. It smelled of stale cigarette smoke and, faintly, spoiled food. A battered, cluttered cedar dining table which seemed to double as a desk was centered beneath the overhead light in the main room. Weary sofa, matching chair, big radio console. One bedroom, one bath, a small kitchen with dishes piled high in the sink. The bed sloppily made, the spread pulled over the sheets but not tucked in around the pillows.

Back in the main room, my skin prickling with anxiety, I went through the mail and papers piled on the dining table. Bills, advertising circulars, old newspapers, a *Life* magazine. It wasn't my style to pry into other men's secrets, but this was something I had to do. I was careful to leave everything exactly as I found it. That day's *Times* was opened to the crossword puzzle. Dumb shit should read the *Express*, I said to myself.

My eyes lit on a tablet of lined notepaper displaying some idle doodling and a few columns of numbers that had been added up. One of the doodles was a stick figure with knees bent. Didn't see anything I could call important. No names or phone numbers, nothing about bases or factories. Nothing that showed Sickles to be a spy.

Cigarette butts filled a glass ashtray. Hold on. Here was a matchbook. I picked it up. Faint green lettering said "Enrique's, Ensenada." I memorized it. *Enrique's, Ensenada.* Only four matches remained. I put it down exactly as I'd found it, next to the ashtray.

Next, the bedroom. If my nerve-endings were lights, they'd have been flickering. I opened the closet door and found some shirts hanging there, two suit jackets, a light windbreaker, several pairs of trousers and a Navy pea jacket. Stacked on a shelf above were some sweaters and ties and two shirts still in paper bundles from a Chinese laundry. I went through the jacket pockets and found nothing but a pencil stub and a paper clip.

Did I hear something? A sound in the other room? I stood stone still and listened for about a minute, trying not to breathe. No, probably just the creaking of a worn-out house settling.

I turned and spotted a wastebasket beside the bed. Before I could check its contents, my eyes froze on a Colt .45 lying atop the dresser like an evil presence. I shivered, felt the hairs snap to attention on the back of my neck. Now my goosebumps had goosebumps of their own. I never knew much about guns, but that .45 was a big so-and-so.

Finally, I knelt and went through the wastebasket. Besides wads of paper, a smelly blue sock with a hole in the toe, and some used-up tissues, I found a Tidewater Oil Company street map of Greater L.A. It was pretty beat up—most of the folds were torn. I started to slip the map into my jacket pocket but changed my mind. I unfolded it and looked for markings. At first I didn't see any but the light was bad so I stepped out into the main room—where I bumped into Chet Sickles.

CHAPTER 13

Tuesday, March 31, 1942, San Diego.

Percy Benbough pulled out a chair and sat at a table in the bar of the U.S. Grant Hotel. An unlit cigar jutted from his mouth.

"Evening, Mister Mayor," said Harry Woodhead, the president of Consolidated Aircraft.

"Hiya, P.J.," added Reuben Fleet, who had just sold his controlling interest in Consolidated to Woodhead and his partners.

The three businessmen—Benbough was a mortician as well as mayor—were about to have a meeting over cocktails. "Come on, Dewey, we're thirsty here," he snapped at a passing waiter. Benbough had just showered and changed after a late-afternoon horseback ride in Balboa Park.

Fleet had moved Consolidated to San Diego from Buffalo seven years before. With a contract to build Catalina patrol bombers for the Navy, he'd established his plant on Pacific Highway, next to the airport and the bay.

Dewey the waiter trotted up to their table. Benbough and Fleet ordered martinis, Woodhead an Early Times on the rocks.

Fleet started talking about camouflage. Netting had been draped over the Consolidated, Ryan and Solar plants. Chicken feathers, painted in wavy green and brown splashes to simulate farm country, covered the mesh. Fleet pressed Benbough about one small section at Consolidated that hadn't been covered yet.

"I'll kick some ass in the Corps of Engineers," Benbough promised.

"Fine, P.J. Now, there's something else about that camouflage. Kind of embarrassing. Wouldn't want it to get into the papers."

"Don't worry, I can damn well handle the papers."

"Well, the chicken feathers went up in an awful hurry. Seems they weren't fully disinfected. Chicken lice are dropping on our workers. We've had to decontaminate some of our people."

Benbough erupted with laughter and slapped Woodhead on the knee. "You've got lousy workers, is that it?"

Tom laughed, too. "I knew aircraft factories were camouflaged that way during the war. Wonder if a problem like that ever came up."

"Or down," Cass said, also laughing. 'This is on your heads,' a foreman might say."

"This is serious, P.J.," Whitehead insisted.

When his laughter was spent, Benbough said, "I know, I know. No use waitin' on the Army. I'll get County Agriculture on it first thing in the morning."

"You know," said Reuben Fleet, "that the president's son is over at North Island. John Roosevelt. Young Navy flier. We oughta do something with that, maybe get him over here for a Chamber of Commerce luncheon."

"Good idea," the mayor said. "Score some points with FDR."

Rumors had spread in town that Japan was planning to seize the harbor at San Quintin, two hundred miles to the south in Baja California, and set up a secret air base. From there they'd bomb San Diego's aircraft factories and bases.

"I keep hearing reports of a radio antenna in a remote mine shaft down there," Fleet said. "The locals say the antenna is raised briefly, then lowered out of sight when it's not in use."

"Army intelligence can't find anything like that," Benbough said, "and they've searched like crazy. Or so they tell me."

Ladera Heights.

At the distance of two feet, Sickles was even bigger than I'd remembered. I dropped the map.

"How are the wife and kids?" I said with a smile that had to be lame. I wondered if I looked as scared as I was.

Sickles grabbed me by the shoulders. "Who the hell are you? What are you doin' here?" His huge hands squeezed. I almost yelped.

"O'Brien, L.A. Water & Power. Had a call from one of your neighbors, possible gas leak. Had to check it out. Gas leaks can be big trouble, sir." I hoped to hell my Alan Ladd sounded convincing. The only good news I could think of was that I was between Sickles and that big Colt .45 in the other room.

"Neighbor? Which neighbor?" His voice like exploding dynamite. "Give me the name."

"Don't have it. My supervisor does. They just hand me an address and send me out."

"Horse shit." The voice hadn't lost a decibel and that iron grip hadn't slackened. "What are you, a cop?"

"Cop? No, Water & Power, like I tol' ya." My Pappy Yokum taking over from Alan Ladd. "Do I look like a cop?"

"Where've I seen you before?" Sickles squinted. I prayed he wouldn't remember that we'd sat side by side on barstools at the Bomb Shelter in Long Beach six weeks before.

"Don't think we've ever met, sir."

"Identification. You're from Water & Power, show me some ID."

He was still trying to place me, but he took his hands off my shoulders as I reached in my back pocket for my wallet. I pulled it out, without a clue as to what I'd do next.

Sickles demanded: "Rivera! Did Rivera send you?"

"Don't know any Rivera, sir."

I ducked past him and darted for the door like Pete Reiser chasing a drive to deep center. The big man was right behind me. As I threw open the door, he got a handful of jacket but couldn't hold it.

I broke away and sprinted across the small yard in the opposite direction of my car, doing my best Jesse Owens impression. I hadn't run like this since my track days at Catholic High. I heard Sickles' footsteps following, then stopping. The bastard's gone back for his gun, I thought, realizing I still clutched my wallet in my hand. I turned left at the corner and kept running. Almost knocked down an old man in a suit and hat. I glanced back. Even in the dark, I knew he was staring at me with astonished eyes.

I pictured Sickles in his bedroom, in a fury, the pistol in his hand, but hesitating. Then he'd realize he had no chance of catching me (maybe I was out of shape but I was smaller and faster), that running through the streets carrying his .45 would get him nowhere.

After three full blocks, I stopped running and switched to what I hoped looked like a normal walking stride. My heart was pounding like a jackhammer.

I slid my wallet in my back pocket and told myself, You ain't the man you used to be. Maybe you never were, an inner voice answered. (Smart ass.) I also said something about drinking less.

Rivera. He asked if Rivera sent me. What was that about? I'd have to remember that name. I looked over my shoulder every few seconds to see if I was being followed or if any strange cars were coming up from behind. I also said to myself, "Enrique's, Ensenada."

L.A.'s blackout was being well observed out here—Ladera Heights was close to the ocean, where lurked the Japanese menace. I blessed the darkness. I stayed away from my car for twenty minutes and then drove out of the neighborhood below the speed limit.

I was still shaky, but exhilarated, too. By God, I'd stared the Reaper straight in the face and survived.

CHAPTER 14

Wednesday, April 1, 1942, Arcadia.

Mori Kawahara and his girlfriend, Sumiko, left the parking lot at Santa Anita Racetrack and started across the broad, lumpy racing surface. Carrying a brown paper sack, they ducked beneath the white wood rail, walked around the long green Totalizator board to the infield, and approached a high wire fence. Guard towers loomed every hundred yards along the fence.

Mori had once won twenty-two dollars at this place. There were no horses to bet on today. The Army had commandeered the lavish racetrack, only eight years old, as a temporary staging area to collect Japanese-Americans before shipping them out to camps in some godforsaken backwater.

"Hey, you," a khaki-clad MP shouted. "You within twenty miles of home?"

"Don't worry, soldier boy, we live in San Gabriel."

Sumiko tugged at Mori's arm. "Don't get into trouble again, please." She tried to guide him away from the soldier, one of hundreds patrolling the acres of fencing.

"Got some veggies there, sweetheart?" another guard taunted.

"Have an important job, don't you?" Mori yelled back.

"Mori, please!" Sumiko tugged harder.

"You're really fighting for *our* country, protecting us from *our* enemies."

"Shut your lip, Jappo. You'll be in here soon enough."

Mori sneered, but knew it was the truth. He had less than a week left. He took Sumiko's hand and turned to the faces of the men milling around inside the fence. Sad Asian faces. Some angry, some stoical, some defeated. All sad.

He soon found his father among them. Mori opened the sack. Through a tear in the wire, he handed him some carrots, celery and oranges. This was permitted.

"I can't even go inside to see you, father. This is so stupid."

"We will endure this, my son. Try to keep your spirits up."

For three weeks, Mori had been coming to the Santa Anita evacuation center, speaking with his father through the fence and slipping him food.

Eichi Kawahara wore the dark suit he'd put on the night he was hauled into custody. Then it had been clean and pressed. Now it was sagging and rumpled. He slept on a hard Army cot in a tent and had only the one suitcase of belongings with him.

"You could still repatriate to Japan, father. I've checked. The International Red Cross is arranging passage to Tokyo on neutral ships."

"No, son, I could not. This is our home. I will abide the war here."

"I knew you'd say that, father. The Tanaka family is going. They're the only ones I know of."

"The Tanakas, yes. They would." Eichi Kawahara paused, then looked into Sumiko's eyes. "I have something to tell you, Sumiko. I know you and Mori are thinking of marriage."

Sumiko clutched Mori's hand tighter, communicating her anxiety.

"I had hoped to pick a bride for my son in Japan. It is the custom. But I am an American now, and that is not the practice here. I have come to see that I could not have found anyone better than you for my Mori. I will honor whatever you decide."

He put his hand against the fence. Sumiko hesitated, then did the same, touching his fingers.

Back in their room after a quick supper at a Mexican restaurant, Cass said, "All that stuff really happened. Sending Japanese-Americans off to camps, breaking up families, taking their property. What were we thinking?"

Tom just shook his head.

"I'm going with you tomorrow," she said. "I want to see this mysterious place and the old crone in the cape."

"Great. It'll be good to get your take on all this."

Cass went to the dresser and pulled out something pale yellow and very sheer. "Read for awhile," she said over her shoulder as she strode to the bathroom. "But not too long. Me and this new nightie don't want any competition."

"I'll be ready." Tom gave a hungry smile to her back. When the bathroom door closed, he turned to the book, happy that her anger at the sexual escapades of Jake Weaver and Corky Held hadn't transferred over to him for very long.

The Eastern Pacific.

One more day of steaming and the Japanese would be in position to attack. They'd come all this way without being detected.

Swinging north of Hawaii into latitudes that spawn most of California's winter storms, they'd hoped to find some foul weather. They did, on March 28, running into a broad low-pressure area sweeping down from the Gulf of Alaska. For three days, the ships "rode in under the low," secure from snooping patrol planes as they approached California.

Lieutenant Kaz Okada and his fellow pilots spent parts of those dreary, rainy days doing calisthenics on *Akagi's* hangar deck. They hadn't flown in two weeks and wanted to keep in shape. Each night they studied the battle plans. Many of them asked Okada about specific geographic features. Some climbed into their planes to feel the controls before going to their quarters.

Los Angeles.

I was in a great mood as I dialed the telephone. Surviving Chet Sickles and his big .45 will do that. The landlady answered on the third ring and went to get my new friend. "Rosa, is there a fella named Rivera working at the consulate?"

"Yes, *Señor* Rivera is the deputy consul."

"Listen, honey, what's he like?"

"What do you mean, Jake?"

"What kind of person is he? What kind of personality? Do you trust him? That sort of thing."

"Well, he's not a warm man. I think he's selfish, mostly out for himself. It seems like—how would you say?—he always has an angle. Why do you ask?"

"I'll tell you in a day or two. Thanks a lot, Rosa, that's a big help. Say, there's something else you could do for me . . ."

When could I write this? The Japanese were going to attack. I knew it, they knew it, and this guy Sickles knew it. That's why they had him collecting all this information. If you were the Japs and you had a dozen carriers and you were at war with us, wouldn't you sail over here and try to blast hell out of the aircraft factories and shipyards? But when? Gus Dobson thought I still didn't have enough to hang a story on. But tomorrow, I thought. . .

I took a break that afternoon and went to Gilmore Field where the Hollywood Stars beat the Oakland Oaks 3 to 2 in the season opener. They have to play day games this year because of the blackout. Charlie Root, the Stars' player-manager, pitched. Root had left me a ticket; he was a pal of mine.

San Diego.

Jack Benny and Mary Livingstone performed that night for the troops at Camp Callan, an Army base at Torrey Pines, north of San Diego. They were housed for the evening at the officers' club at the Marine Corps Recruit Depot. The club refused to admit a member of their company, Eddie Anderson, a Negro whose stage name was "Rochester."

Benny was livid. He argued for his man, threatened to cancel the show, and succeeded in getting the club's whites-only rule waived for the night. Anderson would never forget this example of American apartheid or Benny's response to it. Anderson told me this story himself, right after the war.

CHAPTER 15

Thursday, April 2, 3:00 p.m., Los Angeles.

I could have drowned in those deep chestnut eyes with their long lashes. This was one good-looking woman.

Our upholstered booth sat next to a hardwood dance floor, flanked by musicians' chairs, drums, and a five-foot microphone stand. They looked eerie in the afternoon sunlight, slanting dimly gold through smokeglass windows.

Rosalinda's twenty-two-year old profile was classic mestiza, eminent cheekbones and a slightly aquiline nose. Thin gold hoops dangled from her ears. In a lacy, high-necked blouse and her working-girl skirt, she looked both demure and sexy.

We were in between the noontime rush and the afternoon crowd. The little club downtown near Olympic and Grand sat empty except for the two of us and a patient bartender.

"You're a fine lady, Rosa," I said. Far brighter woman than my ex-wife, Dixie Freitas. "And I'm never gonna forget the fine thing you've done today for me and my country. Say, how's about us celebrating with a special dinner tonight, then we could slip over to your place for a little while?"

Over the past week I hadn't lied exactly, I'd just allowed her to draw some false conclusions. If ever the end justified the means, I told myself, this was the time.

"Oh, I don't know, Jake. I just don't know." Slender fingers, the nails lacquered scarlet, gripped a cocktail glass. "I feel funny this afternoon. I hope I have done the right thing."

"You have, darlin', you have." I gave her my full-bore smile. "I've had them photographed, and tomorrow you just slip them right back in the files like nothing happened. Nothing'll be missing, nothing's been stolen. They were just borrowed for a little while. Everything's fine. I've got something that's going to help my country—our country—and help my career, too. And you've got yourself a little spending money and—"

Her dark eyes flashed. "I told you, Jake, I do not want any money."

I realized too late that offering her money was a mistake. Dumb, dumb.

"—and a good, good friend. That's the important thing, Rosa, I'm your friend. I'd never do anything to hurt you or betray you." I meant those words. I took her hand, held it to my lips and gently kissed it.

Rosa flushed. "I do trust you, Jake. But the money—"

"Have I insulted you? Dang me forty ways to Sunday, Rosa. It's just that I sometimes pay for information that helps me with a big story. Expense account, you know. And you earned it, you deserve it. But if I'm insulting you, we'll say no more. Last thing I'd ever wanta do is tromp on your feelings." I smiled again. "When you said you trusted me just now, that made me feel awful good."

I tried to read her thoughts. She probably wondered what her mother would think of this red-haired gringo. I was Catholic at least—that much would please her.

"You know, I'm mighty happy right now," I said. "I'd rather break a big story and get my byline plastered across the front page than anything else in the world. Being a reporter is fine, and I enjoy most ever' day of it. But a chance to break a story like this doesn't come along very often. Most people never get it in a lifetime. But I got me one."

I could just picture it. "How did you get hold of that?" my city editor would ask. "Trade secret," I'd tell Gus Dobson with a wink.

"And Rosa darlin', the last piece is in the puzzle now, thanks to you."

She smiled and our fingers intertwined.

"These papers are that important then?"

"They sure are. They prove what I thought I knew all along. They give me the story of a lifetime, something most reporters'll never get."

"Then I'm happy for you, Jake."

"And you're not feelin' so bad about helpin' me out?"

"No, not so bad. As you say, there should be no harm, when they are back in the file. I wish they were in there already."

Again I kissed her hand, as tenderly as before.

"You are so unlike the kind of man I have known," she said. "Until this week, I had never taken an afternoon off from work, or even considered such a thing."

"I love you, Rosa," I said. And immediately regretted it. I'd been misleading this little beauty for a week. Why did I have to go and say that?

I knew the timing would be a little tricky. I had a big story to write, the biggest, and adding special plans for the evening complicated things. But she was so good looking and she *had* turned out to be my most important source.

"Now whadda you say we have one more drink and then settle on what time I pick you up tonight."

"I don't know, Jake. I felt kind of—what do you say, guilty?—after the last time."

I squeezed her hand and laid on my lovely smile.

"Well, dinner would be nice, Jake."

3:30 p.m., the Eastern Pacific.

Three hundred miles off Point Loma, Eddie Santos and the *Loma Queen* were searching for yellowtail and halibut. It was too early in the year for albacore.

On his previous trip, Eddie and his crew had sailed south to Mexican waters in the company of several other San Diego boats. This time, playing a hunch, he went northwest. Alone. He'd prospered in these waters in 1939 and he had a feeling he'd do well here again.

Eddie had felt edgy when he'd left port four days before. The Navy had issued the usual warning about being alert. It was reassuring to pass through the Yippee Fleet and wave at old friends who were now part of the Navy.

The tension returned when the *Queen* got farther offshore, leaving the friendly patrols behind. One day, a rookie fisherman making his first trip yelled out that he sighted a Jap sub. Turned out to be a big porpoise.

Eddie climbed down from the wheelhouse, nodded to a fisherman leaning against the stern gunwale puffing an Avalon cigarette, and ducked into the galley. A girlie calendar from Sunset Tool hung there. It reminded him it was Thursday, April 2. The next day would be Good Friday. Easter was coming up. He was sad to realize he wouldn't be coloring eggs with his little boys. And Shirley, well, he didn't want to think about Shirley.

"Hey, yesterday was April Fool's Day," he called to Tony Andrade, who was nursing a mug of coffee at the small wooden table.

"The radio's working fine," said Andrade, adding with a wink, "April Fools."

That CW radio set was definitely shot. The new condenser was on order but still hadn't arrived. Only the military could get stuff fast these days.

Eddie pulled a can of Aztec beer from the small refrigerator, pierced the top with a church key, and swung himself back out on deck.

He scanned the horizon and listened to the thump-thump of the little Western Enterprise diesel engine. He saw nothing but empty sea. A bright spring afternoon, a few puffy clouds lazing in the sky like balls of cotton. A rainstorm had passed the day before and another was expected tomorrow, but for now the barometer was up. The *Loma Queen* lifted and dropped rhythmically on calm swells, making almost eight knots.

He finished his beer, climbed to the wheelhouse and nodded at Uncle Charlie Silva. The old fisherman gripped the wheel and studied him, which made Eddie nervous. He knew Uncle Charlie was saddened to see him moping around with a long face. But, damn it, nothing like this had ever happened to him before.

"She's a fool," Charlie said. "Men get more appealing as they grow older, but not women. It's all downhill for them after thirty. She'll never do better than you. In a few years, she'll have a damn tough time finding a good man at all. Only thing around will be the usual assholes and a few married lechers looking for something on the side. But you'll be a mature, good-looking guy who knows the score. You'll have your pick of all the little flowers. I tell you, Eddie, any woman who dumps a good man is a fool."

The pep talk embarrassed Eddie, but he appreciated it, too. "There's no fool like a female fool, is that it?"

At the same instant, they sighted a small, dark silhouette on the northwest horizon. So did the lookout above them. As it grew larger they could see it was a ship bearing in their direction.

It began to look like a destroyer. Funny place for a destroyer, Eddie thought. He often encountered Navy ships off the coast but usually closer to shore and farther south. Must be on some kind of maneuver, or else coming in from Hawaii.

It was a destroyer all right. As it got closer, he saw faint flashes. Signals. But not directed at the *Queen*. Partially obscured, the flashes obviously were being sent in another direction.

Then another tiny silhouette came into view. Another destroyer, a few miles behind the first one. Must be a column of ships. This would be interesting.

Eddie recalled the many times as a kid on Point Loma when he'd watched Navy ships emerge as tiny dots on the horizon. They would gradually evolve into destroyers or cruisers or fleet oilers before they entered the channel and steamed past Ballast Point into the bay.

The first vessel drew closer. It appeared to be a darker color than the light gray of the U.S. Navy.

"Hope they don't think we're a Jap sub running on the surface. We're about the right size."

Suddenly he saw a yellow flash on the ship. Heard a rumble in the sky like a freight train passing right overhead. A second or two later a geyser of water spouted up a few yards behind the *Queen*.

"My God, they *do* think we're Japs," Eddie yelled, grabbing the wheel from old Charlie.

"Wave something at 'em. Do something! Wait, Charlie, shine the spotlight at 'em. You know Morse. Can you click that thing on and off fast enough to make dots and dashes they can understand?"

Eddie spun the wheel frantically. The *Queen* lurched to starboard. "What the hell they doing over there?"

Then he saw something strange: a chrysanthemum painted on the bow. He didn't know the chrysanthemum was the symbol of the reign of the Showa emperor, Hirohito. (Showa means "enlightened peace." Ironic, eh?) A second later Santos saw something he *did* recognize: the Rising Sun flag fluttering on the ship's stern.

Aboard the destroyer *Mitisio*, Commander Uzi Omori had been coming to a decision.

Omori was proud of his first command. A Hataharu-class destroyer, *Mitisio* had five 5-inch guns and six 21-inch torpedo tubes. She'd been built in the Hudinagata boat works in 1937. She was small, fast, and she was a killer.

Mitisio was the advance ship in a little convoy that was approaching its destination, a point three hundred miles above the 30th Parallel and the same distance due west of Los Angeles. They were to reach this spot in a few hours, at 9:30 p.m., California time.

When his sharp-eyed young lookouts with their Kowa binoculars sighted a small fishing boat in their path, Omori had hesitated. Trained to battle military foes without question, he'd never expected to face a decision like this one. His own family had been fishermen. It wouldn't be *Bushido*-like to fire on a fishing boat.

His mental conflict ended fast, though. The boat undoubtedly had a radio and could report the presence of Japanese warships to the mainland. It had to be silenced.

On the *Loma Queen*, Charlie Silva had turned the light toward the destroyer and was feverishly flicking the switch.

"Never mind the light, Charlie," Eddie shouted. "They're Japs."

There was another burst of light on the destroyer, followed by another roaring splash beside the *Queen*. Eddie jerked the wheel back and forth, trying to maneuver the wildly rocking boat this way and that.

"Left two," the gun director shouted in Japanese and a young sailor made a slight adjustment on his reference grids. "Fire." The gunner pulled the lanyard. His 5-inch gun belched thunder and flame.

The third shell from *Mitisio* arched into the sky, reached its apex, and looped downward.

A moment later, it tore through the *Queen's* deck just in front of the cabin, slammed into the diesel engine and detonated. The high-explosive shell was designed to ruin steel warships twenty times larger than the *Loma Queen*.

A momentary fountain of fire and scrap rose from the ocean and fell back into it. Ragged orbs of smoke raveled above the spot for a few seconds, then eddied and vanished in the breeze. The water stopped roiling in concentric circles; the ever-changing ocean settled back into its ancient undulating patterns.

CHAPTER 16

IN THE MORNING, there was a message at the desk from Pam Wells of the *Sacramento Bee*, answering Tom's request for information. "Sergei Kadinsky, physicist, died in 1982. Survived by wife Alexa. Fell into disfavor with Kosygin because of controversial theories about time. What's this all about, Cavanaugh?"

"That much of the woman's story holds up," Tom said to Cass, sticking the note in a pocket. They had breakfast at the hotel, did some window shopping, then arrived at A TIME AND A PLACE a little after 9:30.

As they approached the door, he said, "After all the weird stuff yesterday, I was wondering if this place would even be here."

"The Brigadoon of clock shops?" Cass said.

Inside, Tom introduced her to Alexa. Instead of the black cape, she wore a loose-fitting maroon dress that almost reached her ankles. Her silvery hair was pulled back and tied in a bun. She smiled warmly at Cass. "What a charming lady. Welcome to my little establishment."

"I wouldn't have missed it," Cass said.

"Have you finished the book?" Alexa asked Tom, as Cass started scanning the many clocks.

"Not yet," Tom said. "About two-thirds of it."

"It sounds remarkably realistic," Cass added.

"Oh, it is," Alexa said, and proceeded to repeat what she'd told Tom yesterday: an unusually powerful sun storm in 1924 emitted such a blast of radiation that it split the earth's space-time continuum, setting up a separate time track, one in which the Japanese attacked Los Angeles, an event accurately recounted in Jake Weaver's book.

Cass listened attentively and asked several questions. "I've read enough quantum mechanics theory," she said, "that I'm not rejecting this out of hand."

After their discussion, Cass browsed throughout the shop, admired the vast array of clocks, then went into the back room.

Looking at the calendar on which Dizzy Dean proclaimed he'd walk a mile for a Camel, she said to Tom, "You're right, there really is a devilish look in his eyes. Seems to know something the rest of us don't. He had a great curveball, didn't he?"

She spent a long time reading the glass-encased front page of the old *Herald-Express* blaring that the Japanese had bombed L.A.

"I believe it," she said, stepping back and looking into Tom's eyes. "Sure. This happened in some kind of a parallel reality."

Tom pursed his lips. "Hmm."

An hour later they were back in their hotel room.

Thursday, April 2, 5:30 p.m., Los Angeles.

I shuffled through my notes and took a look at my watch. My cardigan was unbuttoned and I wasn't wearing a tie.

A cleaning woman mopped the floor at the back of the almost-empty newsroom. A couple of night editors were deep in conversation at the copy desk and somewhere a radio played Benny Goodman. I always got a weird feeling at times like this when all the typewriters were silent. Like sitting by a rushing stream and not hearing the water.

I opened a manila folder and pulled out photostatic copies of two documents I'd obtained that afternoon from Rosa at a price of nine days of personal attention to a kind, beautiful and gullible young woman.

They were bank drafts, each for one thousand U.S. dollars, drawn on the Japanese Embassy in Mexico City. Written in

Spanish, one was dated the previous *dos de Octubre*—October 2—the other, October 16. They were payable to Arturo Rivera of the Republic of Mexico's Los Angeles consular staff and bore the words *servicios de consulta*.

On October 3 and 17, one day later in each case, five hundred dollars had been deposited in Chester Sickles' account in the First National Bank of Los Angeles, Ladera Heights branch. The branch manager verified this for me after I insisted this was a huge national security issue and promised him anonymity. Promised on my mother's grave. (My mother, God bless her, was very much alive and had no need for a grave just yet.) A fifth of Jim Beam helped convince him, too. The guy even said his teller recalled that the deposits were made by a Mexican gentleman, not Sickles. He remembered because it was unusual in that little branch for a Mexican to come in with a lot of money and do something like that.

So I had what I'd been looking for: verified proof that money from the Japanese government was being passed through to Sickles. This was the greatest day of my life. I grinned smugly and slipped a piece of gray copy paper in my 1930 Underwood upright.

I picked up the telephone and started to dial Gus Dobson at home in Santa Monica. It was a Crestwood number. I dialed the C-R, then put the phone back on its cradle. An inner battle raged. I could taste the delicious evening I could have with Rosa.

"That woman really came through for me," I murmured. "Thought it might take three or four weeks to get her to do something like that for me, and I'd been afraid there wasn't that much time—I *do* think they're gonna attack. You got her to come around fast, you crazy-ass reporter. Be a crime if we didn't go out to dinner tonight like we planned."

On the other hand, I had the proof right there in my hands. And if I was right about an attack? Pulitzer Prize, bub! And a tremendous scoop for the *Herald-Express*. The journalist in me begged to write it now, for tomorrow's first edition. I'd already done the story over and over in my head. It could almost write itself. The words would flow out of my fingertips into the typewriter keys and in an hour or so it would be ready. Of course, I'd have to call Dobson so he'd read it first thing in the morning, tell the other editors the paper had something really big, and contact the FBI.

Again I looked at my watch and thought about Rosa. She would feel crushed and betrayed if I broke this date. This isn't one of your insipid Hollywood starlet types, I told myself. This is a sensitive young woman who's bought the whole package, pal. I'd have to let her down real easy, this one, when the time came, but why not enjoy it awhile?

I always made snap decisions, so why was I agonizing over this one? Write the damn story or take the little honey to dinner, Weaver.

I glanced at the file of notes, then my wristwatch. Still enough time to shower and change.

"Whatcha doing, Mr. Weaver? Looks like you can't make up your mind about something." It was a night copyboy, a pimply-faced teenager who looked as if his mother was still tying his necktie for him.

"Matter of fact, no, pardner, decision's been made. I'm gonna take a dolly out to the dangdest dinner you ever saw. See ya tomorrow."

I tucked the file under my arm along with a copy of the day's last edition and headed for the door.

In the morning I'd show my material to Dobson. We'd still blow the lid off the biggest spy story in L.A. history. Everything would be hotsie-totsie. What difference would one day make? By Saturday, the FBI would nab Sickles and the Jake Weaver byline would be the biggest thing in town.

I had a quick beer with a couple from out of town at the Continental across the street. They asked if I knew General DeWitt. Then, while piloting my Chevy east across the river on Sixth where it turned into Whittier Boulevard, I thought the whole thing through again. I owed Rosa this little celebration. Gus would have written the story tonight, I knew, but then he wouldn't have gotten laid.

8:30 p.m., Los Angeles.

When Rosalinda and I arrived at Perino's on Wilshire Boulevard, I drove past the valet stand and self-parked. I was in a great mood. Rosa was both radiant and awestruck at the surroundings. She spied a handsome touring car occupying two spaces in the far corner of the lot and gushed, "What a gorgeous car."

"That's a Deusenberg," I said. "Twin-cowl Phaeton, 1933 or maybe '34. Could be Gary Cooper's. He drives one like that."

"Gary Cooper!" I thought Rosa might faint.

Perino's was crowded with prosperous-looking civilians and a few Army officers in uniform. Rosa looked terrific in a simple, high-necked sleeveless black dress accented at the bust by a hand-tooled silver pendant on a chain. She made a striking contrast to the Caucasian women in their padded-shoulder jackets.

Flaming chafing dishes were wheeled about, smelling of rich roast meats. Rosa looked around sheepishly at the peach-colored walls. Her fingertips caressed her napkin as if cloth ones were pretty rare.

"Wine steward," I said. "This is a special occasion." Definitely Alan Ladd; Pappy Yokum nowhere in sight (make that earshot). "We'd like one of the finest Bordeaux in your cellar."

"But certainly, sir. May I suggest a Chateau Pichon Lelande? Or perhaps the 1929 Chateau Lafite Rothschild? It was an exquisite year."

"You're right, the 1929 is startin' to come into its own. But I prefer something of proven age and character. Do you have the 1917?"

"The 1917 Chateau Lafite Rothschild?" The steward was astonished. I loved doing that. "Monsieur knows his wines. I shall have to check. If we do have it, it will not be, ah, inexpensive."

"Money's no object. This is a special evening. Fetch the 1917."

While this was going on, Rosa had sneaked a peek at the wine list. When the steward left, she gasped, "Ten dollars? Ten *dollars* for a bottle of wine! Jake, I have never seen a bottle of wine for more than eighty cents."

While Rosa was properly impressed, I was sure she was still subconsciously on guard, wondering what the devil she was doing with this crazy, free-spending newspaperman who'd just tumbled out of her sky the week before. A reporter who'd drop a sawbuck on a bottle of wine.

A bottle of 1917-vintage Chateau Lafite Rothschild was located, dusted off, and brought to our table. I told the wine steward it would have to breathe for fifteen minutes before he could pour it.

"Oh my goodness," Rosa gushed. "There's Cary Grant. Over there in the corner. I hope I'm not staring. Who's that he's with? Is that Barbara Hutton?"

"Believe it is. Hey, Rosa, I just remembered, Cary Grant drives a Deusenberg, too."

Meat courses were rolled out on huge chafing dishes. I devoured some prime rib and Rosa feasted on good veal. Later we danced at the Knickerbocker. It was nearly midnight when we reached Rosa's flat.

Tom got up and walked around the room. "Don't know why, but the fact that Dad was at Fort MacArthur at this very time bothers me."

"I know why," Cass said, putting the book aside. "You suspect this may have happened somehow." She gazed directly into his eyes. "You're afraid the old woman is right, and if she is, your dad could be in harm's way. By the way, remember that old photo of your father, that one in his uniform? I saw a painting that looked a whole lot like him. Young soldier in uniform, boarding a train. There was a strong resemblance. His eyes seemed to look right into mine. Gave me a real eerie feeling. Funny that should happen the same day you found this book, and got you to thinking about your dad in those days."

Tom nodded.

"Another thing," Cass went on, "this book rings true to you, just like it does to me. I felt as if I'd been transported to 1942, had been at the next table when your Uncle Jake upstaged the wine steward."

"Hmm . . . You know, I think Perino's may still be in business."

CHAPTER 17

WHEN THEY MET Cass's parents in the lobby, Tom asked, "Is there still a restaurant called Perino's? Somewhere along Wilshire."

"Why, yes," said Edith Nesbit. "It's a wonderful old place, but I hear it's going out of business soon."

"I'd love to go there before it does. My great uncle Jake ate there sometimes, back during World War II."

"You have a great uncle here in Los Angeles?"

"Did have. He died a long time ago."

"We didn't have definite plans," said Ty Nesbit, "so why don't I just call Perino's for reservations."

"Thanks, sir."

"Ty, the name is Ty."

"Right. Sorry . . . Ty"

Ty Nesbit went to a phone and dialed some numbers.

An hour later they were being seated in Perino's. As they slid into a booth, women on one side, men opposite, Tom said, "I wonder if this is where Jake and Rosa sat."

Edith Nesbit looked puzzled. "Who, dear?"

"Oh, just some people I know about."

Cass winked at him; he hoped her father hadn't seen it.

"Wasn't Jake the name of your great uncle?" Edith said.

"Right."

"And Rosa was your great aunt?"

"No, just someone Jake knew, in between marriages, I believe."

"Oh, the family gadabout, was he?"

Tom shrugged and smiled simultaneously. He glanced

around at the grand dowager of a restaurant, the silvery wheeled chafing dishes, an elderly wine steward. *Wonder if he—,* Tom thought. *No, he couldn't be.*

"Oh my goodness," Edith Nesbit said. "There's Clint Eastwood. Over there in the corner. I hope I'm not staring. Who's that he's with?"

"His wife, let's hope," said Ty Nesbit.

"I'm not sure he's married," Edith Nesbit replied.

A sense of déja vu washed over Tom. He wondered if Clint Eastwood had a Deusenberg in the parking lot.

Thursday, April 2, 10 p.m., Los Angeles.

As it turned out, I wouldn't have been able to reach my city editor that night. Gus Dobson took his son David to see a movie, "High Sierra," at the El Capitan Theater. Humphrey Bogart and Ida Lupino.

10 p.m., San Gabriel.

Mori Kawahara tied a sturdy knot, securing a piece of rope around a package of belongings. They included his small collection of lacquered ceramic birds, a textbook on the geology of the Western United States, Erskine Caldwell's *Tobacco Road*, and a book of short stories by Akutagawa in the original Japanese, for Mori could read *kanji*. He was glad the FBI hadn't found them.

Mori was tired. He'd just loaded a sofa and other furnishings in the bed of the old pickup. Even for a strong young man, loading the truck without help had been a struggle. Tomorrow, he'd try to sell off the furniture.

He glanced ruefully around the little San Gabriel house. His father had come to America in 1917, at the age of twenty-eight. He'd bought this house two years later, when his wife was pregnant with him, Mori. A year after that, he'd acquired acreage at Coyote Pass and begun growing tomatoes and cabbages on the hillsides above Montebello.

Their property had been registered in little Mori's name.

Under the Immigration Exclusion Act, native-born Japanese weren't permitted to own land, but their American-born offspring could.

Then, in 1930, Mori's mother had died after a short struggle with pneumonia.

In 1936 Mori had entered agricultural school at Cal Poly in San Dimas, graduating two years ago. During that time, cousin Kaz Okada had come to live with them while he earned his degree from USC. The young men had become close.

Mori stared at the package he'd just tied up. Cold black foreboding swept over him.

10:15 p.m., Burbank.

Lieutenant Colonel Dean Thompson, U.S. Army Reserve, had just endured a long meeting of the Burbank Civil Defense Board. Tired and frustrated, he pulled his 1939 DeSoto Airflow II into his driveway on Angeleno Avenue.

Stepping out into the chill spring night, he shambled up the front steps, beneath a large second-story balcony supported by pillars that extended over the porch.

Inside, his wife Emily greeted him with a cup of tea. "How was the meeting, Gunner?"

Thompson sagged into his favorite overstuffed chair. "I guess I just don't work well with civilians."

He sipped from his cup. "Good tea, Molly." He called her that because he thought his gray-haired wife resembled Molly McGee of the "Fibber McGee and Molly" radio program.

Gunner Thompson had served in the 129th Field Artillery in the First War under a captain named Harry Truman, who was now a U.S. senator. At the age of sixty, Thompson had been put in charge of personnel and instruction for the Burbank Civil Defense. As a gunnery expert, he was the perfect choice for the Civil Defense job, but it was tough going.

"Want to talk?" Emily said.

Thompson picked up his brier pipe from the end table, fussed with it, then put it back down. "The damn city manager and city engineer think they're such experts."

"Heavenly days, those two again?"

"Yes, and they wasted at least two hours tonight. I want to organize this like a front-line unit, the most capable people in the line positions, but they fight me at every step. They're packing it with a bunch of their political cronies. The program should be in place by now, ready to function. We're weeks behind schedule."

Thompson yawned, got up and walked to the telephone. "Got to call the leader of the nightly patrol."

Two minutes later he was back in his chair. "Fairly good out there, considering. Blackout's up to about ninety percent . . . Oh, thanks, hon," he said as his cup was refilled. "Say, you got your hair permed."

"So you finally noticed." She put a hand to her hair. "Like it?"

He didn't, really. "Very much, Moll. How was your day, hon?"

"Nice. I went to the Holy Thursday services at Forest Lawn after the hair dresser. Very inspiring."

"The hair dresser or the services?"

"Gunner!"

"Sorry, but you left yourself wide open . . . Me, I visited the local anti-aircraft battery. Nice boys there. Say, our new radar-controlled gun will arrive in three weeks."

11:30 p.m., Los Angeles.

I walked Rosa to the front door of her apartment building. My hormones were warming up in the bullpen.

"Thank you for a lovely evening, Jake," she said. I took her hand. It was stiff and icy cold. "It was wonderful—but I'm sorry, very sorry. I feel funny inside. Guilty. I was brought up differently than you, no? This lovemaking, it is not right." She kissed me quickly on the cheek— the cheek!—and said, "But I *am* glad you invented 'stop the presses.'" Then she rushed inside.

I reached after her. "Rosa, wait!" She was gone. I rattled the door. It had electric locking, wouldn't open. I kicked the concrete landing, glared at the traitorous door. Pounded on it with my fist. Kicked it for good measure.

I was one droopy man as I straggled back to the car, I can tell you that. She was crying in there—I'd bet on it—as she got ready for bed. Alone.

"How the hell do you figure?" I shouted in a black gloom driving home to Compton. "Women! Why can't they just be people? *Men* are people—women are some other species."

Would I ever learn? Why hadn't I just written the story? *Oh, I am fortune's fool*, I told myself. My high school Shakespeare again.

I'd screwed up every which way, made a mess of things with Rosa, and hadn't written my big story for tomorrow's paper. What a loser.

It was scary how tempted I was to ram the Chevy at full throttle against that bridge abutment up ahead. I must have actually thought about it. Geez, was I that depressed?

Zipping past the bridge and finding I was still alive, I asked myself why I took that bitch to dinner. No, I didn't mean that, Rosa was not a bitch, definitely not. I thought of Stella, and I thought of my first wife, the sexy but obtuse Dixie Freitas. But mostly I thought about Rosa, the beautiful young thing, Rosa. She was better than both of them put together. I was truly fond of her.

Now hold on a minute, I told myself. I could still write the story. So what if it was late? I'd worked all night many a time. I detoured over to Figueroa, drove to the paper and did what I should have done hours ago. The place was quiet as a crypt as I sat down and slipped two sheets of copy paper, with some carbon paper in between, in the typewriter. The words came fast and easy. The keys flew and the bell pinged out in rhythm to the old Underwood's racing carriage.

An ex-U.S. naval officer living in Los Angeles is a spy for the Japanese, the Herald-Express has learned. The man, who was cashiered from the Navy for stealing supplies, has been feeding the Japs sensitive information on area military bases and defense plants.

This newspaper believes the enemy, making use of the spy's information, plans to attack Los Angeles, and urges the War Department in the strongest terms to take this warning seriously.

This writer has learned that Chester Sickles, 49, a former Navy commander who lives in Ladera Heights, dispatches his information through a go-between in the Mexican consulate. His payments from the Japs also are funneled through this agent.

The words flowed on and on. I seldom had to look at my notes. I could smell the Pulitzer. Finished at last, I re-read it, penciled in some corrections, and stuck it under the paper guard on Dobson's typewriter. On top I put a note saying, "Gus, read this first, then call your buddy at the FBI."

CHAPTER 18

Thursday, April 2, 11:30 p.m., Inglewood.

"Will you be all right driving? I could make some coffee," Valerie Jean Riskin said to Corky Held as he laced his shoes.

Clad in a purple silk dressing gown, her hair a little tousled, Valerie waited till he finished buttoning his shirt, then put her arms around him. She gazed on his face. Their eyes were almost at the same level.

Earlier, Valerie and Corky had been to dinner at a little English place in Santa Monica and afterwards had strolled hand in hand on the pier. She always enjoyed the pier, with its fish odors and the surf crashing rhythmically against the pilings beneath their feet. It had a certain charm at night, and since Pearl Harbor the dark Pacific held a special sense of mystery and menace that was somehow exciting.

They shared a kiss. Then Valerie stuck an index finger to his chest and said, "Happy trails, bub. Have to punch that clock in less than eight hours."

"Sleep tight, tool designer. I'll call you tomorrow."

Valerie had decided to walk the few blocks to North American in the morning, as she did most Fridays.

Even though she'd just spent a nice enough evening with Corky, there was that nagging sense again that something was wrong. She had no real love for Corky and not much trust, either. Corky was probably lying when he said she was his one and only. She had no proof, only her instinct. He said it too often. Then a realization struck her like a thunderclap: she didn't care. She didn't feel angry or betrayed, she just didn't give a damn.

For the first time in months, she longed for her dead husband Jim, longed to have his arms around her.

Minutes later, brushing her teeth, Valerie stared at the woman in the mirror and said, "Well, well. Progress."

My emotions at that moment were a lot different. Doubts and guilt plagued me, and I knew where they were coming from. Normally when I felt blue I'd have a beer. I opened one and took a sip. It didn't help at all. I put the bottle down, thinking of the extravagant wine we'd had earlier.

What had I done to Rosa, a truly fine young woman? *Young*, that was the key. She'd gotten in over her head with this conniving old reporter and was smart enough to see it. Maybe it hadn't been a total lie this afternoon when I told her I loved her. I'd conned Rosa but then that terrific little woman had gone and got herself under my skin. Maybe I'd go to Confession at All Saints. (Well, no, probably not.) But I vowed that tomorrow I'd send her flowers, along with the kindest note I could conjure.

11:45 p.m., Los Angeles.

Two tiny slashes of light escaped the Ford's headlights through slits in their blackout shields. The coupe slowly passed the Home for the Aged and Evergreen Cemetery, turned, went two more blocks and stopped under a blackened streetlamp in Boyle Heights.

Chet Sickles switched the headlights off and killed the engine. He sat behind the steering wheel for a few seconds, his eyes adjusting to the darkness.

He opened the door, reached down and got hold of a department store mannequin lying on the passenger seat. It was only half a mannequin, just the torso, adorned by one of Sickles' shirts and a corduroy jacket. He propped it up behind the steering wheel, took off his felt hat, placed it on the dummy's head and adjusted the brim.

He closed the door, made a quick scan of the neighborhood, then walked half a block. A few random patches of light spilled out onto residential yards, but overall the L.A. blackout was fairly effective. With little competition from city lights, the stars were brilliant.

Sickles veered into the shadows and stopped in the blackness beneath an old oak tree. Silence cloaked the neighborhood. Minutes passed like days.

Then a shadowy form appeared up the block and advanced toward his car. The footfalls on the sidewalk were quick but inconspicuous.

Arturo Rivera had a .22 in his coat pocket. He didn't know why Sickles had called this midnight meeting. What was the *Yanqui* fool up to now?

He stopped at the car, put his hand on the door handle and tried to see inside. Someone was in there.

"What is it, Sickles? Why have you called me out here? What—"

He felt the wire cut into his neck.

Jesucristo, how could I—always so careful—have failed to anticipate something like this. To let Sickles take me from behind like—

Pain surged hot and deep. He flung his left hand to his throat, desperate to pull away the garrote. The wire was too tight. He got his fingers on it, but couldn't work them underneath. His body jerked savagely. Fire blazed in his neck. He clutched at Sickles' face. Felt his nails gouge deep into the cheek.

His other hand went to the revolver in his pocket. He couldn't grasp it and pull it out. His damned fingers wouldn't work. Vertigo pulsed in his head.

The garrote bit deeper. His vision turned blood red as if a thick veil had fallen over his eyes. Those eyes seemed to be exploding. His mind flashed on the beating his father had given him in Guadalajara when he'd got caught ditching school. Then on the first *señorita* he'd ever bedded. He'd been fifteen.

His strength ebbed. It was almost gone. She'd been thirteen, hadn't she? That first girl.

Sickles felt Rivera's convulsing slow to a shiver. He heard a gurgling sound, then a sharp crack. Rivera's neck collapsed, like a beer can crushed underfoot. The spasms stopped; the body went limp.

"Double-crossing little son of a bitch," Sickles muttered, "squeezing me outta my cut." He didn't relax his death grip on the garrote handles for another ten seconds.

Then he dragged the limp body to the rear of the car—"Time for you to take a powder, *amigo*"—opened the trunk and pushed it inside. He tossed in the garrote as well.

He clambered into the car too fast, bruised his shin on the running board. He shoved the half mannequin aside, fumbled for the keys. He'd started this Ford in the dark a thousand times but just now his brain took an extra second or two before ordering his foot to the ignition pedal. "Hurry up, hurry up."

His heart raced. The starter motor churned for three grinding seconds before the V-8 engine caught and roared. The car squealed away, Sickles downshifting to second like a drag racer. He drove three blocks before turning the headlights on.

In his lifetime, Chet Sickles had gone from minister's son to naval officer to spy, and from disillusionment, divorce, grand larceny and high treason . . . to murder.

"Thou art dust and to dust shalt thou return," he whispered, then repeated, "Double-crossing little son of a bitch."

It was midnight, and Thursday dissolved into Friday. Good Friday.

CHAPTER 19

The Aircraft Carriers.

Through the almost moonless night the four Japanese ships raced toward the coast at a speed of twenty knots.

Kaz Okada sat before a small mirror aboard carrier *Akagi* and raised a pair of scissors before his eyes, but his gaze went miles beyond. Several seconds passed, then he shook his head. The eyes refocused. He reached up above his right ear and cut off a small tuft of his thick black hair.

Before the attack on Pearl Harbor, he had made out a will and placed it in a small box along with some personal belongings, fingernail clippings and a few locks of hair. If Okada were killed and his body lost, these would be sent to his family and used in the funeral. Now he felt compelled to add another lock of hair.

He closed the box and spent a few minutes in meditation. Then, seating himself at a small steel desk, he got out brush and paper, and wrote a *haiku*:

> "I wonder how far
> "The wanderings of fate will carry me
> "In the fresh morning breeze."

Okada placed the verse in a drawer next to the box of personal effects and slipped into his flight gear.

He had risen a half-hour before his roommates, who'd scrambled out of their bunks and hammocks at four a.m. They ate a breakfast of rice, fish, *misoshiru* (beancake soup), pickled vegetables and tea. Ever since his college days at USC, he much preferred bacon and eggs, but he ate without complaint alongside his comrades.

After they received their final briefings in the ready room, Kaz Okada took a look at the ship's plan for the day:

0400 - Call Air Department and Squadrons
0445 - Early Breakfast for Air Department Officers
0500 - Call Plane Handling Crews
0520 - Call All Hands
A few lines down:
0600 - Launch Attack Flight

Okada stopped. After the long weeks of preparation, this was the day. Launch Attack Flight! His eyes lingered on those words for several seconds. Then they skipped down to the bottom.

0845 - Recover Attack Flight Planes
Would he be alive to carry out that order?

The ships had reached a point 150 nautical miles off California, almost due west of Redondo Beach. They were as far southwest of the Channel Islands as northwest of Catalina Island. Striking distance.

Akagi's speakers squawked flight quarters.

Minutes later, the eastern sky was melting from black to purple as Okada climbed into his plane. The sea was fairly calm and the pitch and roll of the decks was acceptable for air operations.

A flight-deck hand climbed on his wing, clasped his hand and wished him "Good fortune." Okada smiled grimly, slid the canopy shut, and turned to the instrument panel in front of him.

The Target.

Let me tell you about this fairytale land, this Southern California the Japanese were about to descend upon that Good Friday morning. Most Americans only glimpsed it from picture postcards or movie shows, and imagined there were film stars on every corner. Orange and lemon groves and large ranches sprawled across valleys and foothills. The railroads' iron legs ran past Spanish Colonial-style stations under red tile roofs with names like San Juan Capistrano, Azusa, Ventura, Del Mar.

The outward look of permanence and stability was a falsehood. A vast migration from the East was in motion and was starting to generate huge physical and social change.

On a recent drive to the Army fighter base at Ontario, I was shocked to see how fast the citrus groves had been sliced up for housing tracts and military bases. A whole mountain was shaved away by construction companies to make rock and gravel. Jackrabbits and coyotes were being chased from the hills and valleys to make room for people and their houses, schools and stores. The clamor of steam shovel, bulldozer, hammer and saw filled the air. Developers bent on creating a South Sea island setting had been digging up palm trees around the world and transplanting them—until Pearl Harbor. For the duration, all construction was now focused on the military.

On cold winter mornings in the inland valleys the sky would be smoky dark from smudge pots lighted in the groves at night to keep the oranges from freezing. Combining smoke and fog, locals coined the word "smog." It wasn't till later that its meaning came to include the exhaust from cars and smokestacks.

Gas-rationing stickers had just started to appear on windshields. I had an exemption, being a military writer. Lucky me.

I was loyal to my neighborhood grocer, Ollie, but his business was getting hurt by something new called the supermarket. They even sell toothpaste and aspirin; you didn't have to go to the drug store for that any more.

At Ollie's store the other day, a quart of Lucerne milk cost me thirteen cents and my pound of Hills Brothers Coffee was a quarter. (I could've got it for twenty-one cents at the Piggly Wiggly.) Ollie was listening to "Captain Midnight" on KHJ. It was a show for kids, but Ollie said it was his favorite serial. Me, I was partial to "Jack Armstrong, the All-American Boy."

San Diego and Long Beach were big naval centers, thus prime targets. Battleships and heavy cruisers were based in Long Beach, which had become a sea of shipyards.

San Diego bristled with destroyer, submarine and seaplane bases, along with huge training camps. The war had transformed San Diego into a bustling city of 200,000. Servicemen crowded its streets and its railroad station; hotels and apartments were jammed. New bases and aircraft plants sprang into being. Older bases were expanded.

During the night, San Diego police booked a Marine Corps two-star general, who later would become a hero in the Pacific, for felony hit-and-run drunk driving. He'd run down a sailor at Broadway and Pacific Highway, shattering both his legs. He'd driven off but the cops stopped him a few blocks away. The *San Diego Union*'s police reporter told me about it. The cops and Marines tried to hush it up, but the reporter wouldn't have it. Good man.

That general would never be a hero to me, no matter how many islands he took.

But I'm getting ahead of myself. The night was almost over. A thin overcast lay along the coast. There had been a slice of moon, but it had been down for hours. The sun would rise over this fairytale land at 6:39.

The Aircraft Carriers.

Kaga turned her old hull into the wind. Kaga's planes had the farthest to go—to San Diego—so they were first to depart. The attack flag was run up her mast. Chocks were pulled from the planes' wheels and one by one they growled down the flight deck and clawed into the murky sky. The Nakajima torpedo planes went first, followed by the dive bombers, the horizontal bombers, and last, the Zero fighters.

The Takeoff.

On *Akagi's* flight deck, Kaz Okada, minus a small lock of hair, cranked the engine of his Aichi dive bomber. It coughed to life, throbbing with sound and energy. He turned and glanced behind him at his radioman and gunner, Kai Iguchi, who was checking the belt feed of his machine gun.

Okada was fourth in line. The takeoffs of the first three planes seemed to take forever, but actually less than two minutes. His turn. The Kinsei engine, warm now, purred smoothly. Intent on the flagman ahead of him, Okada revved up the RPMs and snapped his goggles down over his eyes.

The signalman had been twirling the flag above his head in circles—now he flung it downward. Okada released the brake, pushed the throttle forward. The plane lunged ahead, crossing the huge red sun painted on the rough planks. The slab end of the deck grew enormously, beyond it, a gray nothingness. Just before reaching that void, he pulled back on the stick. He was up. He climbed fast, raising his flaps and turning left.

Following the faint blue lights on their tails, Okada caught up with the other planes in his squadron, took the lead position, and brought them to a heading of zero-eight-five.

Takeoffs and landings were dangerous. Flying in formation wasn't, not for experienced pilots like these. The minutes rolled by and Okada looked down at the sea a mile and a half beneath him. It was a deep blue in the gathering light, almost as dark as a navy uniform, speckled with dots of white where swells crested and fell. He sensed a splendor in the combination of sky, sea and airplane. He was in the company of the gods.

He sighted San Nicolas Island to the south and knew he had the squadron precisely on course, slightly north of due east. He hoped the barren lump of island didn't have radar.

He thought about his cousin Mori and was glad San Gabriel was miles from their target. He wondered if he would ever visit the United States peaceably again.

Perhaps this raid would convince the Americans to sue for peace, so they and the British could get on with their white man's war against Germany, leaving Japan free to assume its proper role of leadership in the Far East.

His adrenaline was pumping. The Rising Sun would blind the Americans with its brilliance on this morning, eh? "*Taiyo ha nishi ka ra no bori*," he shouted to Iguchi. Sunrise in the west.

Okada's friend, Squadron Leader Tatsu Matsumoto, was in position on *Soryu's* flight deck. The fourteen pistons of his Sakae radial engine clamored. Vibrations quivered the "22" stenciled on the rudder in the Zero's tail. The whole plane throbbed, a colt eager to run.

Because they were faster and had greater range than the

dive bombers and torpedo bombers, the Zeros took off last.

Matsumoto adjusted his goggles, tugged at the orange scarf around his neck, the one his wife had given him, and glanced at his instrument panel to check the RPMs. He fingered the white cloth *hakimaki* bearing the red Japanese insignia, an unconscious ritual. The headband circled his flight cap just above the goggles. Matsumoto rubbed the right sleeve of his badly frayed leather flight jacket, another old habit.

Minutes before, he'd been thinking about his wife and son. He hadn't seen them since November, before Pearl Harbor. He hoped to get some leave after this mission. He longed to go kite-flying with his son along the Sea of Japan beaches, and to fish again off the rocks.

Now, though, he was all concentration. The plane ahead of him had just lurched into the sky. It was his turn.

Soon he was leading his squadron toward the coast. He listened to the hum of the engine. The air-speed indicator danced just above the 200 mile-an-hour line. He smiled grimly. Target: Long Beach.

CHAPTER 20

Good Friday, 5:50 a.m. Los Angeles.

Gus Dobson parked in a lot at Pico and Figueroa. He walked along Pico, past the trolley barns of the "LARy," the Los Angeles Railway, and turned up Trenton.

Across the street from the gray stone and brick *Herald-Express* building, he went into a joint called Moran's and bought a paper cup of takeout coffee—black, no sugar—for a nickel. His morning ritual.

Coming back out, the city editor hesitated and looked around, drinking in the quiet. He'd worked here for years. The rough and lusty neighborhood was home.

His gaze took in the Okie bars along Trenton. Country music had blared from their jukeboxes most of the night but now they were closed and still. There was the Continental, where thieves, ex-cons and newspapermen drank and shot pool with white-shirt guys from Bekins Van & Storage in the afternoon. He glanced up at the *Herald-Express* and the little penthouse that had been added above the third floor for the Associated Press.

Inside, the graveyard shift cleaning woman was dusting Dobson's office. A black fabric cover usually encased his Remington typewriter. This morning it didn't. Pages of copy tucked under the typewriter's paper guard started with, "An ex-U.S. naval officer living in Los Angeles is a spy . . ." A note paperclipped on top read, "Read this first." The woman paid no attention. She emptied an ash tray, then found the cloth hood and put it back in place over the typewriter.

Coffee in hand, Dobson crossed the street and went in. It was almost six. The early crew had already started laying out the first edition. There were three full editions and five replates, meaning that eight variations of the day's paper would be printed before he'd leave in the afternoon.

He glanced at his desk, where nothing caught his eye, and called in the night ACE (assistant city editor), who'd been there for hours, and the day ACE, who'd just arrived. They began going over the list of stories. Looked like a slow news day. Some Councilman thought Mines Field out on the coast near Inglewood should replace Glendale as L.A.'s main airport after the war . . . To save fabric, the War Production Board was banning cuffs on men's pants. Dobson laughed at that.

A new war contract for North American . . . From the police beat: a Mexican official was found dead on the steps of the consulate. Neck crushed, no suspects.

Dobson paused. "On the front steps?"

"Yep," said the night man. "Sittin' there, propped up like he was waitin' for the place to open. But stiff as my cock on a good night."

"Some sick bird out there's got a weird sense of humor," Dobson said, but then something clicked in the back of his mind. "Mexican consulate, huh? Murdered. Let's look into that. Get his name and call it down to Weaver. Wonder if Jake's thing . . ." He let the sentence hang and went back to the list.

More people had moved into L.A. in March than any single month in history . . . There'd been a minor earthquake during the night. "Let's check that out," Dobson said. "Call Caltech. Find out where it was centered. Check on damage. Earthquake story could be a good change of pace."

The rest of the list was nothing. Brooklyn Avenue might be renamed MacArthur Boulevard to honor the general . . . The stock exchanges would be closed for Good Friday.

Dobson glanced at the agate fillers that would run between stories:

One leak can sink a ship. Don't talk.

Let's can Japan.

That friendly chap may tell a Jap.

A slip of the lip may give a spy a tip.

He needed a good story. Hearst papers always scrounged for a sensational headline, trying to beat the pants off their rivals on the afternoon streets.

Sitting around the rim of a desk shaped like a horseshoe, copyreaders penciled corrections and wrote headlines for stories that had been hammered out by reporters or produced by wire-service teletype machines. The sleeves of their white shirts were rolled up, their ties loosened at the necks.

Dobson was dragging on a cigarette and telling a joke to a copyboy.

Palos Verdes.

As the boy laughed, a Watanabe float plane sputtered toward the Palos Verdes Peninsula, flying low over the water. The Japanese pilot was shocked to see a lighthouse beacon flashing and red aviation lights shining brightly on a radio tower. How could a country at war be so lazy as to leave harbor lights on? he thought contemptuously.

The biplane with two large pontoons beneath its wings had been catapulted from the deck of I-27, a large *Kaigun*-type submarine. Japanese subs had been patrolling the U.S. Pacific Coast for four months.

He pulled the stick back as he approached the fat peninsula that shields the L.A. and Long Beach harbors. He'd come in low to avoid radar but he needed altitude to scout the harbor. He began to climb above Portuguese Bend and Point Fermin.

One of the radial engine's nine pistons was misfiring. The pilot knew his engine, had heard its ratty throbbing and guessed the cause of the problem: a worn piston ring, drowning the sparkplug in oil. There was nothing to do for it. His duty was to report on the situation in the harbor.

The little plane climbed. The sputter increased. The high ridge loomed up fast and the pilot suddenly realized he was in serious trouble. He pulled back harder on the stick, raising the elevators.

The engine coughed more. He wouldn't clear the hill. Quick. Reverse course. He kicked all the right rudder he could and the plane banked a hard fifty degrees to the right. Then the engine quit altogether. He tried to steepen the turn, but the plane stalled.

The nose fell. He was out of options. Unable to clear the ridge and without power to complete his turn and get back out to sea, he was a dead man. He silently apologized to the Emperor for his failure, then said a prayer asking his ancestors to make a place for him in the afterworld. *Ima kara go-senzo-sama no moto mairimasu.*

The falling plane slipped past the Point Fermin Lighthouse, then slammed into the first few feet of the San Pedro Bay breakwater, exploding into flames.

The orange blaze was visible all over the harbor. A fireboat and a Coast Guard cutter soon were on the scene. The firemen had been throwing streams of saltwater on the plane for two minutes before one of them noticed the faint Japanese "meatball" insignia on a charred wing.

Compton.

Twenty minutes later, I was awakened by the call from the public affairs guy, Deke Rickey. I'd been asleep only four hours, after my night out with Rosa. I reached for the switch on the bedside lamp, knocked over the alarm clock, cussed, rubbed sleep from my eyes.

This was going to be a big day. First, I'd go to Dobson to see what else he might need for the Chet Sickles story. The phone rang three times before I could answer. I knocked it around a bit, finally got the right end to my mouth. "Yeah?"

"Jake, it's Rickey."

"What's up, Deke? My God, man, what time is it?"

"Listen, Jake, a Japanese plane just crashed on the breakwater. Things are pretty hot around here."

"What? Jap plane. You sure? This better not be another 'Battle of Los Angeles.'"

"Affirmative, Jake. I can see it burning from here. There's no doubt."

"Thanks, Deke, you're a pal. You told anybody else?"

"Negative, you're the first, but I gotta call the others right away."

I was wide awake now. "Yeah, I know. What kinda plane

was it?"

"Scout plane of some kind. Amphibious biplane."

"Where the hell'd it come from?"

"A sub, we think."

"A sub, Deke? Can Jap subs carry planes like that?"

"Their big fleet subs can. The planes' wings are removable."

"On the breakwater? Where, exactly?"

"San Pedro side. Near the lighthouse."

"Pilot killed?"

"Must've been, Jake. It's still burning. We've got fireboats out there now."

"The Japs ain't scoutin' the harbor just for practice. Whadda ya make of it?"

"We don't know. Maybe some kind of sub attack was planned. This crash might have screwed it up. We're closing the submarine nets now, I think. I gotta go. Remember, you got it first."

"Thanks kindly, Deke. See you soon."

I put down the phone for a split second, long enough to disconnect, then dialed the city desk.

"Gus," I told Dobson. "Jake. Jap plane just crashed in the harbor. Some kinda scout plane. Pilot's dead. I'm gonna get right down there. Looks like some subs may be off the coast. I'll call you back."

"Let me know soon as you get anything else," Dobson blurted.

"Gus, about my spy story. Did you—." I was talking to a dial tone. But I was sure he'd read it. I dressed in record time and drove south on Atlantic, a hell of a lot faster than usual.

Los Angeles.

"Hot damn," Dobson called to the news editor. "We got a story! Jap plane down in the harbor." He turned to the picture editor and snapped, "Get a couple of photogs down there fast."

Next, he called over two general assignment reporters, one of whom had been phoning mortuaries for obit notes. "Go straight to Terminal Island. Get all you can on this. Use your police passes. They give you any shit, tell Weaver. He's in charge. He'll already be there. Quote Navy officers, witnesses, Coast Guard, cops, Army. Find out what happened and what they think will happen next. Call in every few minutes. Don't write anything; we'll put it together here at rewrite. Give us all the dope you can. Now haul ass. Do a job for us." It was a pep talk Knute Rockne could appreciate.

San Diego.

A similar biplane circled over San Diego Bay, the pilot flying low because of an overcast. The water was calm and flat in Spanish Bight, a shallow inlet that separated the North Island air base from the village of Coronado. There was no traffic on the causeway between the base and the village, but the rotating beacon atop Building Eight was shooting out its alternating shafts of green and white brilliance.

The only other signs of life were an old ferry chugging across the water to Coronado, and the flickering of welders' torches at the Navy repair yard.

A sailor pulling watch on the quay at North Island heard the engine's drone. He thought nothing of it. Aircraft noise was commonplace.

In his quarters, the commanding officer, Captain Ernest Gunther, hadn't slept well. He was anxious about meeting an order for aircraft tailhooks, urgently needed in the Pacific.

Two young sailors watching a new radarscope saw the Watanabe as a small blip practically in the center of their screen. One of them stepped outside for a visual sighting.

"Civilian aircraft," he said. "These private jockeys oughta know better'n to fly over the harbor with a war on."

The Japanese pilot searched for warships and planes. One old four-stack destroyer was tied up at a base south of town, and two freighters were berthed at North Island. A submarine tender lay at anchor, subs lined up alongside like baby ducklings. A transport was tied up at Broadway Pier. No battleships or aircraft carriers. Several Army P-38's and Navy Wildcats were parked beside North Island's asphalt runway. Seven or eight cable-dangling barrage balloons looked like fat silver sausages. They'd have to be shot down.

He turned, crossed Point Loma, headed out to sea, and sent his report by coded radio message. It was the first use of radio by anyone associated with *Operation Seifuu* in two weeks.

Fighters would have to come in, he reported, splash the barrage balloons and attack the planes at North Island. Dive bombers, coming in at high altitude, could hit the Consolidated plant and the destroyer base simultaneously with the fighter strike at North Island.

While he was sending his report, word reached North Island that a Japanese plane had crashed in the L.A. harbor. All bases in San Diego were alerted. Within a few minutes three Catalina amphibians took off from the water and two Wildcat fighters were sent up from North Island.

One of the Wildcats was flown by Lieutenant Clovis Hill, a replacement pilot chomping at the bit for duty in the Pacific with the *Enterprise* or *Yorktown*.

Ordered to search offshore, Hill climbed above Point Loma. He skimmed over the military cemetery, camouflaged Army buildings and scattered gun batteries before reaching the ocean. At 3,500 feet, he flew into a chain of puffy clouds.

He broke out of them and suddenly there in the pink-gray light was the Japanese biplane, straggling out to sea at about ninety knots. He clearly saw the red circles on the fabric-covered wings. This would be too easy, he thought.

Hill dived from above and behind the fragile craft and squeezed the fire button for his .50-caliber machine guns. The enemy surprised him with a tight climbing turn to the right. The Wildcat's greater speed carried him past the biplane, which snap-rolled and plunged away, coming out of the dive just above the waves.

The agility of the ponderous-looking craft with its twin floats amazed Hill. He could dance all around it, but getting in a clean shot was not so easy.

He couldn't dive on the plane now—it was too low—so he turned back and tried a low-level attack from the side. But the enemy ducked away with a tight turn, making good use of his short turning radius.

Hill was frustrated. The Jap was fighting for his life and doing a damn good job of it.

On his third pass, Hill was still too fast and overshot his jitterbugging quarry. He made a wide turn and approached yet again. He throttled well back and lowered his flaps. His plane slowed to little more than stall speed. This time he got the enemy in his gunsights long enough to hammer home a three-second burst.

Flames blossomed and the biplane tumbled into the sea. It made one terrifying bounce and shattered into pieces.

Hill circled and took a long look at the floating debris. He'd just killed a man who'd been one hell of a flier. He'd been preparing himself for months to kill Japanese. Where was the elation?

Finally, he pressed his radio transmit button. "Green Five to Green Base. Green Five to Green Base. Made contact with bandit. Destroyed same. Position, five miles west-northwest of Point Loma. I say again, Green Five has splashed enemy patrol plane. Do you read?"

They read. A warning was sounded to bases up and down the Coast. *Two Japanese planes confirmed destroyed. All bases on first stage alert.*

But at two of the bases the radio shack was unmanned. At a third, the radio operator was in a card game.

Inglewood.

Heading down Freeman Boulevard toward North American Aviation, Valerie Jean Riskin was lighthearted, almost skipping. The sky was blue, the early morning shadows long and distinct across the sidewalks. It would be a good day.

A brisk, chilly breeze toyed with the raven locks of her hair and swirled the loose skirt of her beige suit.

Seated beside Tom in their hotel room, Cass put a

hand to her short auburn hair. "Did you feel that?" she said, wide-eyed.

"That cool breeze? Yeah. Weird. Wonder if there was a sudden surge in the air conditioning for some reason."

"Tom, the AC's not on."

Ahead of Valerie, two girls and a boy laughed and skipped along on their way to school, jumping over cracks in the sidewalk. Their cheery voices triggered a memory. Valerie's thoughts slid from the romantic evening she'd spent with Corky Held to an incident that occurred in Illinois twenty years before.

She had been playing with her younger sister and brothers in the long twilight of an early July evening. She'd looked away for a moment and then saw stars as a baseball bat cracked across her head. She was certain her brother had hit her deliberately and, when her head cleared, she punched him in the face. He ran crying into the white frame house, shrieking that she was a monster, that the bat had whacked her accidentally.

Valerie had never believed that until this instant. For some reason, marching down a street in California on an airy April morning, she accepted at last that her kid brother had told the truth. Of course it was an accident.

She felt the spot on her head where the lump had been so many years ago and decided to write her brother in a day or so.

She smiled broadly as she passed a small girl in a green pinafore, her hair braided in twin pigtails. The girl was skipping and singing, "Mairzy doats and dozy doats and little lamzy divy . . . ."

Lieutenant Kaz Okada was leading a flight of dive bombers straight toward them.

The Brentwood Hills.

Pfc. Bob Divine's face reflected yellowish-green in the glow from his radarscope. He studied the screen just as he had one night six weeks ago, before the Battle of Los Angeles. That night a blip appeared, which he reported, and soon the "battle" was on. The bandit turned out to be a runaway weather balloon and Divine caught some real hell after thousands of anti-aircraft rounds had been fired into an empty sky.

"Holy cow, bogeys again. Lots of 'em. More than last time. Hell of a lot more. These gotta be planes." With each sweep, the blips were slightly closer to the center of the screen.

"Mother of God, why me? Maynard, come over here and look at this," he shouted to a sleepy corporal half-coiled in a chair with an open copy of *Collier's* magazine covering his face.

CHAPTER 21

Inglewood and El Segundo.

Okada's D3A and the other dive bombers crossed Dockweiler Beach just west of Mines Field at 8,000 feet. It was 7:06 a.m.

Wild oats, still wintergreen, swayed in the morning breeze on both sides of the asphalt runways and on the hills to the south. Scattered among them, California poppies, just budding out in orange bloom, turned the seaside fields into blankets of color.

Okada gave them only a glance. His eyes focused on the rooftops of the North American plant, just beyond the runway, covered with camouflage netting. It was good camouflage but he knew exactly what lay beneath it.

The mission of the *Akagi* planes was to attack North American and Douglas, just to the south. When their thousand-pound bombs were gone, they would swing south and fire their cannon and machine guns into Standard Oil's refinery at El Segundo.

Okada led his string of planes straight over Mines Field. To the south of the runway stood a small, Spanish-arched terminal building that looked like a miniature Catholic mission. He reflected that he'd once been inside that building. The irony of the moment hit him. His stomach fluttered. What a paradox that he should be leading these bright young peddlers of death over a city he knew well and toward which he bore no malice.

A single plane climbed to contest them. Okada knew the experienced Zero pilots, hovering protectively, would deal with it. A few black bursts of anti-aircraft fire from the El Segundo Army barracks began to smudge the sky.

Dead ahead lay North American, its long rows of buildings

hidden beneath netting painted in a pattern of dappled browns and greens to resemble open countryside. A couple of guns fired through openings in the netting.

In Tool Design, Valerie Riskin had been on the job only a few minutes. She was working on a tool to be used in producing a modified gun turret for the H model of the B-25 bomber. Next to her sat Warner Dixon, a thirty-four-year-old draftsman.

Valerie unrolled a sheet of vellum and adjusted the arm of her drafting machine. At her fingertips lay a T-square, plastic triangles, a pink eraser and a small book of trigonometry tables. She placed a fresh cup of coffee next to the drawing table.

"Did you have a nice evening?" she asked Dixon as she reached for her slide rule.

"Yes, pretty nice. We took a drive with the kids before dark. Can't wait till the days get longer. With the blackouts, I like to get the car in before dark. Then we had a little supper and listened to the radio. Did you hear 'Ellery Queen?' It was really good."

Valerie smiled. "No, not last night." She'd been testing bedsprings with Corky Held.

"It was quite a plot. The wife had it figured out, but not me. Her mind's more devious than mine. If she ever decides to do me in, she'll have it planned out so well they'll never be able to hang it on her." Dixon laughed at his little joke.

"How about you? What did you do last night?" Dixon was looking down and drawing while talking.

"Oh, not much. Had a quiet evening. We went down to the Santa Monica—"

Air raid sirens whined. She and Dixon stared at each other. What was this, a drill?

She heard the drone of airplane engines. "What!" she cried. The roar grew louder and louder and mixed with the urgent clamor of the sirens.

Okada rolled his plane over on its back and dived. With a glance over his shoulder, he saw the others following him down in precise formation. They dived at five-second intervals, their technique perfected in hours of training and honed at Pearl Harbor and half a dozen other places in the Pacific.

The bomber hurtled earthward, its air-speed indicator quivering back and forth well beyond the 300 mark. The altimeter spun madly counterclockwise. G-forces pressed against him but still he called back through his voice tube, telling gunner Kai Iguchi to have his camera ready. He wanted good pictures of the attack. At eight-hundred feet he squeezed the bomb release. A small displacing gear on the bottom of the plane freed the missile. The thousand-pound bomb plunged downward. With such a straight, steep dive, there was no missing the target.

A company official burst into Tool Design and shouted above the din: "Air raid! Take cover! Air—"

An explosion threw him halfway across the room. Terror froze Valerie Riskin. Fluorescent tubes crashed down from the ceiling along with chunks of plaster and jagged shards of glass from the skylights.

Okada's head pulsed with blood rush. His bomb had been aimed perfectly. He glanced back, caught a flash glimpse of the fountain of debris he'd created. Several yards behind him, the second plane released its bomb. So did the third. Okada flattened out at three-hundred feet and began a steep left-turn climb. The engine screamed.

Valerie's first ridiculous thought—had broken glass got into her coffee?—vanished in a fraction of a second. A ragged piece of wood glanced off her head and tossed her to the floor like a rag doll. A thousand hornets buzzed in her ears; hot pain filled her head. She looked around, dazed. Blood trickled down her right arm.

Tremendous, shuddering concussions jolted the buildings of North American, one after another. Explosions ripped through ceilings and walls. Chunks of sawtooth-angled roofing twisted and fell. Air-raid sirens had been screaming for several minutes, but few workers made it out of the plant.

Flaming pieces of roof slammed on unfinished B-25 Mitchell bombers on the assembly lines. Cranes and scaffolds toppled like toys.

More explosions. One, two, three. Fifteen of the sixteen large bombs from Okada's planes detonated in the factory. Six, seven, eight. Eleven of them hit the production building and four struck Engineering and Tooling next door to Valerie Riskin.

As the planes circled away to the left, another flight of Aichis bombed the fabrication and sub-assembly area. Machinists and fabricators scrambled out of the burning building in panic. The camouflage net became a flaming tatters.

A lone fighter plane, a P-39 Airacobra from the 4th Interceptor Command, took off from Mines Field and was quickly gunned down by a Zero. It crashed pathetically on a dune at the beach.

A flight of six P-40 fighters from the Army's training base at Glendale raced in from the north, coming in over Ladera Heights. The Zeros spotted them and jumped the formation above Lincoln Boulevard. The green American pilots found themselves over-matched and outnumbered against the Japanese veterans in their fast, nimble Zeros.

Ladera Heights.

In the hills to the north, Chet Sickles gazed out blankly from his apartment window. Smoke rose black and ugly from Mines Field. The twisting, turning, diving warplanes, though tiny in the distance, were easily visible. He watched without expression. Sickles knew what was happening but something inside him wouldn't accept it.

Inglewood.

One American P-40 survived the dogfighting north of the field and reached Okada's squadron as it angled back to the west. Okada saw it, coming in low at five o'clock. He caught a brief flash of the American in his gunsights. He pressed the fire button for his .50-caliber machine guns. Six or seven holes crept up the American's right wing. Okada kicked the rudder hard to the right.

The P-40 blurred past underneath. Before it could turn for another pass, two Zeros jumped it.

Okada swung to the left and pulled back on the stick to climb. Feeling flush with success, his ambivalence forgotten, he led his planes south to the Standard Oil refinery.

When he sighted the rows of steel chimneys belching smoke and tongues of yellow flame spitting from the burn-off stacks, he knew the refinery was in operation. There hadn't been time to shut it down. It reminded him of the Dutch Shell refineries he'd attacked on Sumatra in February.

Los Angeles.

A reporter answered a phone in the *Herald-Express* city room. A caller screamed, "The Japs! The Japs are bombing North American!"

"What? Who the hell is this?"

"Bombs are going off! I'm looking at Jap planes."

Distinct sounds of explosions spurted through the phone line.

"Hey, Mr. Dobson!" the reporter cried.

Inglewood.

Tool Design occupied the second floor of the Engineering and Tooling building. A lunchroom sat directly below. Okada's bomb tore through the skylight above Tool Design, plunged on through the floor, and detonated in the cafeteria. Its explosion wiped out the lunchroom and caved in part of the floor beneath the tool designers.

What the hell had happened? Valerie Riskin didn't know. The stench of smoke and cordite filled the long room. It took her a moment to realize she was half-covered by something heavy and gooey. Another moment to realize it was part of Warner Dixon. Most of the blood on her arm was his. *Holy God*! Nausea choked her. She almost passed out. She'd seen animals slaughtered on the farm in Illinois, but this was a whole different thing. She crawled a few feet and shook off most of the goo, her ears buzzing like a power saw.

She saw a huge hole had been ripped out of the roof. Through it, she made out planes flashing in silhouette against the morning sky. She was only partly aware of other explosions in the plant.

Her head began to clear. "Ow," she whimpered. She felt a lump on her head, saw a shallow gash in her arm. Her hands were cut by broken glass. She pulled herself to her feet and decided she was pretty much okay, considering, but that angry buzz-saw still whined in her ears.

Warner Dixon had been right beside her. *Dear God, why was he killed and not me? Well, I haven't time to feel sorry for myself—or him. These guys need help.*

Though limping, she pulled at dazed, coughing men, and helped them to their feet. Several had serious lacerations. Blood spurted shockingly far from the worst of them. Two men had trouble breathing; maybe they'd suffered heart attacks. Others were dead, but there was no time to be horrified.

She began to shout orders.

"Joe, give me a hand with Ralph here. Chuck, lift that table off these fellas. C.J., check if the stairs can be used. Clint, see if you can get to the nurse's office. Get some first-aid kits, and some gauze or towels, something to make pressure bandages."

Their looks of surprise faded. They jumped at her commands.

North American was not out of the woods. The dive bombers were gone but now six Zeros swooped over, having finished with the American fighters. Each Zero unleashed the 132-pound bomb it carried.

When the concussions subsided, Valerie pulled herself out of a crouch, shook her clenched fist at the heavens—"You bastards"—and resumed helping her battered companions. Dust and bits of glass littered her black hair. Half the wall was now blown away; she could see across the littered parking lot. Flames leaped from blackened cars. The camouflage netting was nothing but shreds of burnt fabric.

Washington, D.C.

The man's face was one of the best known in the world. The jaunty smile the public saw so often was nowhere to be seen in this private meeting. The large cheeks sagged with age and the eyes were hollow, tired, rimmed with dark circles.

He tapped a cigarette into a holder, clamped it in his teeth and said something to Secretary of War Henry Stimson. They'd been discussing the shipment of bombers to Britain. Stimson unrolled a map of the Atlantic on the Oval Office desk.

The secretary buzzed from the outer office. The President flipped a toggle on the speaker box and continued to gaze at the reports and maps spread before him.

"Grace, I asked you not to interrupt—"

"Mr. President, the Japanese are bombing the West Coast."

"Merciful God, are you sure? There's no mistake?"

"Afraid not, sir."

His eyes closed. His jaw slackened its grip on the cigarette holder. His strong shoulders and chest sagged.

"All right, my dear. Thank you. Get General DeWitt on the line as quickly as you can . . . Henry, forget about B-24s for England."

El Segundo.

Okada's dive bombers had worked over North American and Douglas. Now they and the Zeros were strafing tank farms at the Standard Oil refinery. Immense blazes broke out.

A P-40 materialized and suddenly shot up one of Okada's planes. From the corner of his eye, he saw it gush into a ball of flame. He grimaced—the two crewmen had been friends of his.

He made a pass at a large oil tank, his wing guns flashing. Behind him, Kai Iguchi ripped into it with his .50-caliber rear gun. Ugly yellow fires raged. Swirling columns of smoke clawed at the sky.

Just about out of ammunition now and starting to run low on

fuel, Okada knew his planes had been over the target long enough. They'd done an excellent job and he was proud.

He made a quick calculation. Seven air miles in, seven out. Six to eight minutes' flying time. He glanced at the fuel gauge. Should be enough. Just.

"Take over the squadron and lead it back to the carrier," he radioed his wingman. "I will be along in a few minutes." He told the surprised Iguchi they would go looking for a power plant and give it some machine gun fire.

Okada flew northeast, skimming low over Manchester Avenue and Hyde Park. A couple of minutes later he was over Vermont Avenue. They'd seen no power plants, nor had he been looking for one.

"Get the camera ready, Iguchi-san," he called to the gunner. "I want to get some pictures over here."

The plane sailed over the huge Memorial Coliseum, the Museum of Science & Industry, then the University of Southern California. He banked low, skimmed over Bovard Hall and the columns of Old College, wagged his wings. Down below, a tiny man ran for cover.

Iguchi snapped several pictures. Okada took a long look. There was the building in which he'd gotten a D in calculus. Riddle it with .50 caliber, an inner voice said. Instead, he took a last glance, then turned and headed for the coast.

"Iguchi-san, say nothing about what we've just done." Okada glanced at the class ring on his right hand, the hand that had released a thousand-pound bomb that morning.

The Aichis and Zeros scored forty-nine bomb hits on the North American plant, destroying twenty-six B-25s and killing fifty-nine workers.

Flames raged in parts of the nearby Douglas plant, its assembly line wrecked. Twenty-eight Dauntless dive bombers were destroyed and forty-two Douglas workers killed.

At the Standard refinery, four million barrels of oil were lost and twenty-two storage tanks destroyed, as well as pumps and equipment. It would take a year to rebuild. The death toll: sixty-four.

Eight of *Akagi's* sixty-two attacking planes were lost. Twelve U.S. planes had counterattacked and ten of the pilots perished.

Inky plumes of smoke from the ruptured tanks at El Segundo would still be fouling the sky on Easter Sunday.

CHAPTER 22

"**I CAN'T EXPLAIN** it, Tom, but I do believe all this happened back there, somehow, some*where*."

Tom stroked her hand and studied her eyes. "In a parallel time path, the one that split off in 1924?"

"Maybe. I've read about the power of those eleven-year sun storms. Alexa's husband and those other physicists weren't idiots. Maybe they discovered something pretty phenomenal. People laughed at Marconi, you know. 'Sending messages through the air? You must be mad'."

Tom nodded.

"Whether I believe it or not," she said, "it's a great story. Read on, MacDuff."

"It's 'lay on, MacDuff,' not 'lead on,' but I don't want to spoil your play on words."

"You just did, turkey."

Burbank.

Above Will Rogers State Beach, Lieutenant Kengo Yorobe led a flight of Zeros from the light carrier *Junyo* toward Burbank. Target: Lockheed Aircraft.

Yorobe's column droned over Beverly Hills at 9,000 feet and entered the San Fernando Valley. He passed above palm-lined streets and empty schoolyards, got a glimpse of early morning golfers on the fairways at Lakeside Country Club. Some of them waved. Ahead he sighted San Gabriel Peak, rising up behind Glendale. Its summit dusted with snow, it slightly resembled Fujiyama, the holy mountain near Tokyo. The crown of snow was rare. He didn't know that.

*   *   *

While Colonel Dean Thompson shaved in his upstairs bathroom, Emily was busy in the kitchen. Bacon-and-egg smells drifted up. Gunner Thompson stared at himself in the mirror. The years had faded his blue eyes. Can eyes, like hair, he mused, turn gray? He scraped beneath his nose with the fine old straight razor he'd bought in 1919 on his return from the Great War in France.

Thompson's most enjoyable hours were those spent at Burbank's new ack-ack unit. The Headquarters Battery, 75th Regiment, Anti-Aircraft Artillery, was based in the northwest part of town near Lockheed. Thompson liked to tell his war stories to the GI's there, and they in turn would describe their weapons and firing tables.

Despite his troubles with City Hall, Gunner Thompson had made a good start in setting up his unit. Give him six months and he'd give Burbank a first-rate civil defense structure.

As he wiped off his razor, the rest of the town began to stir for the day. Churches were getting ready for Good Friday services. Film workers passed through the gates of the Warner Brothers lot. Delivery trucks bound for grocery stores rumbled down Olive Avenue. A milkman worked his way up and down the residential streets off Magnolia Boulevard.

Down the street, a housewife opened her morning *Times* and read a huge black headline:

YANKS TRAP JAP FORCES IN BATAAN

She'd been duped. The *Times* had headlined a minor temporary success by General Wainwright's doomed Army in the Philippines. (I wouldn't let the *Herald-Express* touch that. We might have been a potboiling Hearst paper, but I knew our starving boys were just about finished by the Japs swarming over the Bataan Peninsula.)

The phone rang downstairs. Thompson looked at his watch.

6:57. Emily rushed up the stairs, her voice preceding her.

"Gunner. Gunner."

She reached the landing out of breath. "Western Defense Command." She put a hand on her heaving chest and continued. "Two planes down . . . along the coast. Japanese, they say. They're alerting all units."

Thompson tossed his towel in the direction of the sink and bounded down the stairs two steps at a time.

Seconds later, he was on the phone, first to the captain of his fire wardens, next, his chief fire guard. Then he kissed Emily and headed out the door.

"Gunner, what about breakfast?"

"I'd better skip it. Probably isn't anything," he called back over his shoulder, "but you never can tell. If any of my people call, tell them to ring me down at the communications center."

But Thompson was worried. He bit his lip and spun the steering wheel hard as he backed his black DeSoto squealing into Angeleno Avenue. He wished he'd been able to start organizing his civilian volunteers months earlier.

Two minutes behind Kengo Yorobe's Zeros, nineteen Val dive bombers from *Junyo* crossed the Santa Monica Mountains, bearing in on Lockheed. They pushed over and screamed downward, the pilots pulling five G's. Altimeters madly unwound.

The 75th Regiment's gunners fired. Black smoke puffs erupted around the bombers. A 75-millimeter shell blew away one plane's right wing.

"Got the bastard," the gunner yelled, squinting through his range-finder eyepiece. "Load, load."

The plane plummeted into Glenoaks Boulevard and exploded, cratering the roadway, shattering windows in houses two blocks away.

The other eighteen bombers got through, released their thousand-pounders at seven hundred feet and leveled off, skimming low over San Fernando Boulevard to the northwest.

Although the CO of the P-40 squadron at Glendale had labeled the first stage alert a gag and gone back to sleep, some of his pilots had suited up. Seven of them, the ones who actually had ammunition in their planes, attacked without orders. One of them flamed a Zero, which dived into a tool-and-die shop at Lockheed. Huge fires broke out.

Yorobe, tailing a P-40, had just begun to squeeze off his first shots when a line of holes stitched across his right wing and up the plexiglass in front of his face. He peeled to the left, trying to circle behind his enemy, but lost him.

Yorobe's eyes popped wide when he noticed his oil pressure gauge falling off to zero. He dropped down over Lockheed and shredded a parked P-38 Lightning with machine gun fire. He skimmed over the factory so low he could see crazed expressions on the faces of workers dashing pell-mell from their blazing plant.

Yorobe's engine was freezing up. He skimmed over residential rooftops. Barely cleared them. He believed he'd done all he could but that it was pointless to die for the Emperor if nothing were accomplished by it. Still, it was his duty to destroy his plane. He mustn't allow the Americans to capture an intact Zero. Firing his flare pistol into the fuel tank would take care of it, would turn this machine into a fireball.

But he had to get down first. Would the Americans torture or kill him, he worried, as he lined up on a street that was rising fast to meet his dying plane. He made an almost perfect dead-stick landing in the center of Vanowen Street. As he rolled to a stop, the right wingtip struck a power pole and the plane flipped up on its nose, knocking him unconscious.

He awoke an hour later, looking up into the face of an American doctor. The flare pistol had never been fired.

Mori Kawahara had two days left before he had to turn himself in. He had arranged through a merchant friend to sell some of his family things to a second-hand furniture dealer in Burbank.

The previous night he'd loaded a sofa, two living-room chairs, a lamp and a kitchen table into the '34 Chevy pickup, the same truck in which cousin Kaz Okada had driven to college. It was dented now, gray primer showed through the paint in several spots, and it was caked with the dust of the San Gabriel fields. It had more than 130,000 miles on it.

Mori had made plans to meet the dealer early, before store hours. The man often bought from Asian minorities but, Mori knew, didn't like being seen with them.

Driving across the north side of Burbank toward the store, Mori was listening to a farm report on the staticky radio when an announcer broke in:

"This is a KNX news bulletin. The entire city is on war alert. A Japanese plane has been forced down in the harbor. The Western Defense Command urges everyone to remain calm. Keep this station on and obey instructions from uniformed officials. This is not a drill. And now back to our regular programming.

"No frost is expected in the inland valleys tonight. This week's rains were beneficial to . . ."

Mori clicked it off. What now? It was tough enough getting through a day—his father imprisoned, his Caucasian friends avoiding him—without bulletins like this stirring up even more trouble for the *Nisei*. What more can happen to us? he wondered. Maybe he and Sumiko could run off to someplace like Brazil and start over.

He crossed the Southern Pacific tracks and turned onto San Fernando, following the shield-shaped road signs of U.S. 99. As he neared Buena Vista, the radio still off, he heard the crump of distant explosions and the scream of sirens.

A block ahead of him, an olive-drab plane with a red circle on its wings streaked across the highway at low altitude. Then he saw another, a brown fighter with U.S. markings, bursts of yellow flame spitting from its wings. Mori pulled the truck to the side of the road and stopped. He was less than three blocks from his destination. He got out, ran around and crouched behind the truck.

Another plane roared overhead, a green one with red rondels for emblems. Explosions punched at his eardrums. Smoke billowed up from where he guessed Lockheed would be.

For one of the few times in his life, Mori didn't know what to do. What fools these people are, his mind screamed, all of them, American and Japanese alike. For the first time he permitted himself a bad thought about his cousin Kaz. Why did he get himself caught up in this insanity?

At that moment his cousin was fewer than twenty miles away, leading the attack on North American Aviation.

A harsh voice pierced the cacophony of sound. "Look! A Jap! Over there."

"He's signaling those planes," another shouted.

Mori turned and saw three men running toward him. They wore blue coveralls and carried lunch pails. The hate in their eyes sent fear shivering through his bones.

Riverside.

The 4th Interceptor Command at March Field directed fighter control for the whole region. Hastily set up after Pearl Harbor, the command post occupied a spartan clapboard structure sixty miles east of Los Angeles. The command's emblem, an eagle clenching lightning bolts in its beak, glowered down from above double screen doors.

It was a madhouse inside. Urgency sparked in the air. Phones rang with reports of sightings. Radio reports crackled in.

Fighter control officers had never expected action. The war was far out in the Pacific; this was a backwater, a training area. Now they were trying desperately to get current, accurate information to the few squadrons and lone pilots scattered from San Diego to Ventura. Orange crayon on a large wall-hung map marked clumsy arrows at San Diego, Long Beach, El Segundo and Burbank.

A lieutenant, cupping his hand over a telephone mouthpiece, shouted, "Major, I've got General Kepner. Says we've got to get more planes to Mines Field. Wants to talk to you, sir."

"Dammit, I've been trying to get B Squadron up to Mines for ten minutes, but they're scattered all over Long Beach. What's he think we're having here, an ice cream social? He want us to dream up a few extra squadrons?"

"Sir, he might hear you."

"Okay, lieutenant, I'll talk to the old man. Gimme the phone."

Burbank.

Mori Kawahara ducked a savagely swung lunch pail, made a fist, threw it at the first attacker. Caught him squarely in the jaw. Sharp pain shot through Mori's hand. The man fell backward. As a lunch pail glanced off his temple, Mori threw his arms around the second man and head-butted him into the side of the truck.

A fist caught Mori in the back of the head. Another smashed into his kidney. He twisted and kicked the face of a man who was trying to get a grip on his knees. The man reeled backward, howling. Blood seeped from his mouth.

"Get that dirty Jap." From behind, someone took a grip around Mori's neck. Another man ran up, then another.

Well, this is it, he thought, I'm going to be lynched, without even selling off my furniture. He flailed out with his aching right hand, plunged it into the solar plexus of one of his attackers, the belly surprisingly soft. He jabbed his elbow into the ribs of the man who had the bearhug on him, felt the grip loosen slightly. Then a fist smashed into his ribs. Once, twice. A sickening agony in his gut, then a sharp pain in his left calf. *My God, somebody bit my leg.*

Mori smashed again with his elbow, but another fist caught him squarely in the nose. His vision went black for a milli-second, then a galaxy of stars exploded in his eyes. He felt blood oozing from his nose.

"Kill the yellow bastard," someone shouted, and a stick or maybe a wrench cracked down across his head. He was almost finished. Go ahead, plunge the knife into me and get it over with, he thought, when a loud roar drowned everything out. The grip slackened on his neck. An airplane screamed directly overhead, lower than the previous ones. He even saw the rivets along its fuselage.

"Get down. They'll get us."

Dizzy and hurting from eye to ankle, Mori realized most of his attackers were flattening out on the ground. He called on the last of his reserve strength. He turned and jammed his shoulder into the only man still standing, the one who held him. He broke free, rounded the truck, leaped in and started the engine.

"The Jap's getting away. Stop that fucker."

He jammed the gearshift into low and squealed away, scorching rubber. A crashing sound. The cab's rear window cracked. Something thrown. A rock? A crowbar? Mori swiped at the blood from his nose and lip with the back of his left hand.

He drove only two blocks before he ran into a National Guard roadblock and was arrested.

Nineteen minutes after it started, the furious battle above Burbank was over. The targets had been hit and the surviving Japanese planes crossed the Santa Monica Mountains and fled back to their ship.

Ten of fifty raiding Japanese planes were lost, while five of the seven P-40 Warhawks that counterattacked had been shot down.

Lockheed was badly damaged, but not destroyed. There was nothing that couldn't be repaired in a few weeks. Fifteen workers had been killed.

CHAPTER 23

Inglewood.

Stubborn fires blazed at North American, some buildings demolished, others untouched. The Army had been installing concrete bomb shelters. Half finished, they sat empty and useless, their existence now farcical.

The classes Valerie Jean Riskin had taken as Tool Design's designated first-aid person had once seemed a waste of time. Not now. Though cut and bruised, she was the least panicked person on the floor. She continued to shout orders, directing those, like herself, with only minor wounds. "Pull David there into a sitting position. Looks like he's had a heart attack. Loosen his shirt; it'll help him breathe."

She pushed a strand of hair from her eyes and fashioned a pressure wrap from a necktie to stanch the bleeding of the worst of several laceration victims.

A man had suffered compound fractures, jagged pieces of bone stabbing through his forearm. "Shut up," she snapped as he wailed in a half-cry, half-laugh. "Hold still." She covered the fracture with somebody's suit coat. "That'll keep it clean till we get a doctor here."

Twenty minutes later, one came at last. A young, red-faced man in shirtsleeves dashed in carrying a black leather satchel. Blood and dust coated his arms and face and hair. He nodded at Valerie, a quick, affirmative head jerk, and looked around to assess the situation.

Los Angeles.

In the middle of the city room, Gus Dobson stood on a desk and shouted, "Who knows someone who lives in Baldwin Hills?"

"Yeah," a copygirl called. "My mom."

"Quick, call her. The Japs are bombing Mines Field. I want her to tell us everything she can see from up there."

Burbank.

Gunner Thompson bit his lip and wished he were somewhere else. He and his fire warden worked from a large wall map in the Burbank Civil Defense center. Red pins indicated fires and there were plenty, most of them near Lockheed. Residents were trying to flee to the foothills by car, creating hopeless traffic jams.

A National Guardsman jogged up to Thompson. "Colonel, we've got a Jap prisoner in the holding cell. What are your instructions? Will you interrogate him?"

"Jap prisoner? A pilot?"

"No sir, civilian."

"The hell you talking about?" Thompson's eyebrows flared. "I'm damn busy here."

"A civilian, sir, man in his twenties. Picked up near Lockheed. Could be a spy or something."

With a resigned shrug of his shoulders, Thompson followed the guard down a corridor to a small holding cell in the rear of Burbank's city hall.

"Leave me alone with him." Thompson shooed the guard away with a hand gesture.

Through the bars, he looked into the young man's eyes, obsidian disks glowing with anger and determination. Red and purple bruises discolored his cheeks. His nose and jaw were swollen.

"What's your name, fella?"

"Mori Kawahara."

"From?"

"San Gabriel. I'm an American citizen."

"What are you doing in Burbank?"

"I'm an American," the *Nisei* repeated, then told his story. The internment of his father and the order to surrender himself. The furnishings he'd been trying to sell. "What are you going to do with me?" he demanded.

"Do with you?" An ironic half-smile crossed Thompson's face. "I've got a city on fire. A population in panic. I'm not set up to handle civilian prisoners. When do you have to turn yourself in?"

"The Fifth. Two days from now."

"You've got troubles enough," Thompson said. He summoned a guard and ordered the cell opened.

"Get out of here," he said to Mori. "Get back about your business." He paused, then added, "Keep your head down."

"Sure," Mori said. Their eyes linked for a few seconds. Thompson thought the young man was about to offer his hand, but he didn't. Mori turned and walked down the corridor, briskly but with a limp.

The guard looked at the colonel as if he were mad.

"Get the hell back to work," Gunner Thompson snapped.

Inglewood.

After a quick look-round in Tool Design, or what was left of it, the doctor told Valerie, "Okay lady, okay. You're doing fine here."

He knelt and ripped open a man's bloody shirt.

"That first-aid kit there," he called over his shoulder, "you can toss it away for all the good it'll be, with the kind of stuff we have here. What's your name?"

"Valerie."

"Nice to know you, Valerie. I'm Art Wimer. Turn that guy on his side—that guy there, the unconscious one. Quick now! On his back he could drown in his own vomit . . . Good. Now, put coats or blankets on anyone who looks to be in shock. Keep the poor devils warm."

Valerie knew that! Had been doing that. But she was relieved to have a pro take charge.

The pro handed her a jar of morphine and a hypodermic from his bag. "Inject those two. There. Give them each a quarter of a grain."

Now she was less happy. She swallowed. "Doctor, I don't think I can. I don't know—"

"Do it! The hypo is calibrated, see?" He examined the eyes of a man with a bloody head as he spoke. "Just a quick jab in the arm. It's like sticking a dart in an orange. Then tag them. Know what I mean by that? Put a tag of some kind on them, write down the time of injection and the amount, so they'll know at the hospital."

Valerie took a breath, filled the syringe, and did as she was told. *Sqump*. Dart in an orange. *Sqump*.

Later. "Okay, now"—he pointed to a jagged hole in the wall—"if anybody's still ambulatory in that room, get them over here. Try to keep them warm."

Later still, Valerie herself was treated, when Wimer found time to clean and wrap the cut on her arm.

Ladera Heights.

A half-drained glass of gin and a crossword puzzle from the *Times*, only four words filled in, sat on Chet Sickles' shabby dining table. So did his Colt .45 semiautomatic. Sickles cupped his chin in his hands and gazed mournfully from the window of his apartment, looking down on Mines Field.

Four fresh, deep scratches, courtesy of the late, departed Arturo Rivera, marred his left cheek. He touched one of the scabs. "Bastard got what he deserved," he mumbled. "Sticking him on the consulate steps was a nice touch, though."

The view took in Barnes City and Venice. Nearby the jaws of oil derricks along Stocker worked up and down like hungry monsters, untouched by the Japanese bombing. To the south lay Inglewood, Hawthorne and El Segundo, and the North American and Douglas plants, where snaky ribbons of smoke stained the sky.

Sickles had watched with almost detached interest as the planes attacked the factories. Some shutoff valve in his mind had closed to the terror he'd helped to make possible.

Somewhere deep below his consciousness he'd known this day would come. When the raid took place, it wasn't an entirely clear reality, more like the second playing of a bad dream.

Sickles had always tended to be gloomy. In bars, the first drink mellowed him, the second made him happy, but the third and fourth brought depression and anger. The cloudy part of his personality had become dominant after the court martial and his wife's walkoff. After his March 22nd trip to Ensenada with his information and maps, his moods grew even darker. He hadn't spoken to any of his neighbors for days.

His large jaw supported two days' growth of beard. He continued to cup his chin in his hands, the deep brown eyes staring blankly toward the rising smoke. The ice in the glass of gin—gin in the early morning—had melted half an hour ago.

CHAPTER 24

San Diego.

Shirley Santos didn't know she was a widow. Her husband Eddie was the unlucky tunaboat skipper killed by an enemy destroyer the day before.

A few minutes before seven, carrying her lunch pail, Shirley climbed down from a bus on Pacific Highway. She crossed the street on a footbridge with fifty other workers and entered Consolidated Aircraft's Plant One.

Shirley was a rivet sorter. It had taken her about five minutes to learn rivet sorting, and six minutes to hate it. She'd turned down a transfer to the assembly line and was applying for a job as receptionist in the front office where she could wear her hair down and put on feminine clothes.

She punched the time clock and walked to her work bench in the sub-assembly building. She opened her lunch pail, poured coffee from her Thermos, stirred in some sugar. She placed the box on the bench and said her good mornings to the four women around her. Their hair, covered by scarves, was stacked tightly on their heads or pulled back into severe buns, like Shirley's, to keep it from tangling in machinery.

The seven o'clock whistle blew. The shift began. When a well-built male worker sauntered by, one of the women whistled and said, "Hubba hubba." Shirley knew that was how women workers got back at the men who were threatened by their new presence in the work force, narrow-minded dopes who called them "the lipsticks" or "the crack outfit."

The woman on her right was telling about a sailor she'd been seeing. "He's got a nozzle that just won't quit," she said when a siren finished her sentence like an exclamation point. One of the others burst out laughing.

They looked at each other. They'd never had an air-raid drill so early in the shift.

A loudspeaker crackled on. "Attention. Attention. An enemy attack is expected any minute. This is for real. Put tools away. Shut down machinery. Find shelter. Get under heavy benches or tables. Cover your heads. This is not a drill. Take cover." No one laughed now.

Shirley's lunch pail crashed to the concrete floor as they scrambled under their bench. *Shoot.* Her Thermos must have shattered.

A minute later, the whine of airplane engines filled the air. The women gaped at each other, faces scrunched in puzzlement and fear. A few seconds later a thunderous explosion shook the building. Another and another. Glass and wood and steel showered down. More explosions.

"My boys!" Shirley cried. Her two small sons were staying with her mother. Mom lived four miles away in Hillcrest. They wouldn't be bombing Hillcrest, would they? *Please God, let them be okay.* She pictured their faces. The freckles on little Danny's nose.

As the bombs began to scream down at the destroyer base, Commander Reed McBride ducked into a shelter. Horrified, he caught a glimpse of an explosion on one of the destroyers, tied up not three hundred yards away. An orange and black burst of fire and steel shot skyward. The concussion hammered at his ears.

He instantly thought of Chet Sickles. Now he knew what Sickles had been up to that afternoon of boozing and shooting the breeze over at Sixth and B. McBride hated himself for having been so open. He tried to remember what all he'd said to Sickles. How much *had* he revealed?

McBride vowed he'd personally see to his former friend being shot as a traitor. He might just do the shooting himself. *If* he survived the next few minutes.

*   *   *

The thunder finally stopped at the Consolidated plant. The women stared blankly at one another, shock etching frightened faces. The explosions were gone but the clatter of gunfire and straining aircraft engines swirled around them for several minutes more.

At last, the long, shrill all-clear sounded. Shirley and the others got up and stretched stiff muscles. They'd spent an eternity under that bench. Smoke and dust filled the air. Strange acrid smells accosted their nostrils. Blackened steel beams twisted grotesquely; pipes and funnels overhead were bent and broken.

One of the women made the sign of the cross. "Thank you, dear Jesus, I'm alive."

Shirley noticed a cut on her left arm. She'd been nicked by flying glass or something. Hadn't even realized it.

The carrier *Kaga* planes that raided San Diego seriously damaged Consolidated and disrupted production of B-24 Liberator bombers. They also sank an ammunition ship and a submarine, and damaged a destroyer and a sub tender. They wrecked thirty-two planes on the ground. This despite a counterattack by Army P-38 Lightnings from North Island. Marine F4F fighter pilots at Miramar got the word too late. The radio hut hadn't been manned.

Near the end of the raid, a Zero crashed into a lumber storage shed at India and F streets. Flaming aviation fuel started a fire that soon devoured six square blocks, mostly warehouses.

Autos choked intersections. Streetcars, immobilized by power failures, sat idle in the streets, thwarting firefighters and their trucks. Panicked office workers and clerks, many of them on their way to work when the attack began, clogged the streets. Among them was a seedy little fellow named Rifty LaPlante, a snitch for the *L.A. Herald-Express.*

Long Beach.

Early that morning, a small earthquake rumbled beneath Long Beach.

Millie Simpson was one of the people it woke up. Lately, she'd been having trouble sleeping anyway. She'd just experienced her first earthquake. Alone. The good feelings weren't there any more. She hadn't heard from Corky Held in a week and she needed him desperately.

Corky couldn't lose interest. He just couldn't. They were in *love*. Where *was* he? Not even in the first weeks after Jason was shipped to Hawaii—before being comforted by Corky—had Millie been this alone. She felt hot panic. She thought she couldn't even go back home to Oklahoma. How could she face her parents?

Her period was three weeks overdue.

After getting the call that would change my day and, to some extent, my career, I had hurried to Long Beach to check out the tip on the crashed plane.

I didn't know it, but Commander Tatsu Matsumoto, who liked flying kites on the beach with his son, had the same destination. Only he was going a hell of a lot faster than I was.

The carrier *Soryu* was attacking Long Beach. Primary targets: the new Douglas factory and the Texaco refinery. The plan called for the dive bombers to cross Torrance and Carson and strike the Douglas plant on Lakewood Boulevard. Just to the south, Nakajima B5N2 horizontal bombers would hit the Texaco refinery along the Pacific Coast Highway.

Instead of covering the bombers, the Zero fighters would swing around the tip of the peninsula, drop their small bombs on the Bethlehem and Navy shipyards, then strafe Terminal Island and Fort MacArthur in San Pedro. It was a complex plan, but it would work if the bombers didn't run into much opposition. Using *Soryu's* limited number of Zeros as attackers instead of bomber cover was a calculated gamble Admiral Yamaguchi felt he had to take.

Tatsu Matsumoto sighted the Palos Verdes Peninsula up ahead. The sun was peeking over the Santa Ana Mountains. He made a small correction in course, veering to the south. To the left, waves slashed against the rocks at the tip of Point Fermin.

The spray arched high and white, then fell away. The cliffs rose jagged and steep up to the guard rail along Paseo del Mar.

Ah, the lighthouse, a landmark he'd been told to watch for. The lighthouse, blinking innocently, told him he was on course. Adrenaline pumped as he neared the target. Combat always exhilarated Matsumoto.

North of him, the horizontal bombers approached Douglas. These were single-engine jobs, similar to the dive bombers but without diving flaps.

If the Japanese have an equivalent of Murphy's Law, it was about to engulf those fliers in spades. First they ran into F2A Brewster Buffalo fighters from Daugherty Field. The aptly named Buffaloes attacked clumsily but eagerly. The Japanese couldn't get drawn into fights, not with their bombloads aboard, but their formation got scattered as they twisted and dodged in evasive action. Two bombers were shot down but one of their rear-seat gunners flamed a Buffalo.

This cut the bomber column to eight planes. Two of them got separated, mistook a smaller refinery near the Dominguez Hills for their Texaco target, and released bombs there. That left only six planes to hit Texaco. Just when they reached their drop point, a squadron of P-38 Lightnings from Santa Ana jumped them.

The Lightnings overwhelmed them. Only two of their thousand-pound bombs actually hit the refinery, where a storage tank gushed into flames.

The two lost planes that bombed the wrong target survived these first moments, but their luck ran out, too. Following their battle plan, they headed into Long Beach to strafe, but they were caught by Lightnings and blown down in flames. The entire squadron of ten horizontal bombers was wiped out while causing insufficient damage.

I'd reached the Naval Station. The crashed scout plane sure as hell wasn't the story any more. "This is the real thing, Gus," I yelled to my city editor through the phone. "Can ya hear that shootin'? And those planes? The goddamn Japs are here."

"Okay, Jake, they must be bombing the whole damned area.

We just heard North American's getting hit, too. For godsakes, don't get yourself killed. My photogs should be there by now. Have 'em shoot everything they can, some Jap planes in the air, if possible. How bad is it, Jake, can ya tell?"

"Don't know yet. It's big all right. Like Pearl Harbor. These bastards are from carriers, that's for sure. This thing won't last more'n half an hour. They'll be gettin' back to their ships PDQ."

"Hang on a second, Jake, I'm getting something else in here." A pause. "Christ, they're bombing Lockheed, too. In Burbank. Stay on it, Jake. Keep that line open. Anybody tries to take that phone, bust their arm. I'll put a rewrite guy on this end. Give us all you got as fast as you can. We're gonna get the One-Star out early. Here's Harry Bauer. Give him what you got so far. And get those damn pictures."

A photographer—I wish he'd been one of ours—took his Speed Graphic to the roof of the *Press-Telegram* building on Pine. He looked into his viewfinder, focused, and clicked off a shot of a Nakajima bomber bursting into flames with a P-38 on its tail. The shot would flash nationwide as an AP wirephoto and become one of the most famous photographs of World War II.

Los Angeles.

Gus Dobson stormed into the editor-in-chief's office, calling for the managing editor and news editor as he went. A black telephone, an old Underwood typewriter, and several editions of L.A. papers cluttered the wooden desk.

"The Japs are bombing Mines Field, Long Beach and Burbank. We need everybody working on this. I've already sent—"

The head copyboy burst into the office. He never did that.

"They're bombing San Diego, too, Mr. Dobson."

The boss leaped to his feet. "Gus, it's your show. You run this. We'll put out extras, replates, whatever we need. Johnny," he snapped at the managing editor, "tell the composing room we'll need a real effort from them today. I'll call Mr. Hearst. This meeting's over." The editor picked up his telephone as Dobson and the others sprinted off.

Long Beach.

The dive bombers were doing better than the horizontals. They found the new Douglas plant only partly camouflaged. All fourteen planes pushed over, barreled downward and released their bombs.

Meanwhile, Tatsu Matsumoto brought his fighter squadron into Long Beach Harbor. Suddenly I could see him from the Naval Station. I didn't know who he was then, of course, but found out after the war. I clearly saw a "22" on his tail.

His squadron tore over the harbor, fast and low, hungry green birds of prey, a scary sight. He might have got a flash glimpse of people lined up at rail cars at a loading platform near a pier. He wouldn't have known they were Japanese-Americans being sent to the Santa Anita evacuation center.

An American P-39 Airacobra flew in from the east, probably from the Los Alamitos fighter strip. Matsumoto pounced on it, squeezed off a burst with his 20-millimeter nose cannon and blew away most of the P-39's left wing.

I'd never seen anything like it. I was stunned but perversely thrilled, like seeing a bad crash at the auto races. "Get pictures, get pictures," I yelled, even though my photographer on the roof couldn't hear me. The Airacobra wobbled, stalled, and plunged into an oil-drilling platform near the Long Beach Auditorium. A yellow-orange fireball blossomed from the platform.

The formation split, planes darting this way and that, seeking targets. Matsumoto leveled off, reached the Navy shipyard, and dropped a small bomb. It wobbled down onto what looked like an unfinished destroyer. Debris flapped upward, then a brown-gray billow of smoke hid the ship. Other planes bombed the shipyard, some strafed ships and oil platforms, orange tracer fire spitting from their wings.

A few minutes later, Matsumoto wheeled west, his minions following. They disappeared from sight. I didn't know they were racing to their secondary target, Fort MacArthur.

CHAPTER 25

San Pedro.

Approaching hot and low, Matsumoto saw one- and two-story buildings, beige with red tile roofs, surrounding a grassy parade ground, fat date palms, and tiny men running for their lives.

He made a strafing run. Cones of fire streaked from his wings, raking the base in front of him. Chunks of stucco burst like sand from barracks walls, gobs of turf fountained up from the lawns. Men dropped. "Well, I am a professional killer," he said to himself. "This is what I do."

Long Beach.

I was on the phone again, dictating from notes and memory. I hadn't had a moment all morning to think about my spy. I spoke fast. Alan Ladd.

I knew the rewrite man at the other end of the line had the phone cradled between his shoulder and ear, his hands free to type. His fingers would be a blur, typing the words almost as fast as I said them. Sometimes he said, "Hold it, Jake" or "Gimme that last line again" or "You want a comma there?"

When I finished, Gus Dobson told him, "Get that stuff to the desk fast as you can. Let it go in takes of three, four 'graphs at a time. We're getting the One-Star out in ten minutes."

In the composing room, three and a half inch wood letters, the largest type we had, were set up in a metal form that would become Page One. The makeup man spelled out the words:

JAPS BOMB L.A.

San Pedro.

Some P-38 Lightnings caught up with Matsumoto's fighters near Fort MacArthur. He'd only seen the strange P-38s, with their twin engines and booms, in photographs. They were fast, as fast as his Zeros.

A blur of howling, twisting dogfights broke out. Bullets hammered the air. Several planes on each side torched. Matsumoto thought he counted six of his own eighteen fighters gone. He pursed his lips. He wasn't fighting the Dutch colonial air force any more. If the other raids were hitting this kind of trouble, the entire attack could be failing.

Long Beach.

In her apartment, Millie Simpson heard explosions and straining aircraft engines. She pulled aside the curtains to look. A brown plane flashed past. Four black puffs of smoke followed it. She couldn't believe it. It was just like the newsreels.

The light went out. Her electric clock stopped. She ran into the little bedroom, squeezed under the bed. "Momma," she sobbed. "Momma."

Fingering his lucky orange scarf, glad to be alive, Matsumoto led his remaining Zeros over Signal Hill toward the Douglas plant. He glanced down on a forest of oil derricks, then found several dive bombers from *Soryu* fighting wildly with a group of P-38s above Douglas.

The line of fighters broke up. It was each man for himself in a chain of dogfights.

A P-38 attacked him from seven o'clock, its nose cannon hammering. Matsumoto rolled, swung around and, engine screaming, knifed almost straight up at the P-38's left belly. His plane stood on its tail, held aloft solely by the power of its fourteen Sakae pistons. Only a Zero could do this, he thought.

The American looped tightly but Matsumoto remained glued to him and opened up with his nose cannon. The American fighter flamed and plunged into an empty lot beside a boulevard.

It was Matsumoto's eighth air victory—two this morning.

I was on the phone again. "Bauer, this is Jake. Got paper in that machine? Okay, here we go again. New lead." I started dictating.

"Army Air Corps fighters shot down at least ten Japanese planes over Long Beach harbor this morning as the Imperial Navy made its first big raid of the war on the U.S. mainland. Paragraph.

"More than fifty enemy planes attacked in the Good Friday raid. Their prime target appeared to be the Douglas factory. First reports there were sketchy but several bombs ripped into the war plant. Paragraph.

"Fires raged throughout Long Beach as Jap dive bombers and fighters pressed the attack. Navy officials said the incoming attackers had been discovered by radar minutes before reaching Long Beach. Radar is a new invention that uses radio waves to detect aircraft. This gave pursuit planes time to take off and enabled anti-aircraft gunners to load their weapons. No, make that 'arm their weapons.' Sounds better. One more 'graph.

"American losses were not immediately known, but eye-witnesses saw at least two U.S. planes go down in flames. The Red Cross alerted Long Beach Memorial, St. Mary's and other local hospitals to be ready for a big load of emergencies."

I'd been dictating from a Navy building at Terminal Island. When I hung up, another of our photographers showed up. "Climb up on the roof and get some shots," I told him.

"Against Navy orders," he said, winking, as he scrambled for the stairs.

"Attaboy. Get your ass up there." I already had one guy on the roof. A newsreel cameraman from Warner-Pathé was up there, too. Both were filming the combat, excited as schoolboys.

Matsumoto didn't see the P-38. Not until its fifty-caliber slugs tore into his Zero. He knew at once he was badly hit. Pain seared his back. He banked sharply left, then right, even though he had trouble gripping the stick. Either those moves lost the P-38 or the American broke off. The controls turned mushy. He knew the tail section was badly damaged. Flames streamed from the side of the plane. Hot pain surged into his shoulder blades and across the back of his neck.

He thought of his young son and the beaches of western Honshu. He knew he'd never go fishing from those rocks, nor ever see them again.

The Zero that had always responded so beautifully to his touch was dying, too. He used the last of his strength to try to keep the plane in trim. It was no use. He continued to lose altitude.

This is my time to depart, he realized. His plane couldn't reach the sea and he had no parachute. He wasn't sad. He knew what he had to do.

"Goodbye my dearest wife," Matsumoto said, touching the orange scarf one last time. Now he would join his ancestors. He dived the plane into a wellhead, taking seven workers to the next world with him.

Inglewood.

At North American, two buildings down from Tool Design, parts inspector Corky Held had been thinking about the steamy night he'd had with Valerie Jean Riskin—what a Don Juan he was—when the attack began.

Now he was congratulating himself on being alive. The glass had been blasted out of the giant window above his work station, but that appeared to be all. He was racing for an exit. He wasn't running away, he told himself, he was rushing to see if he could help in the harder-hit parts of the factory. Wasn't he?

That's when the second wave of the attack arrived.

Suddenly a Zero was overhead. For an instant, its small bomb hung in the air. Then with a deafening roar it exploded on the roof.

The blast burst an overhead steam pipe. A jagged piece of it shot into Corky's chest like a spear. He fell back against a wall, clutching at the pipe with both hands. He had trouble getting his breath. Felt a funny stinging deep inside but no great pain. Blood bubbled onto his chest around the pipe. He didn't know it had crushed a rib, pierced one of the ventricles of his heart, and severed the pulmonary artery.

His knees buckled. He sagged toward the floor. This is ridiculous, he thought, growing drowsy. I'm too young. I can't die now. I won't. I'll get out of this somehow. I've got a great car and I'm screwing two swell girls.

But he visualized only the face of Valerie Riskin.

He was on the floor now, still clutching at the pipe but with less strength. His lifeblood continued to course from his chest. The grogginess deepened. "Valerie," he moaned.

Air rushed through the mucus in his lungs with a whoosh and his hands went limp. Corky Held was gone.

Signal Hill.

I was in the oilfields thirty minutes later. Knowing the angles, I'd come with a Navy rescue team, my surest way of getting past Army roadblocks. Now the team was helping civilian firefighting crews.

Along with my photographer, I poked in bits and pieces of rubble, stopped occasionally to scribble a note. Stumbling on tatters of airplane metal, mixed with bits and pieces of oil-well rigging, piping, and torn bodies, I almost chucked my cornflakes. Then I saw the "22" on a scrap of aluminum. This was the plane I'd seen blowing an Airacobra out of the sky less than an hour before.

Amid pathetic fragments of flesh and leather and bone and aluminum, the smoky morning sunlight illuminated a scorched orange scarf. I gazed on it for a moment. It must have belonged to the pilot of Zero 22. I thought of taking it as a souvenir, but then kicked it away as if that could wipe the agony of flaming death from my mind. Man, I was queasy. I had to get the hell out of there.

CHAPTER 26

THE JAPANESE FAILED at Long Beach because they tried to do too much, not because the American defenses were so great. Using his Zeros as attackers instead of protecting his bombers—Admiral Yamaguchi lost that roll of the dice.

Meanwhile, B-17s from the 22nd Bombardment Wing at March Field, sixty miles east of Los Angeles, flew out to search for the enemy ships. So did some Navy Catalinas. Only two planes sighted any ships, I later learned, and their bombs missed. Hitting a moving ship with an aerial bomb was a lot tougher than the movies made out.

At the time, though, we thought this glorious counterattack by our young bomber crews was pretty heroic. They'd surely sunk some Jap ships.

In late morning, with that in mind and the attack over in Long Beach, I cranked up the jalopy and headed out to March Field. Besides getting the dope on the counterattack from the B-17 boys, I wanted to get some info from the 4th Interceptor Command, see why our fighter defense hadn't been more effective. If I could. Army censorship was tough as bricks in those days.

I was on my way to March when it hit me. Like a Japanese bomb. Hell's bells, the spy. My mood darkened like a thunderstorm. My great spy story, my scoop of the year, had been upstaged big time. A far bigger story had broken.

Whether 'tis nobler to suffer the slings and arrows of outrageous fortune, or to take arms against a sea of troubles . . .

I drove right through a red light in the little town of Orange. I had to talk my way past two Army roadblocks on U.S. 91 in the Santa Ana Canyon. Told the sentries the world was waiting to read about our B-17 heroes. Handed out some passes to the

Russell Brothers Circus I'd gotten from their advance man.

Farther out on 91 I passed a string of Burma-Shave signs, spaced about three-hundred yards apart. I liked those couplets, wondered who wrote them. IN THIS WORLD, went the first one. OF TOIL AND SIN, said the second. YOUR HEAD GOES BALD . . . BUT NOT YOUR CHIN . . . BURMA-SHAVE. This lightening of my mood was brief. Toil and sin, I thought. Yeah, there'd been a whole lot of that today.

At March, I learned that one B-17 never came back, presumed lost in a midair collision.

The radio boys monitoring their frequency said that crew had encountered a Zero from the enemy's combat air patrol a hundred and fifty miles offshore. The B-17 was trying to evade in the clouds. Then they heard, "Oh, shit! Bank hard right. Help me with the rudder." They thought they'd heard just the start of a volcanic noise—like a thunderclap cut off in mid-roar—when the transmission cut out.

Inglewood.

Valerie Riskin worked feverishly for hours beside Arthur Wimer, the doctor. Never felt so tired in my life, she thought. Got to keep going.

The tasks were endless. Give water to burn victims. Clamp oxygen masks on the faces of heart attack victims. Douse antiseptic on gashes before Dr. Wimer sewed them up.

They had some help now—ambulance drivers, paramedics, volunteers—but not enough. Ambulances came and went, sirens blaring, hauling away the injured. The pace never let up.

"I need your help doing a cutdown," Wimer barked, making an incision in a man's ankle. "A cutdown. This man needs fluid therapy. I need a vein so I can insert a tube for plasma."

"Give plasma through the ankle?"

"Normally the thigh, but there's no time. Ankle's faster, easier to find a vein. Now, hand me that—no, not that—yes, that's it." His fingers probed for the vein. "Ah, there's the little devil. Hand me that tube. That's it. Now that cloth."

On and on it went.

By eleven o'clock the dead were removed and most of the injured treated, tagged and taken to Inglewood Hospital.

"Valerie, now I want you to . . . Valerie? Valerie?"

She stared blankly at the doctor. Then she started to giggle.

"Well, I'll be damned," Wimer said to an ambulance man. "Hysterical behavior like this sometimes occurs in the midst of disaster. Something like battle fatigue. Take her off to the hospital on your next trip. This woman's earned her pay today."

A glassy, faraway gaze in her eyes, her hair a mess, pretty beige suit ruined, Valerie Jean Riskin was led to an ambulance.

Arcadia.

Gloomy and shamed, Eichi Kawahara drooped in a seat aboard a dirty gray Southern Pacific passenger train as it pulled out of the Arcadia station. He was jammed in with other forlorn Japanese-Americans squeezed two or three to a seat. The shades were drawn.

Army guards with automatic rifles stood at each end of the coach as the train clacked down the tracks toward the orange groves of Redlands, the pass at Banning, and the great desert beyond.

Eichi Kawahara didn't know that he and nine hundred like him were heading for a crude new camp at Poston, Arizona.

Ladera Heights.

Chet Sickles held his head in his hands. His mind drifted in a black region somewhere between self-pity and despair. He hadn't moved in fifteen minutes.

The day before, he'd gone to the Hyde Park post office to mail an alimony check to his ex-wife in Ohio. He'd wanted to include a note, something he seldom did. He struggled with the words, then gave up. Crumpled the paper, tossed it at a waste basket. Missed.

He checked the post office box to see if there was anything from his daughters. Or the Mexican consulate. An old Navy buddy.

Any *thing*.

Any *one*.

Did anybody in the world want to communicate with him?

That night he'd gone out and kept his midnight appointment with Arturo Rivera. Since giving that double-dealing bastard what he deserved, Sickles hadn't slept.

Sometime during the early morning he got up and went to the bathroom. Then he slumped down on the sofa, flexing and unflexing his fingers, remembering the feel of Rivera's body as it had gone limp. He occasionally touched the gouges on his cheek. That damn dead little Mexican had had sharp fingernails. He wondered if anybody had found him yet on the steps of the consulate.

Just after sunrise, Sickles went to the cedar dining table and lit a Twenty Grand cigarette. Below his window, La Cienega Boulevard weaved through a canyon toward Culver City, down toward MGM and RKO.

At 9:02 a.m., sitting at the table, he made his decision.

At 9:07, he put his right hand on the wooden handle of the government issue Colt .45.

"'For I know my transgressions, and my sin is ever before me.'"

He put the barrel of the weapon to his right temple. "Wonder if He'll let me in." He chuckled mirthlessly.

He squeezed the trigger. Nothing happened.

His body shuddered convulsively.

The moment for which he'd prepared himself had come and gone.

He stared at the drab wallpaper and the dusty light fixture as if he'd never seen them before. The whole room seemed foreign. His breathing wheezed like a bellows. He waited for his hand to stop shaking.

Although he'd handled the .45 often, fired it many times, he'd forgotten to release the safety at the top of the handle. Now, still gripping the pistol with his right hand, he flipped the safety off with his thumb.

He placed the gun to his head again, taking care to hold and clasp the handle lightly so another device, the grip safety beneath his hand, wouldn't keep it from firing.

He squeezed the trigger. It pressed against the sear, which moved back against the hammer and released it. The hammer fell against the firing pin, which leapt forward a sixteenth of an inch through the breech, striking the primer of the cartridge. All of this took place in the smallest scrap of a second.

With a loud explosion, a piece of lead less than half an inch in diameter sprang from the cartridge. The recoil drove the slide to the rear of the pistol where it mindlessly reloaded and cocked for a second shot that would never be fired.

The piece of lead, weighing slightly more than two hundred grains, tore through the right side of Sickles' skull. Shattered the muscle above the ear. Drove a groove through the cerebral cavity. Splattered most of the brain. Spurted out of the skull three inches above the left ear.

Sickles toppled forward, knocking the gin glass to the floor. A stream of blood soon soaked the crossword puzzle from the *Times*.

CHAPTER 27

Inglewood, Friday evening.

Valerie Jean Riskin is afloat in a dreamy cosmos. An eerie white light glows everywhere, but brighter at one point. A rural railroad crossing and a crumpled car appear. She hears a rhythmic *thump-thump-thumping*, like the steady beating of a muffled drum. There's a man. He's carrying flowers. It's not her father, her dead husband Jim, or Corky Held. She's never seen this man before, but she has nothing to fear from him. She knows that.

The dream fades. The *thump-thump-thumping* becomes the beating of her own heart.

Inching out of drug-induced sleep, Valerie sees a ghostly white blob. The blob gradually becomes a light fixture on the ceiling of her hospital room. She has no idea how long she's been out.

She lay motionless for a long time, trying to focus her mind and her eyes. She wasn't sure what was reality and what was dream.

The attack on North American wormed its way to the forefront. Had it really occurred or was it a nightmare? She looked around. Steel bed posts. Venetian blinds in the window. A woman asleep in the next bed. Two Army cots, also occupied. Small mahogany table beside her bed. Shaded lamp on the table. No man with flowers.

Yes, the attack had been real. She was sure now.

The day, which had started so light-heartedly with her walk to the factory, had changed her. She knew that. She'd seen men die. Friends, co-workers. She'd kept a few alive, thank God for that.

Pain began to insist. Her left shoulder and arm throbbed. She noticed fresh bandaging below her elbow.

She lay quiet, thinking. Finally she chanced some movement and found she could adjust her position without making the pain any worse. She opened a drawer in the small table and found a pencil and writing tablet. She looked at the paper for a few minutes, then began to write.

"Dear Mom and Dad: Guess who's alive and reasonably well in California?"

Los Angeles.

A strange feeling knotted my insides as I walked into the city room at five o'clock. I'd been working for twelve hours straight—hadn't stopped once, not even for food.

I'd done a hell of a job, if I do say so myself. Phoned in new leads and vast amounts of information all morning, given directions to photographers and other reporters. Gone to the remains of the oil rig where Tatsu Matsumoto had crashed. Hauled myself out to March Field where, against Army orders, I'd sneaked interviews with some of the B-17 crews that had counterattacked.

I'd been brilliant, honestly, but the Good Friday Raid had gypped me of a bigger prize.

I thought Gus Dobson would be mad at me, have me covering the City Council in Barstow. But it turned out he was madder at himself. "Jesus H. Christ, man, why the hell didn't I believe you on this Chet Sickles? And why couldn't you have got this evidence a day or two sooner?"

I was about to say I'd been working as fast as I could, but stopped short. Too damn tired to make excuses.

Dobson called the FBI. He knew the special agent-in-charge, Warren Grimsby, and gave him a complete fill-in. Dobson got a promise out of him that the *Express* could come along in the morning when they put the sleeve on Sickles.

"At least we'll have that," Dobson said. "*Herald-Express* exposes Jap spy, leads FBI capture," he said, visualizing the headline.

Long Beach.

Millie Simpson's image in the medicine-cabinet mirror shocked her. Hair stringy, in need of brushing. Eyes swollen. Sunken cheeks ghost-white.

She opened the cabinet and pulled out a bottle of sleeping pills. She twisted off the cap, poured a handful into her cupped palm, dropped several. With her other hand she filled a glass with water from the tap.

She jerked her head back, threw the pills into her mouth and reached for the glass. Brought it to her lips. Hesitated a moment.

Thoughts spun. New life in her belly, a life that she had created . . . Her wronged husband somewhere out in the Pacific. But unaware that he'd been betrayed . . . Corky Held, huge mistake, the worst . . . New life in her belly.

She spit the tablets out.

"No, no, no."

It took twenty minutes for Millie to get through to Ada, Oklahoma on the phone.

"Hello, Daddy. Daddy, I've been . . . Yes, yes, I'm okay. The apartment wasn't hit at all . . . I love you, too, Daddy. Listen, I've got a little problem—and I'm scared. I want to come home."

Inglewood.

A steel door clanged shut in the city morgue. Two men in white overalls carried a stretcher into a long room with marble-topped tables. A sheet covered the form on the stretcher. Two bare feet protruded. A tag tied to the right big toe read: HELD, CORCORAN. AGE 27. NORTH AMERICAN. 4-3-42. D.O.A. SUSPECTED CAUSE OF DEATH: ACCIDENT/THORACIC TRAUMA, AIR RAID. DEPUTY CORONER JAMES H. PRATT.

The Aircraft Carriers.

Kaz Okada ate little of the evening meal aboard *Akagi*. His fellow pilots were glad to be alive, but not jubilant as they'd been after Pearl Harbor. They had turned from boyish adventurers into hardened masters of war. The loss of fallen comrades saddened them as much as ever; their victories thrilled them less.

Okada pushed himself up from the table and went out on the flight deck. He stared at the dark sea to the east. The sky was black, starless. A chill wind pierced the leather jacket and rippled his trousers, pinning them tightly to his legs. Beneath the overcast, the sea lay flat and black as ink.

He thought about his cousin Mori.

San Gabriel.

In the house he would vacate in two days, Mori Kawahara sat looking at his packed belongings, two boxes and a tattered old steamer trunk, the same one his father had brought from Japan twenty-five years before.

His neck ached. So did the ribs on his left side. He only half heard a newscast on a small wooden Philco, one of the few furnishings left in the house. H.V. Kaltenborn was reading reports of the Good Friday Raid in a thick, serious voice. Mori folded a blue sweater and put it in the trunk.

He thought about his cousin Kaz.

Los Angeles.

I glanced at the stories we had for tomorrow, many of them mine. Then I walked across the street to the Continental and downed a few drinks before going home. The place was an asylum, a glass in every hand, a theory or a rumor on every lip. The Japanese were about to land invasion forces . . . Their battleships were shelling Fort MacArthur . . . Their planes would be back in a few hours for a night attack . . . Their squadrons had been led by German pilots, because everyone knows Japs have bad eyesight.

I had done one last thing before leaving the paper. Called a florist and ordered two dozen roses for delivery to Rosa the next day. I'd been either too tired or feeling too disgraced to come up with a message I thought was adequate. Finally, I told the florist to put on the card, "For a wonderful woman who deserves the best—from a selfish old fool."

I flashed for a second on the couple from out of town who'd bought me a beer in here yesterday, but today's fresh, hard realities brushed them aside. I drowned the tensions of the day in a lake of bourbon, then had to sober up fast driving down Avalon—a heavy fog had rolled in that night.

If only I'd broken the story a day earlier I could've saved a lot of American lives. The hell with Pulitzer Prizes.

Thoughts of my life swirled like the wet, cottony mist awash in my headlights. I'd made a ridiculous early marriage, and had held various kinds of jobs in preparation for—what? I'd written some good stories, and I believed I was liked by lots of people. I was thirty-five years old, my life half over. What did it amount to?

Rosa was nice, but not right for the long haul. She needed some nice Mexican fella closer to her own age. But I was glad I'd ordered the flowers.

Where was I heading? Life doesn't give you many chances for a real accomplishment. Had I just been cheated out of the big one?

The questions bounced around like corn in a popper all the way home. "Aw, shit," I said, parking the car.

I stumbled to the door, kicked at a riser on the porch stairs, then just sat on the damp steps, chin in hands, for several minutes. Exhaustion struck like a punch. It was all I could do to get inside and yank my clothes off.

"Jake, dear." Rosa's words from the night before haunted me: "I was brought up differently than you, no?" So did Dobson's: "Why couldn't you have got this a day or two sooner?"

I started crying. Can you believe it? I never thought I was capable of tears.

Drained as I was, I was still keyed up. Sleep didn't come easily. But then, just before falling off, I think I smiled.

"We'll get that spy bastard in the morning." It would only be a sidebar to the second-day stories on the raid, but still a pretty fair yarn.

CHAPTER 28

Saturday, Ladera Heights.

The day before Easter. At first light, FBI agents and L.A. police secured the neighborhood and surrounded the triplex. The place had been under surveillance since an hour after Gus Dobson's call to special agent-in-charge Warren Grimsby.

FBI men toting Thompson submachine guns and .30-06 rifles with high-powered scopes ringed the apartment.

Dobson and I huddled with the officers. We had a photographer along. I was all primed to ask Sickles, "Have you ever played baseball?" as soon as the cuffs were slapped on. It would be a great little touch.

Most of the story was already written and typeset—all it needed was the confirming call from Dobson and some details on the capture itself for the lead.

A few minutes before seven, crouching behind an unmarked car thirty yards from Sickles' door, agent Grimsby raised his hand and called out, "Entry team, go." Two G-men—one armed with a short-barrel shotgun, the other a Tommy gun—rushed the apartment, forced the door. They were inside within seconds. I couldn't stand still, kept shifting my weight from foot to foot.

Half a minute later an agent appeared in the doorway. He shouted "Hold your fire" and made a hand signal like an umpire's safe sign. Sharpshooters lowered their thirty-ought-sixes. Grimsby rushed up, followed by the rest of us.

What we found was Chet Sickles face down on the table in a pool of purply-black hardened blood. The walls wore some shreds of his brain and skull. God. I'd smelled too much dead-flesh stench the last two days. It was all I could do to keep my breakfast down where it belonged.

Sickles was almost twenty-four hours cold. So was the story. It made Page One, but below the fold. The second-day angles on the Good Friday Raid were bigger news than the apparent suicide of a suspected spy.

In another story the famous actor James Cagney claimed he was kidnapped by enemy agents the night before the raid and locked in a closet. I hope his wife didn't buy *that.* Looked to me like a pretty lame attempt to cover why he'd stayed out all night.

Over the next two days I helped the Army and Navy compile the casualty lists, military and civilian both. They appear as an appendix to this book. I also conducted a hospital interview that turned out to be one of the best things I ever did.

Aftermath.

Instead of making us quit in the Pacific and leave the Japanese with their newly-won empire, as they'd hoped, the Good Friday Raid got us hopping mad. After Pearl Harbor and now this, we wanted to grind those devils into dust. First off, Roosevelt went ahead with Jimmy Doolittle's carrier-borne raid on Tokyo. It wasn't much, but it was a start.

The biggest impact on our war effort was that we beefed up our West Coast defenses at the expense of the European Theater. Churchill complained like hell, but FDR said that was just tough. The Allies' invasion of North Africa, originally scheduled for November 1942, was delayed four months.

I learned the following facts after the war. If you've read along with me this far, you'll want to know:

- Kaz Okada was shot down near the Philippines in 1944 and was rescued. In later years he was a sales representative for Mitsubishi. His territory included the western United States.
- His cousin Mori Kawahara got out of his internment camp in the Owens Valley in 1943 by joining the U.S. Army. He fought with the 442nd Regimental Combat Team in Italy and France, and won the Silver Star. He married Sumiko Uyeji and they became noted

developers of premium wines in northern California.

- Mori's father, Eichi Kawahara, was a spent and embittered man when he returned from his Arizona internment camp in 1945. He died of heart failure—Mori said "breakage"—a year later.

- Millie Simpson's husband, the Marine, was killed on Guadalcanal. She earned a journalism degree at the University of Oklahoma and became a reporter and then an editor on the *St. Louis Post-Dispatch.* Her son—hers and Corky Held's—was born seven months after the Good Friday Raid. He was killed in 1968 at Khe Sanh.

Inglewood.

A couple of hours after the FBI stormed Sickles' place, I parked the car in front of Inglewood Hospital. I still had another story to run down. "After this interview, I'm gonna get back onto that Nazi plot to kidnap Walt Disney," I told myself.

I entered her room carrying a bouquet of flowers, mostly daffodils and tulips. It was almost 11:30, the morning before Easter. I saw two beds and two cots, all occupied by women, and smelled strong antiseptic. I picked out the prettiest one and hoped she was Valerie Jean Riskin.

"Oh my gosh." Tom slapped his forehead with the heel of his hand. "I should've figured this out sooner."

"What?" Cass asked, looking around the clock shop.

"Tell you in a minute. Let's read on. You'll love it."

I approached the bed. "Miss Riskin? Miss Riskin?" I said softly. It took awhile to get her attention.

"Miss Riskin, I'm Jake Weaver of the *Herald-Express.* Hate to barge in on you like this, but I thought you might like some flowers. Couldn't have a good-lookin' heroine like you without some nice flowers to brighten her room tomorrow on Easter Sunday."

"They're lovely," she managed. Composing herself a little, she said, "This is the nicest thing that's happened to me in two days—no contest. I must look horrible."

She was disheveled and bruised, but looked darn good to me. "You'll have to excuse me," she said. "I've been drifting off. Still pretty druggy. Must have slept fourteen hours since writing to my parents."

"Are you in much pain?"

"My shoulder and arm hurt, but I'm feeling a little better, I think."

"I hope so. I won't keep you long, miss, but we've heard from one of the doctors that you performed some heroic work yesterday at North American. 'Farmer's Daughter Turns Angel of Mercy,' huh?"

"Your eyes are very candid. There's a spark there I've never seen in Corky's."

"Beg pardon?" Obviously, the drugs still had her pretty foggy. "Anyway," I went on, "you're being nominated for a Presidential Citation."

"Presidential Citation—me?"

"Yes, ma'am, doctor said you saved the lives of at least seven men."

"I did?"

"You sure did. The First Lady, old Eleanor herself, usually presents those, representing the bossman. Would you feel up to a few questions? We'd be real proud to run a story on you tomorrow." I got out a pad and pencil. "Now, I know you're tired, I just have a few questions."

"You've really caught me by surprise. I look awful, but if you really want to ask this old wreck some questions, fire away."

"Prettiest wreck I ever saw." I hoped that hadn't come across as hollow flattery. I meant it.

"Thanks, but you'll have to stop calling me ma'am. My name is Valerie. What did you say yours was?"

A week later, we went out to dinner.

Nine months after that we got married.

"Great Aunt Vee!" Tom said. "Valerie Jean Riskin became my Great Aunt Vee."

"You're right, I love it," Cass said.

"My folks never called her anything except Vee. I never knew she used to be named Valerie Riskin. That's why this didn't dawn on me till now. She's still alive, you know."

"Sure. She was at that testimonial dinner last year. Charming old lady."

"And Dad was there too, wasn't he? I didn't just dream that?"

"Of course he was there, and you too. If he'd been killed in 1942, you'd have been nowhere in sight and of course I wouldn't have been there, either."

Tom grimaced. "Oddly enough, that thought isn't comforting."

Cass tousled his hair. "Don't let it bother you, sport. Now, that's the end of the book, right?"

"Yeah, except for the appendix." Tom lurched. His neck turned cold. "The appendix! Military Casualty lists." He opened the book to the back, found the index and a list of people Jake had interviewed, then the appendices. There it was: Casualty List, April 3, 1942. Under "Killed in Action," he thumbed past the A's and B's. There weren't many. It jumped out at him like a flashing knife. "Cavanaugh, Rect. Desmond M., USA, Fort MacArthur."

"I knew it," Tom whispered. "I knew it."

He closed the book. "We've got to go see Aunt Vee."

PART TWO

1 - VALERIE JEAN

CASS TOOK A SIP from the cup of tea Alexa had provided. Tom was still shaking his head.

"It just can't be," he insisted. "My dad is alive and well in Novato at the age of sixty-eight. He couldn't have been killed at Fort MacArthur. As you said, I would never have been born. Michael either."

He slumped into a chair, his heart working too fast. Cass put her hands on his shoulders and stroked them tenderly. "Not to worry, love. Maybe it *is* a made-up story."

"Oh no, you think it's real. And I admit it feels kind of real to me, too."

"Well, let's say it did happen, but in a parallel time path, as Alexa says. If so, just let it be. You're alive and well in this time path, and that's all that matters."

"Just the same, reading that was a hell of a shock, like seeing my own death warrant. I'll grant you," he said, holding up the book, "none of this feels made up: Mori and his cousin Kaz, the poor fisherman who got blown out of the water, and that spy.

"I knew there was something vaguely familiar about that Valerie Jean. No doubt about it, she and my Great Aunt Vee are the same person. But if Jake's book is entirely made up and the Japanese never attacked L.A., why do I even *have* a Great Aunt Vee?"

"Maybe," Cass said, "because the book is not made up."

"Well, Cass, we've got to go and find out if Vee Weaver, a.k.a. Valerie Jean Riskin, was ever an aircraft tool designer, and see what else she can tell us about this. If I remember right, she lives in a retirement home in the San Fernando Valley. She'd be about eighty."

Back at the hotel, Tom called his older brother, commanding officer of a naval air base in Virginia. Michael confirmed that Great Aunt Vee lived in a nursing home north of L.A. He asked why Tom wanted the address.

"Oh, we're putting our Christmas list in order, Mike, trying to get half as organized as you are."

Ninety minutes later, Tom and Cass arrived at the home, a scattering of motel-like buildings arranged in a loose square. They found Vee's room near the rear of the second building, close to a grassy courtyard. Tom knocked.

The door opened. "Tom, come in, come in," said Aunt Vee, gripping a hardwood cane with her left hand, her gray-blue eyes bright and clear. Tom saw a still-lovely face among the wrinkles of age. She bore a strong resemblance to Alexa, although her steel-gray hair was cut severely short.

"It was nice of you to call, Tom, and nicer still that you came to see me," she said in a voice scratchy but strong. "And this lovely woman was with you at that police dinner last year. I'm sorry, dear, I've forgotten your name."

"Cass. Cass Nesbit. We're engaged now."

"Your fiancée, eh? You've got a good eye, Tom, like your late Uncle Jake."

Vee took a sprightly cane-aided step forward, and grasped Cass's hand. They kissed cheeks. Vee smelled like peaches.

"Why don't we talk outdoors?" she suggested. "It's such a lovely day."

As Vee led them down the hall toward a rear door, Cass dropped back beside Tom and whispered, "While their hair and complexions are different, she and Alexa have quite similar faces. Did you notice?"

"Yeah, I did."

Outside, chairs, benches and a couple of picnic tables dotted a grassy yard. Vee went to an umbrella-shaded table. Seating herself, she said to Cass, "I hope for you, Tom here will be your one and only, unlike this old woman. Valerie Jean Riskin Weaver Pancino, that's me, the wearer-out of husbands."

She turned to Tom. "You came to the service years ago, Tom, when I lost my big Ray Pancino. That was so nice of you."

Nearby, three old men and a woman played horse-shoes on a lawn that was losing a battle with crabgrass. The clangs of iron striking iron rang in the air. "That one in the blue shirt, Buster Clark?" Vee pointed. "He's a hustler. Don't play him for money."

"I'll remember that," Tom said. "Now, you shouldn't call yourself a wearer-out of husbands. Two died in auto accidents, I believe."

"Yes." She smiled wistfully. "Jim in Illinois, Jake here in L.A. The damned automobile. Not one of man's best inventions, at least not for me."

Cass touched Vee's hand. "I'm sorry."

"Nothing to be sorry about." She sighed. "That was a long time ago. How different my life would have turned out if Jim hadn't been killed. I still see that tall, beautiful man in the sunlight of my memory."

A Filipino woman in a green jogging suit appeared and Vee asked for glasses of lemonade. When she left, Cass said, "Was that a waitress?"

"No, physical therapist, but she extends some extra little courtesies sometimes, when she feels like it. You wouldn't happen to have a flask of something yummy in your purse would you, dear? They won't let us have anything strong."

"No," Cass said, laughing. "Sorry."

"I'll sneak you a bottle of wine next time if you like," Tom said.

"Wonderful. Now tell me, why are you two here? You didn't just come out to pay a friendly visit on an old shirt-tail relative you hardly know."

"You're right, of course, but first tell us about yourself. Your life, your career. Weren't you with the space program?"

"There's no avoiding it," Cass said, grinning. "This history freak won't leave without getting your story."

Vee laughed. "Sounds like a reporter I once married. Okay, short version. Born in Illinois, married my college sweetheart, Jim Riskin, who crashed his car on an icy road. I took his death very hard. Moved out here, took a job as a tool designer in an aircraft plant. I'd studied mechanical drawing in college, you see. Met and married Jake. Crazy talented screwball, wonderful reporter. He started calling me Vee and the name stuck. He cheated on me a couple of times but I forgave him—in my mind, that is. I never let on that I knew. We fought a lot, but who doesn't?

"All in all, Jake was good for me. He pushed me. I took a graduate degree, became an aerospace engineer. I helped to draw up North American's F-86 Sabrejet, then hooked up with the design team for the Jupiter C rocket. I was with the Apollo Program when Jake got killed jaywalking in the middle of Hollywood." Her face clouded. "That was 1968. He and that gorgeous Bobby Kennedy, same year, gone. Bad year, '68. Jake and I raised a young German girl. I sometimes called him the Louisiana Kid. We had twenty-five good years together. They went too fast."

The lemonade arrived. They all had some before Vee continued.

"Jake always felt some guilt that he hadn't broken his story sooner. He thought his warning might have saved lives. After he died, I buried myself in work for a long time. Worked on the Saturn V at the Marshall Space Flight Center. I worked with Wernher von Braun. Jake had already met him, but that's another story. Met Ray Pancino, who was with NASA. Married him in 1972. I don't really know why—he didn't have a lot of humor or personality. I was just lonely, I guess. I retired in '81, then, after Big Ray died, moved out here so someone else could look after me and cook my meals. Will that do you?"

"A woman ahead of her time," Cass said, touching her hand. "You accomplished a lot. Women like you opened some doors for the rest of us."

"The war did a lot of that but if I did help, I'm glad." Vee took a drink of lemonade, made a face. "A little chardonnay would hit the spot right now." Melancholia swept over her face. "Jake was a connoisseur of wine."

"Chateau Lafite Rothschild, 1917," Tom said.

Vee's eyes popped wide. "How would you . . ." She gripped the top of her cane so hard her knuckles went white.

"The book," she said after a long silence. "That's why you've come. You've read Jake's book."

"Yes," said Tom. "In a little clock shop—"

"Downtown on Grand."

"Then you know—"

"What about Corky Held?" Cass asked. "You left him out of your life story."

"Corky was an all-right kid, but just a footnote. If he hadn't been killed I would have broken it off, whether or not I'd met Jake."

Cass pressed on despite a go-slow look on Tom's face. "But how could Corky have been killed if the Japanese never bombed Los Angeles?" Tom touched Cass's arm, then pulled his hand away. They both stared at Vee, waiting.

She held their gaze for awhile, then pushed up the right sleeve of her blouse and held her arm out. "See that scar there, just below the elbow? April 3, 1942, shrapnel from a Japanese bomb."

Tom and Cass stared, slack-mouthed.

"You'd better explain," Tom said at last. "Start at the beginning, okay?"

"You know about solar storms, right? And Einstein's space-time theories?"

Tom and Cass nodded.

"Sun spots happen all the time, little flare-ups, but there's an eleven-year cycle of big sun storms that hurl extra radiation our way. Very volatile ball of gas up there, the sun. These hot periods can mess with satellite communication, airline flights, radio and TV broadcasting, do harm to pregnant women, things like that.

"One of these came in 1924, surely the heaviest in eons. Must have been huge explosions on the sun, great earthquakes—sunquakes if you will—churning gobs of that gaseous mass around. This upheaval created what is called a coronal mass ejection, jets of flame arching thousands of miles off the sun."

She took a drink of lemonade, pulled a face. "You won't forget to smuggle me in something, will you?"

"Chateau Grand Pontet be all right?"

"Certainly. Or some Beefeater's."

"You got it," Tom said. He leaned closer, elbows on his knees, chin in his hands. "1924, you were saying."

"Yes, they're eleven-year cycles. Next one came in 1935, then '46 and so on. Well, the one in '24 was the granddaddy of them all. What I'm going to tell you next you probably won't believe. You're sure you want me to go on?"

"Absolutely," Cass said.

"You may think I'm just some crazy old woman who's lost her marbles, but what you're going to hear is God's truth."

"Go on," Cass prodded, touching her hand.

"Well, you see, I know the woman who owns the clock shop downtown, Alexa Kadinsky. That's where you saw Jake's book, isn't it?"

Tom nodded.

"There are very few copies around in this . . . ." Seconds lingered.

What was she going to say? Tom wondered. Very few copies in this *what*?

"Her husband, Sergei, was a prominent Russian scientist and a disciple of Einstein and Minkowski. She and I have studied his papers, her husband's, on time and space. It was wonderful work, if not appreciated by all his peers."

"Yes," Tom said, "she alluded to her husband and Einstein." Vee looked Tom and Cass in the eye, each in turn. "You're sure you want to hear this?"

"Yes," Tom insisted. "Don't stop now. 1924."

"All right then. That coronal mass ejection shot forth a huge solar wind, packing such a surge of electromagnetic energy that it buckled the Earth's magnetic field for a moment, long enough to split our space-time continuum. A second time track began."

Tom pursed his lips. He'd heard this from Alexa.

"Two parallel time paths from that point forward," Vee went on. "In one of them Amelia Earhart finds Howland Island and lands safely, the Hindenburg ties up harmlessly in Lakehurst, and the Japanese attack Los Angeles and San Diego. Years later, President Mondale . . . okay, you get the idea. In the other time track, well, you know about the other one—you're in it."

"But how?" Tom insisted. "How could this happen?"

Vee shrugged. "I'm not a physicist. I can only get so far

in Dr. Kadinsky's papers." Vee studied her visitors' faces. They stared back. Tom's smile was thin. No one spoke for a long time.

At last Vee said, "Alexa's husband received so much ridicule that he stopped talking about it, withdrew his papers and calculations. But I'm living proof." Vee glanced down at her arm. "Now Alexa and I are in contact with a physicist at UCLA—a young genius, by the way—who's intrigued by Dr. Kadinsky's theories. She's let him study all his papers."

"This just can't be true," Tom said, slowly shaking his head.

Vee regarded him for a moment, then reached into her purse, rummaged a bit, and removed a small leather-bound book, maybe a diary. She opened it, pulled out a photograph and handed it to Tom. It was faded, cracked in a couple of places, but it showed a Japanese plane spouting flames, with a World War II P-38 on its tail. In the background, very clearly, he saw a large rectangular sign reading, LONG BEACH PRESS-TELEGRAM.

Tom looked in silence for a long moment, then handed it to Cass.

"This is a newspaper wirephoto," Vee said. "Jake gave it to me years ago. The photographer won several prizes."

Tom and Cass exchanged a look. At last Tom said, "If this is true, what is Jake's book doing here, in this time track? And the old newspapers reporting the air attacks?"

"And the scar on your arm?" Cass put in. "Your scar, the book, and this photo should be in the other dimension."

"And *you*," Tom said. "What are you even doing here?"

"I can't begin to explain it, but Alexa came here from the other dimension and brought certain old books and newspapers."

"Why?" Tom asked. "Why would she want to do that?"

"The L.A. economy was stronger here, and Mayor Bradley was giving tax incentives to new businesses. So this is where she established her shop. I met Alexa just after Big Ray died. She convinced me to go with her to this dimension and I'm glad I did. It's better over here."

"Better how?" said Cass.

"For one thing, I get my benefits from North American Rockwell. Over there, the company went bust. Also, D-Day failed and Truman finally had to use the A-bomb to finish off Hitler." Sadness swept across her face.

"Geez," Tom said, and let out a long, low whistle. "Hey, what about Elvis?"

"The King is dead over there, too. In fact, his heart attack came a month earlier. Poor old Elvis never did take care of himself—in any time dimension."

Tom shook his head.

"Would you like to go there?" Vee asked.

"What!" Cass gasped. "You can do that?"

"I not only can, but at almost specific times."

"Specific times? Like, say, 10 a.m. on February 20th, 1957?"

Tom grinned inwardly. He knew that was Cass's birthdate.

Vee nodded. "Within an hour or so."

Tom leaned far back in his chair, putting distance between them. "No offense, Aunt Vee, but now this does sound crazy." Cass shot him a look. "You're talking time travel."

"I hate that term. It's been made to sound so silly by movies and television, but, yes, that's what I mean."

"For the sake of argument," Cass said, "how do you do it?"

"I don't fully understand it—I'm not a physicist—but it has to do with molecular orbitals. Are you familiar with Molecular Orbital Theory?"

"I think I've heard of it," Cass said.

"Every atom in your body contains electrons," Vee said. "Einstein showed that a certain kind of maverick electron called a positron can reverse its direction in time if it loses enough energy."

"Sort of a marriage between biotechnology and quantum mechanics?"

"Yes. Alexa and Dr. Hastings, the UCLA scientist, discovered a way to apply this to control the electron spin in the human body's molecules and reverse your direction in time."

"Oh, come on," Tom said, suppressing a laugh.

Vee held up a hand. "Of course you're skeptical. I didn't believe it either. Who would?"

Tom looked at the old wirephoto. "I can't grasp all this," he said, "but I saw my father's name on a casualty list in the . . . the other dimension. He was killed. I read that. If what you say were true, and—I'm sorry, I still can't accept it—that you could travel in time, hell, I'd go back and save his life—"

"Except," Cass interrupted, "we don't have to." Tom noted the *we*. "Your father," she said, "is very much alive. We can just leave well enough alone."

"*But*," Vee said, lifting her now-empty glass, putting it back down, "the time tracks are merging again. Our young UCLA friend claims his calculations prove it. The recent major sun flares have messed with the space-time continuum once more. The other day, a maintenance shed appeared on campus, a shed that was torn down years ago. A few hours later, it was gone again. The chancellor tried to pass it off as a student prank. So which track will it turn out to be? Will Martin Luther King be a very live and boring old windbag, as he is over there? If so, you'll vanish, Tom, because you'd never have been born. Your father died young."

"Dad mustn't die," Tom said, his stomach cold with shock.

While he and Cass sat in dazed silence, Vee expounded. "Alexa zaps you with a measured electrical charge to alter your molecular orbitals. When the process kicks in, and it takes awhile, these molecular changes cause you to slip through one of the quantum fluctuations in curved space-time, the things Stephen Hawking calls wormholes. After several hit and miss trips, she's been able to calculate just the amount of reverse causation needed to reach a certain point in time, within a matter of hours or minutes.

"When the treatment wears off, you return to the present. The longer the charge, the further back you go, and the longer it takes to wear off. A tiny hit will take you back for awhile, and you'll return quickly. If you go back half a century, you'll stay there two or three days."

Tom had once been plopped down in the middle of the Battle of Antietam, or so it had seemed, for about an hour. It was something he never dared tell his fellow cops. The vivid memory of that weird dream, or whatever it was, still gave him the willies. So did this. He gave his great aunt a bewildered look.

She put a crinkled hand on his forearm. "And, you're thinking, the mad old biddie has only been drinking lemonade. I begged you to stop me."

"What was the longest trip Alexa ever made?" Cass asked.

"She and I went back to the 1700s once. Nothing around but chaparral and cactus and a scrawny band of underfed Indians. They were hiding from the Spaniards who were building missions. They thought we were Spanish and they shied away from us. We were there about eleven days. Nearly died. We were sucking on cactus and eating bitter wild berries before we rebounded."

"My God . . . Have you gone back to see Jake, before he was killed, I mean?"

"Once. It was painful. I knew I'd bounce back here fairly soon, so I just looked at him from a distance. Besides, I was getting on in years and the younger me was around somewhere." Her eyes widened. "I won't do it again."

"Couldn't you have saved his life and had Alexa move

him over here?" Cass asked.

"I agonized long and hard over that," Vee said. "We had some good years, but maybe we'd have been awful together as old people. Might've made each other miserable. I was sorely tempted but, leave well enough alone I decided, me with my memories." She leaned forward and looked earnestly at Tom. "But saving your father, that's a different tub of tuna."

Tom was thinking about all she'd said, but mostly about the time tracks merging. If the wrong one prevailed, he'd just disappear. "I almost believe this," he murmured.

Vee's stare lingered. "You're going to do it, aren't you?" she said at last with a knowing little smile.

The moment dragged. Finally, Tom nodded. "Well, Cass, shall I go and see Alexa? Maybe I should find a coin dealer first and see if I can get some currency from the 1930s and '40s."

"We," said Cass. "Shall *we* go and see Alexa?"

God, she's taking this seriously. But then Tom thought, if there's anything at all to this book and what Vee said about merging time tracks, I've got to get Dad out of Fort MacArthur before . . .

He spent the next several minutes rehashing the whole thing. He barely heard the clank clank of the horse-shoe game, or Cass's conversation with Vee. His mind swirled with Jake Weaver's book, the Japanese attack on California that sounded so genuine, Valerie Jean Riskin who was sitting right here in ancient but quite real flesh as his Great Aunt Vee, and above all, his father's apparent death, years before he, Tom, had been born.

He knew denial was setting in. Good, let it. What was the worst that could happen? They'd get a little jolt of the old lady's shock therapy, have a good laugh, then head home to Sacramento and reality.

He shook his head. "What was that, Cass?"

"Oh, we were talking about what we'd need to do before our trip."

"Our trip? *Our* trip?"

"Yes. Vee was suggesting a place where we can get some old money, and I wondered if she knew any antique clothing shops."

2 - ALEXA

"I KNEW YOU'D be back after you saw Valerie Jean," Alexa said when they entered the shop the next day.

She spent a few minutes explaining. "You see, every electron in your body differs in its spin. Now we know how to regulate that."

Atop a dark oak desk she had a computer connected to a metallic gray apparatus that looked like a cross between a paper shredder and a small microwave oven. Color-coded cables dangled from each end, and green digital numerals were visible through glass panels on the front. Tom had seen this device the other day and had gotten a shock when he'd touched the end of one of the cables.

Alexa took a notebook containing several charts from a drawer.

"Does this always work?" Tom asked. He wondered how a zap of electricity could possibly cut through the fabric of time; but he also remembered his weird experience the other day after touching that cable.

"I've only performed this on myself, Vee, and Dr. Hastings," Alexa said. "So far, we've always succeeded, and with complete safety. One time in the 1700s, Vee and I had trouble finding food and water, but that had nothing to do with the process."

Alexa put down her charts and seated herself at the computer. She asked their weights, then tapped some numbers on her keyboard. "Okay then, April 1, you say, 1942?"

Tom nodded. They had been over this several times already, but while Alexa thumbed through her charts and typed commands, he said, "Listen, Cass, I have to do this, but you don't. I'm not going to endanger you."

She leaned toward him and straightened his collar. "I'm going, too, Cavanaugh," she said with that determined look she had. "We're in this together. You're not going without me."

"But—"

Her look stopped him.

Tom winced in defeat, then nodded to Alexa. She motioned them to sit in old leather chairs by either side of the desk. Tom sank into his seat, thinking, *What the hell are we doing?*

Alexa turned to her device, adjusted dials labeled VOLTAGE and AMPERES, then took the cables, which turned out to be electrodes, and began attaching them. She snapped one on Cass's forehead, saying, "This black one is the anode." She attached another near the collarbone. "Red is the cathode. This will draw off just enough electron energy to activate your reverse causation.

"All right, ladies first. The process will take effect in the next two hours," she said, setting the digital clock with taps on the keyboard. "You'll arrive at approximately four p.m. on April 1, 1942, give or take. You'll get there within thirty minutes of each other."

"How do you know we'll show up in the right time path?" Tom asked.

"Oh, you will. The fixed spatial distribution takes care of that."

"Goes without saying." Tom had no idea what she was talking about. His sardonic grin quickly vanished. "But how long will this last?"

"You'll be there roughly forty-five hours. Your return will activate some time around noon on Friday."

Her right hand poised above the keyboard. "Are you ready?"

"Go for it," Cass said. "Zap me."

Alexa typed a command and the screen flashed with

the words VOLTAGE ON.

Cass quivered slightly, obviously feeling the charge. When it was over and the electrodes were being removed, she said, "Not bad, kind of like the static shock you get touching a doorknob on a dry day."

Alexa then attached the electrodes to Tom, checked her notes and re-set the TIME command. "You need a bit more because you have more body mass. Ready then?"

"Fire in the hole," he said, quoting some old movie or other. The door was open a crack, through which he saw a sliver of the back room and the face of Dizzy Dean on his wall calendar. Dean seemed to be staring straight into his eyes.

". . . *Hear the lonesome hobos call, you're traveling through the jungles on the Wabash Cannonball . . .*"

The vibrating sensation hit. It wasn't sharp or painful, but it surprised him how long a few seconds could take when your whole body was tingling like that.

Alexa removed the electrodes. If this crazy thing worked, he and Cass would soon arrive in the Los Angeles of 1942, a day and a half before the Japanese attack on April 3.

"Go to an open place," Alexa warned, "a sidewalk or a park that existed in '42, to assure a safe arrival. Pershing Square, Union Depot. Otherwise, you could fuse with a wall or building that's been demolished since then. Your molecular structure would be instantly, fatally altered."

Tom swallowed hard. Cass gasped.

Tom knew that the Musso & Frank Grill, which was a still-thriving restaurant and bar in Hollywood, had been around in '42. "My father told me about getting a Coke there," he said, "and Edward G. Robinson's autograph."

Also, it was near Musso & Frank, on Hollywood Boulevard, that his Great Uncle Jake had been killed jaywalking. The historian in Tom wanted to view that spot.

"Yes, that would work," Alexa said. "And be careful otherwise. You'll find that things have changed greatly over the years, even the language. What we call gas stations were filling stations back then. Making love was flirting or pitching woo, not doing the horizontal thing."

She sounds just like Aunt Vee, Tom mused.

"I see what you mean. We'll be careful," Cass said. "Tom, we have to hurry."

He smiled, humoring her.

They left and did some hurried shopping, first at a costume shop Aunt Vee had recommended, where they picked up some vintage clothes. Then they went to a coin shop and bought a hundred and fifty dollars in 1939 silver certificate bills. Tom felt decidedly stupid paying six times their face value with his Visa card. "But I figure I can sell some of them back," he told Cass.

Glancing anxiously at her watch, she insisted they rush to the hotel. While they changed clothes, Tom said, "Should I tell the desk we'll be gone for about fifty years?"

"Quit kidding around and hurry up."

When they hailed a cab, he hated the look the driver gave him, sizing up his fedora and old-style suit with ultra-wide lapels, pleated pants and cuffs the size of rain gutters. Cass wore a snug-fitting red toque and mid-heel sandals with ankle straps, both new purchases as well.

When they reached Hollywood, Tom paid the cabbie and checked his watch. "I figure we have twenty minutes or so before the electron zap kicks in," he said with a funny smile as they stepped onto the sidewalk in front of Musso & Frank. "You know it won't." He didn't mean that. He really believed he'd spent a few minutes in 1968 the other day, but he thought some denial might help Cass from getting nervous.

"Oh ye of little faith," Cass said, not a bit nervous, sounding more eager than Tom, in fact.

Tourists milled around them under a bright sun, cameras at the ready, gawking at pink and bronze stars inlaid in the sidewalk, part of the Hollywood Walk of Fame.

"Look," Cass said, pointing, "Here's Nat King Cole. And

over there's Harrison Ford, right in front of Musso's."

"Nat Cole was great," Tom said, holding his new gray snap-brim hat. "Had a velvet voice."

Cass said, "Come on, chicken, put it on. You've always looked good in your topper." He had a similar hat, beige with muted checks and a tiny red feather in the band, but it was four hundred miles away in Sacramento, so Cass had persuaded him to buy this one.

A teenage girl in low-rider jeans, a tattoo on one arm, navel pierced, stopped and said, "Way cool. You guys like guides or something?"

"Right," Tom said. "Hollywood Chamber of Commerce, at your service."

"Awesome," she said, bopping off.

Cass smirked at Tom as he leaned against one of the decorative concrete stanchions on the sidewalk in front of Musso & Frank. "Nothing's going to happen," he said.

"Tom, it *will*. But not arriving at the same time worries the heck out of me. If you show up first, promise me you'll stay glued to this very spot. And if I arrive first, I'll stick right here waiting for you, right beside Harrison Ford."

Tom grinned. "Sure, Harrison Ford. I don't suppose you could find Danny DeVito."

"Tom, this is serious." Cass glanced at her watch. "We've got to be able to find each other."

"Okay, right here, I promise. Except I'll be by Nat Cole. But, come on, this is an elaborate practical joke some of my buddies worked out with Aunt Vee. Got me to spend a bunch of money, dress up in a fool costume, and get my batteries charged. You're in on this, too, I'll bet."

Cass said, "I suppose I wrote that whole book—"

Tom suddenly felt some queasiness . . .

"—and paid to have it printed—"

. . . then a micro-second of splintering shock. He stumbled, lost his balance. Grew weak and shaky. Couldn't see. He felt himself in some kind of dizzy freefall. Something bumped his body hard.

3 - GINGER

TOM SLAMMED against something.

His vision returned. Thank God for that. Instead of bright sun, scowling clouds filled the sky. He blinked, his eyes adjusting to the changed light, and found himself lying in the street.

A horn honked, a woman screamed, brakes shrieked, and tire smoke swirled. He jerked his head up and found himself staring down the throat of a car: an old-fashioned chromium bumper and a yellow California license plate. Yellow, not the white he was accustomed to, with black numerals.

"Good God, I nearly got you killed," a voice cried. Suddenly a woman was bending over him. "Joel? Joel? God, I hope you're all right. Jesus, that was close."

Realizing he must have stumbled off the curb and almost got hit by a car, Tom looked up into a face that wasn't Cass's. He knew this face. He'd seen most of her movies with Fred Astaire. It was Ginger Rogers.

"Holy—" he gasped.

"Joel," she said, kneeling and taking his arm. "Here I am, leading you down the primrose path again." The actress's big eyes widened. "Oops, you're not Joel McCrea. Anyway, I sure didn't mean to . . . Are you all right?"

Shaky, confused, embarrassed, Tom nodded feebly.

A guy beside her—small, fifties, black hair parted in the middle—had Tom's hat and was dusting it off.

Another man rushed up, out of breath, and stammered, "I, I'm sure sorry, sir. Hit the brakes as soon as I saw you." He was wringing his hands. "You saw it, didn't you?" he pleaded to the small crowd that had gathered. "He fell right in front of me. This wasn't my fault."

"Yeah, yeah," said the black-haired man holding Tom's hat. "Saw the whole thing. You're in the clear, Mac." Then he turned to Ginger Rogers. "Ginger, you know this guy?"

"I thought it was Joel McCrea, Sid. I knocked him down."

"Sorry to disappoint you, ma'am, I'm not, at least I don't think I'm—." Tom shivered. Had he somehow invaded the body of a 1940s actor?

Ginger Rogers brushed some dust from Tom's jacket. "Well, whoever you are, are you all right?"

"I think so, thanks. What was that about the primrose path?"

"That's a picture I made with Joel McCrea, 'The Primrose Path.'"

"Come on, Ginger, give the guy an autograph and let's get outta here," the man said, handing Tom his hat.

"No," she snapped. "I've injured this nice-looking man."

Tom felt a sting of pain from the heel of his left hand and saw some blood. Must have scraped it against the pavement. A drop fell to the concrete. He looked closer at the grille of the car facing him. An ornament depicted an Indian head—looked like the Washington Redskins' logo. Ah, this was a vintage Pontiac.

Tom looked back to the woman. She'd taken his hand and was wrapping a handkerchief around it. Definitely Ginger Rogers. Large lime-colored eyes, mole on her chin, thick black lashes, and full lips, the kind that actresses would fake with injections decades later. The big surprise was her wavy hair. It was reddish, not blonde, as it had looked in black and white films.

An Indian motorcycle whined past, a fat necktie flapping behind its rider like a scarf. He wore no helmet.

"You're hurt," Ginger Rogers said. "I'm so sorry. I'll get

you a doctor."

"No, no, it's just a scratch. It's hardly bleeding. I'll be fine." But he wouldn't be fine till he knew Cass was okay. Where was she? Had she arrived, too?

"Where's Cass? I was with a woman."

"I've only seen you here, bub," said the man, handing Tom his hat as the Pontiac drove off. "Come on, Ginger, let's go."

"Hold on, Sid, don't be rude." She smiled warmly at Tom. "I slammed right into you, knocked you off the curb. You seemed to pop out of nowhere. Thought my eyes were playing tricks. Did you see that, Sid?"

"Nah, I was distracted by that kid on skates. Almost hit us."

"That kid," she said, "must've blocked my view of this—"

"Let's go, Ginger."

"Sid!" she barked.

"Yeah, you're right, sure. Sorry." He extended a hand. "I'm Sid Grauman, mister, and this is Virginia Rogers."

"Tom Cavanaugh. Pleasure. You haven't seen a woman? Tall, little red hat?" Grauman shook his head. Ginger still held his arm, steadying him, getting him to his feet. She wasn't as tall as Tom had thought, maybe five-four. The enormity of all this was setting in.

Tom looked at the streetlights, incandescent bulbs hanging beneath enameled, coolie-hat reflectors. A fat red streetcar rumbled toward them, sparks flying where its trolley pole jolted along a web of wires. The car had twin portholes on the front for the drivers. They looked like giant eyes, staring, questioning his presence here. He shook his head. "Wow, look at that."

"Never seen a streetcar before?" Ginger said. "What are you, the April Fool's joker? You look like Joel McCrea but you talk like Lou Costello. You had a darn close call there. Come on, you need a drink."

"Get back everybody," Grauman demanded. They had

him surrounded, each with an arm, Ginger standing much closer. They started pulling him toward the door of Musso & Frank.

"No," Tom protested, dragging his feet. "I've got to wait for Cass. She'll be looking for me out here by Nat King Cole."

"King Cole?" Grauman asked. "The piano player? The King Cole Trio? He's coming here?"

Tom looked for the bronze stars on the sidewalk. Nat King Cole. Harrison Ford. They'd vanished.

"Uh, no, I might've been mistaken about that. But my friend Cass is definitely coming." He hoped. He prayed.

"We'll get a booth by the window," Grauman said. "You'll see her the minute she shows up."

Tom thought about it, trying to calm himself. "Well, okay then," he said at last.

They settled in a red leatherette booth, Tom sitting where he could see the street. A haze of cigarette smoke hung in heavy layers. The realization that he was sitting down with a movie star of yesteryear gave him one of the strangest sensations he'd ever had in his life. But then this was one of the strangest days he'd ever had in his life. Or *before* his life.

He removed Ginger's handkerchief. "I've ruined this. Sorry."

"Don't worry about that. What's one little hanky to a girl like me? Are you okay?"

His left side felt a little bruised. "Sure. See, the hand's clotting nicely."

A waiter arrived and Ginger ordered a Gibson, Grauman a stinger. Tom asked for a beer, but Grauman vetoed him. "No, no, you need something stronger. Double scotch for this gentleman," he told the waiter. "He needs it."

"What time is it?" Tom said, figuring his own watch wouldn't be even close to right. Grauman said it was 3:45.

Tom re-set his watch. It was two hours off. He'd read about Double Daylight Savings Time, a wartime contrivance to conserve electricity. Still reaching into his memory bank, he asked, "Grauman? As in the theater?"

Grauman looked annoyed. "Of course. It's just up the street here. Ginger and I were just making plans for her ceremony. Going to immortalize her hand- and footprints in cement."

Tom noticed several people around the crowded room staring at them, awestruck. Ginger pulled out a cigarette, a Dunhill, and struck a pose, holding it in front of her face. *Is she doing Garbo?* At last the coin dropped. *She's waiting for you to light it, stupid.* Tom picked up a matchbook he saw beside a glass ashtray and awkwardly gave her a light.

"You don't smoke, I take it." Twin blue plumes streamed from her nose. Tom shook his head No. A shame to dirty up such nice nostrils that way.

"I heard there was a man in Hollywood who didn't smoke." She laughed her lively laugh again. "We've found him, Sid." She was pretty but a bit brassy. Hard years on Broadway and in the movies will do that, Tom thought.

People still gawked. For a moment he wondered if some of them, too, mistook him for Joel McCrea. Tom, a film buff, thought McCrea had been great in Hitchcock's "Foreign Correspondent" and in "Sullivan's Travels" with Veronica Lake.

Music began to flow from a jukebox. "Take the A Train." He loved Duke Ellington, but Cass, not music, occupied his mind. Where the hell was she? What if she arrived yesterday? Or tomorrow? In some other year? Or not at all?

What if that car had hit him, and he'd been taken to a hospital? Cass would show up here and there'd be no Tom around—she'd be frantic. Plus, the hospital people would find no current identification on him, only 1988 stuff they couldn't possibly understand. They might consider him a spy or something. This was turning out to be far more complicated than he'd ever imagined. He should have planned better, taken time to have some fake 1942 ID printed up. He remembered Alexa's warning to be careful, that things had changed greatly in forty-five years.

He thought he saw a guy at a corner table inhaling some cocaine off the back of his hand into a nostril. Snorting coke had been legal in the early 1900s. Tom wasn't sure if it had been outlawed by 1942 or not. He forced himself not to say or do anything. He was way, *way* out of his jurisdiction.

The drinks came. They clinked glasses. "Bottoms up," Grauman said. Tom took a sip of strong scotch. Grauman was right—he'd needed it.

"Are you in the business, Tom?" Ginger asked.

"The business?"

"Pictures, silly."

"No, I'm from out of town." *Far* out of town. "Just visiting. Got some business to take care of at Fort Mac-Arthur. My fath—, that is, a friend of mine, is down there."

"Fort MacArthur," she said. "We shot a scene there last fall."

"A scene?"

"For 'The Major and the Minor,' a picture I just finished."

"Do you remember who the commanding officer is?" Tom took another drink.

"Yes. Let's see, uh, Higgs? No, it was Hicks. Yes, Colonel Hicks. William Hicks, I believe. Nice man, but all business, not a bit gay."

"Gay? In the military?"

"Why not? The Army shouldn't be all drudgery. That's why we do shows for them. With your looks," she said, "you should give the biz a try. I could arrange a screen test." Ginger's smile was definitely coquettish. Was she coming on to him?

"Nah." Tom laughed. "There's already one Joel Mc-Crea."

Suddenly he saw Cass staggering around on the side-walk, her head snapping this way and that, eyes wide and

wild. His heartbeat missed a tick. He jumped to his feet—
"Excuse me"—and raced for the door.

When Cass saw him sprinting up, she squealed "Tom"
and jumped into his arms. It was one of the tightest
clinches they'd ever had—with their clothes on. Were
people staring? Who knew? Who cared?

"Thank God," she murmured after a long silence. "This
thing really worked, didn't it? I don't like taking trips like
that without you. I was blind for a minute. Well, not a
minute, but a couple of seconds. Scared me to death. A few
minutes ago you just vanished into thin air. Darndest
thing I ever saw. That scared me to death, too."

"I was pretty shook myself," Tom said. "My God, I'm
glad you showed up."

"Wouldn't have missed it for the world." Cass leaned
back in his arms and glanced about. "This is unbelievable.
Look at the old cars. And the streetcar tracks. Say, no
stars on the sidewalk. The Walk of Fame is gone."

"Or still to come. When you get your bearings, I want
you to meet Ginger Rogers."

"Ginger Rogers? Yeah, sure."

"No, really. I fell off that concrete pillar—See? Those
posts are gone—and smacked right into Ginger Rogers. Fell
into the street. I've been having a drink with her and—"

"Don't waste any time do you, lover boy?"

"Nothing like *that*, babe. She's with Sid Grauman,
owner of the Chinese Theatre, where they have the stars'
handprints. Up the street a few blocks."

"Hey, what happened to *your* hand?"

"Scraped it a little when I fell. It'll be fine. Come on."
Tom took her arm. "You ready?"

"As I'll ever be, I guess."

Thank God she's here, Tom thought. Okay, it's
Wednesday at 3:45. If we've got forty-five hours here, that's
till around noon or so on Friday. The attack was early
morning. We should be okay on time.

As they approached the table, Ginger Rogers sized up

Cass and said, "So, Joel McCrea's dating a starlet. Wait'll the gossip columns get a load of this."

The look on Cass's face said Huh?

Grauman stood and pulled out a chair for her, while Tom made the introductions. "This fella here is a dead ringer for Joel McCrea," Ginger said.

"The cowboy actor?"

"Cowboy actor?" Grauman said, his brows arching.

Tom whispered, "That was later." Ginger and Grauman exchanged a look.

Cass sat and turned to Ginger. "I hear this lug fell at your feet out there. Thanks for taking pity on him."

"What are you drinking?" Grauman said, waving down a waiter.

Cass ordered white wine, then noticed Tom's glass. "Into hard stuff now, eh, Joel?"

Ginger laughed, then said, "We saw you two out there. Looked like you hadn't seen each other in years."

"You don't know the half of it," Cass said with a sly grin.

"You two married or something?" Ginger probed.

"No, we're—"

"Just friends then." Ginger's eyes looked pleased. "We've enjoyed chinning with Tom here. Don't you think he looks like Joel McCrea?"

"Hmm." Cass studied him. "More like Mickey Rooney, I'd say."

"She's got a mean streak," Tom said, grinning.

Grauman pushed his chair back and stood again. "It's been charming, but I've got to get back—no, please don't get up—back to the theater. Not good for my reputation to stay here too long."

"Right, being an owner of the Brown Derby," Ginger said with a quick wink.

Grauman pulled a twenty from his wallet and chucked it on the table.

"Double sawbuck?" said Ginger. "We can drink all

night on that."

"Be my guest. Best of luck to you two. Glad we met. Ginger, we're all set for the sixteenth? My publicity guy calls yours?"

"All set, Sid. Thanks." Ginger blew him a kiss as he made for the door, slapping a shoulder here, shaking a hand there.

"What do you think?" Tom asked Cass. "Should I take a screen test?"

"Ha, you in the movies. We'd have to change your name. Let's see, how about Kirk Douglas? Think that would catch on? Or maybe Robert Redford?"

Ginger grinned, getting into it. "Kirk Douglas. I like that. Rolls nicely off the tongue. Robert Redford would never work, though. Nobody would pay to see someone called Robert Redford."

Cass's wine arrived and the three of them touched glasses. "If you don't mind my asking," Cass said, leaning forward, "What was it like, working with Astaire?"

"Greatest dancer ever, but a tyrant."

Tom started to say "Great sound bite," but choked down the words. Sound bite was not a 1940s term.

"Fred made us shoot numbers over and over again, even when they were perfect. Never let up. God, my dogs were killing me after a day's work."

"But you like him?" Cass probed.

"Adore him." Ginger's eyes lighted up. "First met in New York back in 1930. I was doing a Gershwin show and we were having a hell of a time with the 'Embraceable You' number. Fred stopped by and straightened us out in nothing flat. I knew right then he was a genius."

"He was, I mean is," Cass corrected herself, "an elegant man."

"He is that." Ginger caught a look in Cass's eye. "But no hanky panky. He's happily married to Phyllis, you know, and I was married to Lew Ayres when we made all the musicals."

Tom noted the past tense. He vaguely recalled that Ginger Rogers had been married several times.

"But it was time to move on," she continued. "Ten musicals with Fred was enough. I think they provided some escapism during the Depression, but it was time to show the world I could act, not just dance."

"You sure did," Tom said. "Academy Award for 'Kitty Foyle.' Well-deserved. Let's see, that was—?"

"Last year."

"Right, last year. Tough Irish lady from the wrong side of the tracks showing up those Mainline bluebloods in Philly. Great stuff. Congratulations."

Ginger's green eyes smiled. "Why, thank you."

Cass, marveling that Tom knew even more movie trivia than she realized, said, "Yes, congratulations on the Oscar. What are you doing now?"

"Just finished a thing called 'The Major and the Minor' with Ray Milland. Imagine me playing a twelve-year-old at the age of, well, at my age." Tom thought she was about thirty-two.

Ginger laughed. "My character's not really a kid, just masquerading as one. It's a funny script." She took a swallow of her Gibson. "Are you a working girl, Cathy?"

Working girl? She takes me for an L.A. streetwalker? "The name is Cass. I'm the governor's chief of staff."

"Governor Olson?"

"Er, yes."

"He came to the premier of 'Kitty' last year. Had quite an entourage. Funny I didn't meet you."

"I wasn't, ah, working for Governor Olson at that time."

A woman came up and pushed an autograph book in front of Ginger. "Oh, Miss Rogers, would you? It would mean so much to my daughter."

"Sure, honey, what's her name?"

On the jukebox, Billie Holiday was singing "Them There Eyes."

After the intrusion, Ginger looked at Tom and said, "So now you're in town to take care of something at Fort MacArthur. What can I do to help?" Another kittenish smile. "What is it you need?"

"I have to see my friend, a recruit, and get him out of there for a little while Friday morning."

Ginger leaned forward, clutching her glass, her fingernails blood red. "Why?"

"For private reasons I'd rather not go into, but it's very important to my family."

"I love a challenge. Let me help."

"Oh no," Cass demurred, "we couldn't impose on your time."

"I hurt your friend, almost got him killed. I feel responsible. Besides, time is something I have right now. I don't start my next picture for three weeks." Ginger thought for a moment. "If you can't tell me the reason, can you tell Colonel Hicks?"

Tom shook his head. "He'd never believe it."

"You *are* mysterious," Ginger said. "This gets more interesting by the second." She pulled out another cigarette. "Come on, give me the Punch and Judy," she begged, as Tom gave her a light.

Looking surprised at the light-up, Cass said, "My, aren't we gallant?"

Along with the playfulness, there was a genuineness about this actress. Tom wanted to trust her. His instinct was that he could—up to a point. No way in hell, though, could he tell her they'd come from the future to save his dad from a Japanese attack.

"We have reason to think something unpleasant will happen there Friday morning," he said at last, "that could adversely affect my friend."

"You can't say that to Colonel Hicks?"

"Nope, he'd never go for it."

"Okay then, we need a ploy. We could say I'm shooting a one-reeler for War Bonds and we need a young soldier."

Tom pictured Ginger at a rehearsal, tossing out ideas to improve a scene. "I'll say I saw your friend when I was there last fall and he's perfect. We have to have him. No one else will do."

Tom frowned. "Great idea. Trouble is, though, he just enlisted. Wasn't there last fall."

"Hmm. Well then, he's my little brother and our mom has suddenly taken ill. He needs to come to her bedside right away. Sometimes I wish my mom *would* take ill. She's a pistol."

Cass looked puzzled.

"The ultimate stage mother," Ginger explained, rolling her eyes. "What about that, then? Our mother's sick."

"My friend Desmond is pretty straight—"

"Straight?"

"You know, not very spontaneous. He probably wouldn't pick up on it. Likely to say something like, 'You're not my sister, and my mother's in northern California.'"

"Maybe we could get him on the phone tonight and tip him off."

"No," Tom said. "You've been too gracious already. Plus, I don't know if recruits can take phone calls."

"Why not give it a try?" Cass interjected, twirling the wine in her glass, studying Ginger's face.

Tom was thinking, suppose I got him on the phone. How would I introduce myself? Say I'm a distant relative?

Ginger flagged down a waiter. "Bring us a phone book, sweetie, and another round of drinks, would you?"

Tom looked at his almost empty glass. "Make mine a Coke this time. One double scotch is my limit."

Just then a big man sauntered in. Tall, thirties, sandy hair, rough-and-tumble face. Tom knew exactly who he was. He approached the table. "Miz Rogers, I'm Dizzy Dean. Big fan of y'all's. Seen all your pictures. Just wanted to say howdy." He smiled at Ginger and Cass, then gave Tom a look of such familiarity it made him shiver.

"What are you doing in L.A., Mr. Dean?" Tom asked.

"Shouldn't you be with your ball club?"

"Playin' days over, pardner. Busted toe messed up mah dang deliv'ry. Only threw one inning last year and got drilled somethin' fearful. Now I'm scoutin' for the Cubs. Out here takin' a look at these Coast League fellas."

"Join us," Ginger said.

"Thank you kindly, but I don't wanta intrude." He slapped a big hand on Tom's shoulder and winked. "Nice to see y'all, pardner . . . Wonder if they got my friend Jack Daniel's here." Dean walked off toward the bar, humming "The Wabash Cannonball."

"He acted like he knew you," Cass said, staring after him.

"I know," Tom murmured, his eyes reaching for the ceiling. "Weird."

The waiter returned with a telephone directory and a white phone attached to a long cord. "Your drinks will be right up," he said.

4 - THE POLO

WE KNOW THIS little beauty works for the governor," Ginger said, leaning close to Tom, ignoring the little beauty. "But what about you, Tom? What do you do?"

"I'm a cop. Sacramento."

"Copper, huh? What kind?"

"Homicide detective," he lied, knowing there'd be few if any narcotics cops in 1942.

Ginger's eyebrows rose. "Oh, you really should take a screen test. Pan Berman would love it, a real live homicide dick who looks like Joel McCrea."

Tom knew Pandro Berman had been a major producer at RKO. He chuckled and shook his head No.

"Big mistake, you'd be great." Ginger picked up the phone book the waiter had brought, stopped at the page headed "FO" and followed her finger downward. "Here we are," she said, "Fort MacArthur. Terminal Four-Five-Seven-One."

"Please," Tom said. "You've done more than enough."

"I owe you this," Ginger said, touching his hand. Cass glowered.

Ginger moved her hand to the receiver, picked it up, then put it down again. "Hold on, I've a better idea. Why didn't I think of this before? General DeWitt, I know him."

"General DeWitt?"

"Yeah, John DeWitt, head of the Western Defense Command. Worked with him on 'The Major and the Minor.' Army's top dog on the Coast. He's Hicks's boss, everybody's boss. Had a big crush on me. Old enough to be my father, but that didn't stop him."

"Hit on you, huh?" said Cass.

"Good gosh, no, he never touched me. I would've walloped him. But he kept on pitching, trying to get me to have a drink with him, or dinner. He'd do anything for me."

"You think he'd—"

"Sure he would. I might have to have that dinner, but now I'll have a safety net: you two. I'll say, 'Do me a favor, John. Couple of friends are in town tonight and it'd be rude to leave them alone. You won't mind if they join us, be a dear.' This would be after we spring your friend, of course."

Yes, Tom could definitely picture her improvising on the set. "Sounds good," he said, knowing he and Cass wouldn't be here for that dinner; they'd be decades away and Ginger would have to deal with the general alone. If anyone could take care of herself with a dirty old man, though, it was Ginger Rogers.

"Okay," she was saying, "we'll go with the War Bonds one-reeler. Tell him I need this Desmond—is that right?"

"Desmond, yes."

"I need Desmond for the shoot. I'll tell DeWitt we need to get him off base tomorrow night, wrap it in three or four takes, and have him back by noon on Friday. Hicks would have to go along with his superior. Would that do it?"

"Perfectly," Tom said.

"Swell, cat's pajamas," Cass added, grinning at her wit.

Ginger gave her a look, took another gulp of her second Gibson, then asked, "Where you staying?"

"Don't know yet," Tom said, holding up both palms. "We just got in. Pretty much wherever we like tonight, but tomorrow we should be in San Pedro, near the fort."

"You could stay with me tonight but I'm temporarily at my mother's apartment. Not much room, and my mom, well . . ."

"We'd never impose," Cass said.

"You might like the Beverly Hills Hotel or the Ambassador." Ginger picked up her glass and found it empty. "Yes, the Beverly Hills. You'll love the Polo Lounge."

"Might be too rich for our blood," Tom said, thinking about the vintage dollars in his wallet.

"Tell you what, Copper, dinner at the Polo Lounge is on me. You take care of the room. It won't be cheap, but I'm sure you can get a nice bungalow by the pool for around thirty, forty bucks."

Cass protested about the dinner, but Ginger insisted. "Won't cost much. I get an outrageously sinful discount. They love having actors in the Polo."

"Good PR," Tom said.

Ginger squinted. "PR?"

"Public relations. Publicity."

"Oh, you bet . . . Now, about tomorrow night, there's a little place in San Pedro called the Adams Motor Court. Studio took over the whole joint for a week during our shoot. Nothing fancy, but it's clean."

"Sounds good. Thanks."

Before parting, they agreed to meet at the Polo Lounge at seven.

As they climbed into a cab, Cass said, "Oh, this'll be a thrill, dinner with Lena Horny. 'Oh, you *should* take a screen test,'" she mimicked.

"She was just being a movie star. They're all like that. We have to be polite, she's been so generous." The driver, reaching for the flag on the meter, peeked at Tom in the rear view mirror.

"She'd love to take my place tonight in our room, you know."

Now the driver stole a glance at Cass. Tom squeezed her hand. "No way, babe." She squeezed back.

As they started down Sunset Boulevard toward Beverly Hills, Cass looked around. "No seat belts?"

"Seat belts?" the cabbie said. "Whatcha think this is, an airplane?" He geared down for a red light and sneered, *sotto voce*, "Seat belts."

The driver turned on his radio. It slowly warmed up, burped some static, then played what must have been the tail-end of a newscast. ". . . Remember, you know plenty that could help the enemy. Talking to a stranger could spell danger. Loose lips sink ships. This is Walter Winchell, saying be careful, Mr. and Mrs. America, and so long for now."

Tom gazed at the sights. All the cars were dark in color, most of them black, although some were blue or maroon. Only cabs had bright colors.

When they arrived, Tom signed the register "Mr. and Mrs. Cavanaugh," figuring it was frowned upon, maybe even illegal, for unwed couples to check into hotels in 1942. No poolside bungalows were available, but they got a second-floor room overlooking a banana tree and a Mexican fan palm in the courtyard below. The rate was twenty-eight dollars. A one percent sales tax bumped the total to $28.28.

After he signed the register, Tom thought he saw Basil Rathbone walking toward the elevator. While the desk clerk rang for a bellboy, a *Herald-Express* lying on the counter caught Tom's eye, the headline reading, BATAAN YANKS PULL BACK AGAIN. It's April 1, he thought. The starving Americans on Bataan will surrender in a week, then face the Death March. *Poor bastards.*

But the Polo Lounge lifted his spirits. Immaculate table cloths, huge windows, pink walls, shaded lamps spilling soft pools of light on each table. In these sumptuous surroundings, it was hard to believe the nation was in a desperate war.

Tom checked his watch. Forty-one hours left. Give or take.

Ginger already had a table. "Damn," Cass hissed, "she showed up."

"How's your hand?" Ginger asked as Tom pulled out a chair for Cass.

"It'll be fine."

Ginger ordered a bottle of pinot noir, 1933. She took out a cigarette, which Tom lit, while Cass smiled hard.

After studying the menu, Cass asked for smoked salmon and Ginger ordered a baked chicken breast. She said she had to watch her waistline. Tom had watched her waistline, too, and thought it looked just fine. He ordered a T-bone steak.

Halfway through the meal, Cass gasped, and Tom saw why. None other than James Cagney was approaching the table. Short, light on his feet, bantam rooster chest, round Irish face, hat tilted back. James Cagney for sure.

He stood between Tom and Ginger, feet apart, put two palms on the table, and leaned forward. "Ginger, I wanted to give you my congratulations on the Oscar. That was a grand piece of work in 'Kitty Foyle.'" He threw a warm but curious glance at Tom and Cass.

"Mr. Cagney, could I possibly have your autograph?" Cass said.

"Sure, sure."

Tom, reaching for a pen, figured Cass had done this just to irritate Ginger. If so, it didn't seem to.

"And who might you be?" Cagney asked, taking the piece of notepaper Cass handed him.

"These are some new friends of mine," Ginger said, "Tom and Cathy."

"It's Cass," the owner of that name insisted. "C-A-S-S."

Cagney pulled out a thick-barreled fountain pen—but not fast enough. He put it down and took the BIC which Tom was already handing him. "What's this?"

"A ball-point pen," Cass said.

"Ball-point pen? That's a new one on me."

Damn. Tom knew he'd made a mistake. The ball-point pen wasn't introduced till after World War II. He hadn't been thinking.

Cagney made a couple of squiggles. "Say, this is swell. Where can I get one of these?"

"I'm afraid you can't," Tom said. "It's an experimental

thing an inventor in Sacramento is toying with. Loaned me one of his few prototypes."

Cagney scrawled his autograph for Cass. "I'd like to buy stock in this." He gazed at Tom, then at Cass. "Big fellow with fair skin," he said, "accompanied by a beautiful, mysterious woman. Perfect models of the master race." His eyes twinkled. Tom's darkened. "Got themselves a special secret pen. I'd keep an eye on these two, Ginger. Could be Nazi spies."

Tom blurted, "Now wait a sec—"

Ginger's sharp laugh cut him off. "The mysterious woman," she said, "works for the governor and the big Aryan is a cop."

"Copper, huh?" Sounding just like he did in "The Public Enemy." "Sorry, Officer, don't be running me in for demeaning the law."

Cagney handed Cass the autograph, gave her a sunny smile, then slowly handed the pen back to Tom. He returned his own pen to an inside jacket pocket. Then, leaning close to Ginger, eyes still glistening with mischief, he stage-whispered, "Cop and governor's aide—perfect cover for a pair of enemy agents." In a normal voice, he said, "Well, congratulations again, Ginger; I mustn't interrupt your meal any longer," and walked off.

While Ginger watched him cross the room, Cass clutched the notepaper and murmured, "Think what this will be worth when we get back. Not that I'd ever sell it."

Ginger swiveled back to face them. "Jimmy's a scream. Forever teasing people like that."

"A real scream," Tom said, unsmiling. Anything pinpointing them as suspicious strangers in this nation newly at war was dangerous.

"Were you making that up about the pen?" Ginger asked. "I know my onions when it comes to acting. I do it for a living."

Tom smiled playfully. "Have I ever lied to you?"

"Oh, aren't you the sweet one," she said, touching his

hand. "Keep your little secret then. We all have some."

Cass winced.

Later, over coffee, Ginger said, "I'll call General DeWitt the moment I get home."

Tom said he'd like to go down to Trenton and Pico tomorrow and see the *Herald-Express's* neighborhood. Ginger asked why.

"Well, I sort of know the military writer, Jake Weaver."

"Jake Weaver? Sounds familiar. I've probably seen his byline . . . Well, I need my beauty sleep and I imagine you two would like some time alone in that room." She gazed directly at Tom. "Unless you—"

Cass's hard scowl stopped her. Tom thought Cass might actually jump across the table and belt her one.

After an awkward pause, Ginger said, "I'll call you later then, or else leave a message at the Adams." She tossed her napkin on the table, got up, arched her eyebrows toward the pink ceiling and said, "Well, home to Momma. I'll call you, Tom."

In their room, Cass said, "God, I've had to pee for hours, but there's no way I was gonna leave you alone there with the Spider Woman."

"Have a little faith, babe," Tom said to her back as she scampered into the bathroom. He figured Ginger Rogers had been amusing herself trying to get a rise out of Cass. And succeeding.

When she returned, they put away the few overnight things they'd brought, all of which had been stuffed in Cass's bag. Placing his pants over a chair, Tom gave her that look he had.

"Mmm," she purred. "When have we had a chance to make love in 1942?" She ran the tip of her tongue across her upper lip and unbuttoned the top button of her blouse. "What Ginger Rogers wouldn't give," she said as Tom undid the others.

Later, as they lay entwined, she murmured, "You got

luckier tonight than Uncle Jake did. Ginger Rogers, too, I hope."

"Yeah."

They listened to each other's heartbeats for awhile, then Tom said, "Say, maybe we should rob a bank. We've got the perfect getaway. The statute of limitations couldn't run for more than forty years."

Cass kissed his neck. "Go to sleep, Sundance."

5 - JAKE

IN THE MORNING, from their room in Beverly Hills, Tom called the Adams Motor Court to reserve a room for that night. He hadn't used a rotary-dial phone in quite a while. It seemed to take forever.

The proprietor answered. "Rate's five dollars," he said apologetically. "Everything's gone up with the war on." Tom laughed, thinking about the twenty-eight dollars his present room was costing.

Checking out of the Beverly Hills, he asked the desk clerk if they had any messages and was told No. "If any come in, ask them to call the Adams Motor Court in San Pedro."

They found a coffee shop nearby on Beverly Drive and went in for a late breakfast. A skinny young man with thick glasses and a serious cowlick at the crown of his head handed them mimeographed menus.

"I'd like a Danish," Cass said. "No, wait. Would you happen to have German apple pancakes?" Those were a specialty of her favorite bed and breakfast inn in Sonoma.

The skinny waiter scowled. "Lady, we don't have anything German."

"Regular pancakes will be fine then, and coffee."

Tom ordered bacon and scrambled eggs with wheat toast, and coffee. "Bugle Call Rag" wailed in the background.

"I wonder if we'll ever get back," Cass said softly after the food arrived.

"Oh, we will."

"But not at the same time. I don't like that at all. What

if your stuff wears off first and you bounce back an hour or two before me? I'd hate that."

"That's something we'll have to face tomorrow, but I know you'll be fine. You're a strong lady."

"Just now I don't feel very strong at all," she said. "This is a scary deal. Who would've guessed that German apple pancakes would trip us up?"

"Or a BIC pen," Tom added, scanning the room. "The world has changed plenty in forty-six years."

The food arrived and Tom took a bite. "These eggs aren't half bad."

On a radio above the cash register, an announcer was urging housewives to make their countertops sparkle with Bab-O Cleanser.

After they finished their meals, the bill came to sixty cents. Tom plunked down three quarters, which the waiter picked up and examined. He dropped two of them into a pouch on his apron, but held up the third.

"Hey, this two bits ain't right," he said. "It's light." He held the coin close to his face and squinted. "1987! What are you, a wiseguy? What this place needs, some palooka passin' funny quarters."

"Sorry," Tom said, reaching for his wallet. "My mistake. I got that at a fun shop." He pulled out one of his genuine 1939 dollars. "Here. And keep the change."

The waiter slapped the coin on the table and shot Tom a look that said "Don't try and chisel me, bub." He dug into his apron and returned the other two quarters, then stalked off.

Tom saw him standing at the cash register, talking to the manager and pointing this way.

A moment later the waiter returned. "Are you sure you wouldn't like something else? Some more coffee?" Tom thought he sounded nervous. Was he trying to stall them?

Tom glanced back at the manager, who held a telephone receiver to his ear. He was squinting at them, his glare cutting across the room like a laser.

"No coffee, pal. We're out of here." Tom grabbed Cass by the arm.

"Huh? What—"

He steered her to the door. Almost sprinting down the sidewalk, he said, "That guy's probably calling the cops. Thinks we're spies or saboteurs. We can't afford to get stopped by any cops. We've got no good ID, no 1942 driver's licenses, nothing." Tom waved at a cab. "We've got to be more careful."

"And watch what money we throw around."

"Exactly. People here are really nervous. Can't blame 'em; they've just been thrown into a horrible war. We're outsiders who've landed in a strange world." A world, he thought, where thousands were being tossed out of their homes and thrown in camps just because they looked different. "We've got to be on our toes every second."

"Right, both of us. Do you really think that guy was calling the cops?"

"Or the FBI."

The cab pulled over. Tom reached for the door handle and they slid into the back seat. "Hollywood and Vine," he told the driver.

"I never should have mentioned German apple pancakes," Cass whispered. As the cab pulled out, a squad car arrived. Cass gave a sigh of relief as the coffee shop disappeared behind them.

Tom glanced at his watch. He often wore a digital watch, but had deliberately brought this one with conventional hands and numerals. At least he'd got that right. People here wouldn't have seen a digital watch and might take it for some sinister German device.

Cass looked at a billboard that said KEEP 'EM FLYING —BUY WAR BONDS, and whispered, "This is *much* freakier than I ever figured on." Tom gripped her hand.

Time was sailing by. He wished he could do something besides pray that Ginger Rogers would come through, would reach General DeWitt and arrange his father's release. What kind of backup plan could he have?

Back in Hollywood, they walked around, trying to be sightseers. Their minds not fully there, they viewed Grauman's Chinese Theater, the Pantages, and the spot where Tom figured Uncle Jake had been killed jaywalking twenty years ago. Or twenty-six years in the future, depending on how you looked at it.

From dangerous-looking "safety islands" in the middle of the street, people climbed on and off fat red streetcars with bells that went *clang clang clang*. Tom had never heard a bell clang on the sleek blue and gold trolleys he was used to.

The traffic signal at Hollywood and Highland had only red and green lights. It turned red and a little sign popped up reading STOP. Tom said, "Look at those sign flags that swing out saying STOP and GO, as if we didn't know what the colors meant."

"Right, and there's no yellow light. That looks so weird."

A squad car, a small Ford with spotlights on each side of the windshield, stopped at the light. The cop stared at them.

"Be cool," Tom whispered. The light turned green and the cop drove on.

Ten minutes later they were in a taxi headed for the *Herald-Express*. Along Figueroa Street, they saw a bill-board featuring a woman factory worker with her sleeves rolled up and hair covered by a kerchief. The sign read, "Do Your Part. Uncle Sam Needs You."

Cass smiled and said, "See that? This was one of the first steps in this country toward Affirmative Action. It's like being inside a history book." In the rearview mirror, Tom saw a curious look cross the driver's face.

Reaching South Trenton Street, they stepped out in front of a juke joint opposite the *Herald-Express.*

As Tom paid the driver, being sure to use the right currency, a maroon Hudson pulled up to the curb and a woman with a mink stole over her shoulders got out. Tom had seen a car like that at the Blackhawk Auto Museum.

He and Cass strolled to the corner of Pico, where a P Line streetcar rumbled past. They went up the east side of Trenton to the *Herald-Express* and contemplated the stone building, three floors with a squat penthouse on top.

"Going in?" said Cass.

Tom thought about it. "Nah, a couple of strangers, what would we do in there? What would we say? It's not a spectator sport." He looked at his watch. "Getting hungry? It's after one."

"Sure, let's try the Continental over there. One of your uncle's hangouts, right?"

As they jaywalked, Cass said, "Look both ways. Let's not end up like poor old Jake."

A man in a double-breasted suit and a hat similar to Tom's came out of a place next door to the Continental called Moran's. The woman on his arm wore clunky heels and a jacket with padded shoulders.

The Continental's plateglass window displayed a yellow neon sign saying BREW 102. Tom held the door open for Cass. Cigarette smoke stung their nostrils. "San Antonio Rose" blared from the jukebox. "Great song," Tom said. "Heard it many times on Country Classics."

Cass spotted the women's room and said she'd be right back. Several men slouched against a long bar, mirror behind it, shelves full of bottles up above. The clack of a cueball from the back of the room, along with lusty shouts, echoed off a stamped-tin ceiling.

He found two open stools and asked for a beer.

"What kind?" said a gum-chewing bartender with a crooked nose. "Eastside, 102, Acme, Regal Pale, Schlitz?" He was running a silver dollar in and out of his fingers like a sleight-of-hand artist.

"Schlitz," Tom said.

"Haven't seen you in here before," the bartender said when he returned with a cold bottle and a glass.

"No, I'm from outta town."

"Ain't everybody these days? Twenty cents for the beer."

Tom's mouth dropped a little.

"Tough luck, mac, that's a good price nowadays." His right hand resumed the silver dollar trick. "Some places get two bits. You want beer less'n twenty cents, go back to Peoria."

Damn, Tom thought. Got to fit in, got to watch myself every second.

Someone yelled for a Brew 102, calling the bartender Shaker. The song ended with Bob Wills crying out, "Ah-ha, San Antone!" Check out that jukebox, Tom thought, a clear-glass Seeburg with purple neon tubing, stacks of shiny black records, and a forest of push buttons. Be worth a lot of money where I live.

Cass returned, took the stool beside him and asked for white wine. The bartender put both hands on the counter and leaned forward. "Got no wine of any color, lady. You can have beer, liquor or soda pop."

"I'll have what he's having," she said with a nod at Tom's bottle."

The place was getting busy. When they finished their beers, he looked around and saw only one open table. They grabbed it, Tom pulling out a bentwood chair for Cass. "I'd love to have these chairs," she said. "They'd bring a fortune today, I mean . . . you know what I mean."

Tom glanced at the scrape on his hand. It was healing nicely.

A well-worn waitress arrived, snapping her gum, pulling a pencil from above her ear. She plunked down some beat-up flatware. Her hair, a blinding shade of red, flopped like loose paper when she jerked her head at a menu printed on white cardboard above the bar. Pastrami or ham sandwiches, hamburgers, cheeseburgers, chili. No mention of salads. "Decided, hon?" Was she addressing Tom?

"Chili and a hamburger, I guess," Cass said. Tom said he'd have the same.

"Well done or not so well done?"

"Not so well done," they answered in chorus.

"Two bowls of red and cows to cover," she yelled toward a window behind the bar. Looking back at her customers: "And to drink?"

Cass asked what kind of soft drinks they had.

"Coke, RC Cola, Delaware Punch, Nehi."

Cass ordered a Coke, Tom a Royal Crown. Then he said, "Do you know Jake Weaver? Does he come in here?"

"The Weav? Only every day. Three, four o'clock."

A few minutes later she was back with bowls of chili and a handful of crackers. Cass sampled hers first. "This is delicious."

Tom took a spoonful and agreed.

The burgers came. They were a different story: stale buns, an ocean of grease. After one bite, Cass said, "Ugh, this has got to be about forty percent fat." She took only one more bite, a small one, but she did pick off and eat her slice of tomato. Tom forced down most of his burger.

After lunch, Tom found a wall-mounted pay phone in the back near the pool table. He dropped a nickel in the slot and dialed the motor court to see if Ginger Rogers had left him a message. She hadn't.

"Time's running out," Cass said, her fingers clenching into fists. "This thing happens *tomorrow*."

"I know."

"Let's just go right down to Fort MacArthur and see this Colonel Hicks."

"I'm worried, too," Tom said, pushing the door open for her. "We've got to make this work, nobody knows that better than me. But going there right now could mess things up if Ginger works out her deal with that general."

Cass squinted in the sunlight. "You really think your actress babe will come through? That we'll even hear from her? Maybe she was just getting her kicks with the rubes from out of town."

Tom shook his head. "She'll contact him. She meant it. We've got to give her another couple of hours."

"Is that cop intuition?"

"If you like."

She touched his cheek. "I hope you're right."

Tom checked his watch. Twenty-three of their forty-five hours gone. By this time tomorrow it would all be over. One way or another.

As they walked back to Pico, Cass said, "None of this exists now. It's all been knocked down for the Convention Center."

"Yet here we are looking at it," Tom answered.

She hugged him. "Too weird. We'll never be able to tell anyone about this. Never."

Trolley car barns took up much of the next block over, on Georgia. Row after row of streetcars hunched there, some of them being serviced or washed.

A bum in shabby clothes, who still looked much cleaner than the 1980s homeless Tom was accustomed to, asked if they could spare a dime. His eyes lit up when Tom handed him a quarter.

"Maybe I should've given him that '87 one," Tom said. "He wouldn't have been able to spend it for forty-five years."

They returned to the Continental just before four. When they stepped through the swinging doors, Roy Acuff was singing "The Wabash Cannonball," which spooked Tom. "Man, that's weird. Dizzy Dean was humming that song yesterday, remember?"

". . . *She's mighty tall and handsome and she's known quite well by all; She's the regular combination, on the Wabash Cannonball.*"

"Grab a table," Tom said. "I'm going to call the motel again."

There was still no message from Ginger Rogers. As he rejoined Cass, someone shouted, "Hey Jake, howsa boy?

Any big scoops today?"

Tom spun in his chair and saw a ruddy-faced, redheaded man about his own age. He intercepted him in mid-wave to someone across the room. "Excuse me, Jake Weaver of the *Herald-Express*?"

"Right, pardner. And who might you be?" Tom liked his great uncle's smile.

"Tom Cavanaugh," he said, "avid reader. And this is Cass Nesbit. Can we buy you a beer?" He gestured at an empty chair opposite Cass.

"That'd be Jim Dandy, *amigo*, never met a free beer I didn't like." He smiled at Cass. "Pleasure, ma'am."

Half a century separates me from my great uncle, Tom marveled as he pulled out a cane-bottom chair for the man. He's been dead twenty years, but here I am talking with him.

"How'd you know me?" Jake asked.

"Heard someone call out your name."

"Well, what can I do for you? What brings you to this charming establishment? Shaker, gimme an Eastside," Jake called over to the bartender.

"Make it three," Tom added, then said to Jake, "Just wanted to meet you. I've read a lot of your stuff." *Stuff you haven't even written yet.* "You're a good writer."

"Thanks, pardner. Would you like to subscribe?"

Tom gave a puzzled look.

Jake grinned. "Just kidding you, friend. I don't sell subscriptions."

Tom wanted to tell him he was right about the spy, right about the Japanese, that they would attack in the morning, tomorrow morning. To blow off Rosalinda and rush right back to the paper. But he couldn't. Couldn't meddle with Jake's destiny, only his father's, here in . . . in whatever nuthouse of an existence this was. His only business here was to save his father.

"We wondered," he asked, "if you knew General DeWitt."

"Sure. Interviewed him coupla times. Why?"

"Is he a pretty straight shooter? Would he help you if you had a problem?"

"You're tryin' to get outta the draft, friend, I wouldn't worry about it. You're too old."

Cass grinned and punched Tom on the arm. The same flame-haired waitress arrived with their bottles of beer. "You're a gem, Daisy," Jake said with a suggestive wink.

"No," Tom went on, after bottles were hoisted and "cheerses" exchanged. "Has nothing to do with the draft."

"DeWitt's got his hands full right now," Jake said. "You prob'ly heard about the big roundup of the Japs. Moving 'em all out of the coastal zone. Huge operation." Jake laughed. "Folks'll have to start mowin' their own grass, weed their own gardens."

"You think this roundup thing is really necessary?" Cass asked.

"Personally no. FDR's givin' in to political pressure . . . But how come the interest in DeWitt?"

"Friend of ours also knows him," Tom said. "Going to ask him for a favor on our behalf. Just wondered what kind of guy he was."

Jake shrugged. "He's old, he goes by the book, and, like I say, he's busier'n a one-armed paper hanger right now. Don't know what else to tell you." He stared at Tom for a moment. "Say, have you ever played baseball?"

"Not much. I'm a basketball man."

"Never played first base? Or second base?"

"Nope. Why do you ask?" Tom knew why. He'd read his book. Christ, did even his own uncle think he was a spy?

"No reason, really. Just bein' a nosy old reporter."

Change the subject, Tom told himself. He found his foot tapping to the sound of a wicked violin. "Who's that on the jukebox?"

"Sounds like Spade Cooley. Great fiddler, Spade Cooley. What kinda favor you looking for?"

"Family matter. A relative of mine is a recruit at Fort MacArthur." Had he said too much? Tom wondered.

"I know the CO pretty well, Colonel Hicks." Jake pulled out a pocket watch on a chain and looked at it. "I'm busy tonight. Fact, I gotta be going."

Right, Tom thought, it's April 2. You're having dinner at Perino's tonight with Rosalinda. Just read about that. God, this is too eerie.

Jake drained his glass and put it down. "Thanks for the drink, friends. Tell you what, call me tomorrow, maybe I can help you with Hicks. Richmond Four-One-Four-One."

That would be too late, Tom thought. Besides, Ginger Rogers was taking care of the matter. He hoped. That was supposed to be resolved tonight, and he still hadn't heard from her.

Jake pulled out a yellow pencil and scribbled a note on a paper napkin. "TCav. Hicks. Ft.Mac." He folded it and stuck it in a shirt pocket, saying, "Just to remind me, case you call. Left my notebook in the office." Then he got up, offered his hand to Tom and flashed his best Alan Ladd smile at Cass.

Tom sat there for a beat, stunned, knowing full well where he'd seen that note before. Then he refocused, half-stood, shook Jake's hand and said, "When the war's over, you should write a book about your experiences."

Jake grinned, said "Yeah?" and left, slapping shoulders and fielding wisecracks all the way to the door.

"Did you see that?" Tom said, sinking back onto his chair.

"I sure did."

They stared numbly at each other for several seconds.

Finally, Cass said, "It's after five; they probably have rush-hour traffic here in the Twilight Zone, too. Let's get down to San Pedro."

Twenty hours left, Tom thought. Give or take.

6 - SAN PEDRO

ON THE CAB RIDE south along Vermont Avenue, Tom said, "So what do you think of Jake now? Still a reprobate, an asshole?"

"No, I like him. He's charming. Still a dirty old man, but I like him."

Cass scanned the sights in silence for awhile, then said, "No tall buildings, no sign of a freeway anywhere. And the sky's a curious color, kind of powder blue."

"No smog," Tom said. "That's what it is."

"You're right. No smog. Nice." Then she asked what they'd tell his father when they got him off the base and there was no movie shoot.

"I don't know, just take him out with Ginger and get him drunk I guess."

"Get him drunk?" Cass said. "He's under age."

"No, he's twenty-two."

They still didn't have a good answer to that when they arrived twenty minutes later. The Adams Motor Court reminded Tom of the small motels from a bygone era along Sacramento's Auburn Boulevard. Well, sure it did. He was in that bygone era.

Tom recognized the desk clerk's voice. Same man he'd spoken to on the phone. "Ginger Rogers finally called," he said, looking impressed. "'Bout half an hour after you last checked. Left a number." He handed Tom a piece of paper.

"Is there a phone in the room?"

"No." The man looked as if Tom had asked for the moon. "But you can call from the office here. You know Miss Rogers? She was here making a picture not long ago.

Swell lady."

Tom went to the desk and picked up the phone. Looking at the note in his hand, he dialed.

Ginger answered on the second ring. "Hello Tom." Her voice sounding flat. "I finally reached DeWitt today," she said apologetically. "It wasn't good. When he asked me out awhile back—remember?—I said my mom was sick and I'd have to stay with her. Apparently a friend of his saw me at dinner with a fella that night. On the phone today, he just blew up. Scolded me pretty fierce. Called me a lying, draft-dodging bitch."

"What'd he mean by that?"

"I mentioned I was married to Lew Ayres? After we split up last year it came out that he's a conscientious objector. Refuses to serve. Caused a lot of bad publicity, PR as you call it. Poor Lew. It's killed his career. So DeWitt calls him a yellow coward and screams at me like I was responsible for Lew's beliefs. 'Hell, give me a gun,' I said, 'I'll go fight in his place.' Anyhow, long story short, DeWitt turned me down flat. Want me to call Colonel Hicks and try 'Desmond's my little brother'?"

"No. Thanks anyway. We'll take it from here. You steered us onto the CO, that was a huge help. I didn't even know Hicks's name. We sure appreciate it." Standing nearby, Cass frowned.

"It was swell meeting you," Ginger said. "You have my mother's number. Let's get together again." Her voice dropped to a stealthy level. "Come back to town some time and show me your badge when the little beauty is busy."

"Sure," Tom said, knowing he never would, or could. Before meeting Cass, he might have gone for a hit-and-run, one-night stand with such a glamorous star. In this case, hit, and then run forty-six years. He hung up, flattered, trying not to let it show.

"Plan A went south?" Cass asked, snapping him back to the serious reality they faced. "You said 'We'll take it from here.'"

"Yeah, DeWitt blew her off."

"I knew she wouldn't come through. Half a day lost. So now what?"

At the counter a few feet away, the clerk leaned toward them, looking like he deserved to be filled in.

"Come on, babe," Tom said, taking Cass's hand. "Let's go to our room and work on it." He shot the man a look that said butt out.

Their cottage, one of a dozen arranged in a "U" around a fat date palm, contained a standard double bed, an oak nightstand, two lumpy chairs, a tiny closet and a claw-foot bathtub. No shower and, as advertised, no phone. "Great tub," Tom said. "My grandfather had one like that."

"Right," Cass said. "But Jesus, Tom, we're running out of time. I saw a diner just down the street. Let's get some supper while we figure out what to tell Colonel Hicks."

Minutes later, as they settled into a booth, Cass said, "Too bad we can't talk some more with your Uncle Jake. Maybe he could help us figure what to do."

"He'd never believe us," Tom said, "but even if he did, he's out trying to score with Rosalinda, remember?"

"Oh, yeah, his hot little source from the Mexican consulate."

A teenage waitress hunkered over a pile of books at a corner table, chewing on a pencil. Homework, probably. She got up and bopped over to their table, intoning something that sounded like "hey-bob-a-re-bob."

"Hello, Joe, whaddaya know?" she asked musically.

Tom, who'd read about jive talk, said, "Hey, keed, you're a winner; we're in need of a little dinner."

The girl chuckled her approval; Cass gave him a look.

After checking the limited menu, Tom ordered a hamburger and a chocolate shake, Cass a chicken salad sandwich and a Coke. The waitress left and Cass said, "One 1942 hamburger was enough for me, thank you."

Tom, toying with a water-spotted fork, said, "Maybe what we could do, I could tell the colonel Dad was a witness to a crime and we need to question him off base."

"Hicks will ask, 'Why off the base?'" Cass said. "Because he has to view a lineup?"

"Dad's from San Francisco. They wouldn't have a lineup down here. How about this? LAPD picked up our suspect. They're holding him at the San Pedro precinct for San Francisco."

"Okay, but you're a Sacramento cop. Why would San Francisco have you involved?"

"It was handy because I was down here visiting relatives. Inter-force courtesy."

"What if Hicks calls the San Pedro cop shop to check our story?" Cass asked, talking over the Andrews Sisters singing "Apple Blossom Time."

"We'd be screwed, but I doubt he'll do that. He'll be busy and we'll make this sound real urgent. Which it sure as hell is. I think he'll buy it."

The food arrived. Cass took a bite of her sandwich, then said, "Play tough cop, no time for messing around. 'This won't take long, we'll have your man back in no time, it's the Army's duty to cooperate.' That kind of thing."

"Right. I'll make him go for it."

Cass pushed her plate away. "I can't eat. Too nervous. Too scared."

Tom put a hand on her wrist. "It'll be okay. It will." He sighed, took a drink of his milk shake. "God, it'll be weird seeing my pop when he was twenty-two."

The tab came to eighty cents. Tom put down a fifty-cent tip. The waitress clapped her hands, said, "Gee whiz," then added, "handsome ransom, happy chappie."

After that bit of entertainment, they left and found a phone booth in front of a hardware store next door. Tom looked up Fort MacArthur, dropped a nickel in the slot and dialed Terminal Four-Five-Seven-One. The operator, probably some enlisted man, handed him off to the night duty officer, whom Tom finally convinced to ring the colonel's residence. He looked at his watch. Eight o'clock. He hoped the colonel wasn't having his dinner. But then the man came on the line.

"Colonel Hicks, my name is Tom Cavanaugh." Lying about his name wouldn't do; he'd surely have to show his shield; good thing there was no date on it. "I'm a detective from the Sacramento police department. I need to question one of your recruits tomorrow morning, off the base. He may be a witness to a crime. Shouldn't take more than an hour or two."

"What this recruit's name, detective?"

"Desmond Cavanaugh."

"Cavanaugh? That's your name."

"Right, sir. Coincidence."

"When do you want to do this?"

"Early, sir." *Tatsu Matsumoto's squadron reaches Long Beach at 7:15, doesn't it*? "Would 6:30 be all right? We can't ask L.A. to hold these suspects too long."

"I'm an early riser, son. Never could break the reveille habit. Come in at oh-six-thirty and we'll talk about it. I'll leave your name at the gate. The sentry will give you directions from there. I'll have the coffee on."

Tom and Cass strode along the darkened street back toward the motor court. A slender moon hung above them, enough to see a four-engine, propeller-driven bomber droning across the sky, breaching the stillness of the night. "That's a B-17," Tom said. "Quite a sight."

"It only emphasizes how far away from home we really are," Cass said, squeezing his hand, "in every possible sense."

"Yeah, just think," Tom said, "somewhere out there in the dark are the *Akagi* and those other Japanese carriers" —he swung his head toward the bulk of the Palos Verdes Peninsula, which loomed large and black in the west like an evil presence—"which haven't existed for half a century."

At Fort MacArthur, Colonel Hicks told his aide, "Get

the Sacramento police department on the line for me."

"Yes, sir."

7 - YANKEE DOODLE

TOM STOPPED to admire a long, sleek Mercedes at the curb, its highly polished finish gleaming a misty red in the moonlight. The hood ornament, a three-pointed star inside a circle, sparkled like fine crystal. Spare tires with deep virgin tread were mounted externally, just behind the front fenders.

"Look at this fine old Mercedes-Benz," he said. "This was one of the great touring cars of the Thirties."

"There's something stuck under the wiper," Cass said. "Looks like a parking ticket."

"Or maybe an advertising flyer." Trying to see the interior, Tom leaned in close to the passenger-side window, absently resting a hand on the door handle. "Can't tell about the upholstery. Too dark."

A voice resonated behind them. "That's quite a car you have there."

Startled, Tom grunted, "Huh?", turned and saw a small man strutting toward them out of the gloom. He looked like James Cagney.

"I've been keeping an eye on you two," he said. It *was* James Cagney.

"What do you want, Mr. Cagney?"

"To know who are you and what you're up to, you and your fancy-dancy German car."

Tom's pulsed quickened."Sorry, but this isn't our car."

"The hell. You were just about to get in."

"Oh no. I was just taking a look. You don't see one of these every day."

"In Berlin you do."

"Berlin? What are you talking about? You're making a

mistake here, sir."

"Not me. You two have made the mistake." Cagney took a step closer.

"Knock it off, please," Tom said. "We're not in the mood to be confronted by some confused actor on a sidewalk after dark."

"Confused actor, no. Patriotic American, yes."

Stay calm, Tom told himself. Cass touched his arm, the gesture sending the same message.

"Who are you and what are you doing here in Los Angeles, the West Coast's major arsenal?" The words demanding, clipped, sounding like Walter Winchell.

Though seriously irritated, Tom figured he'd better play along.

Then Cass spoke up. "We're from Sacramento. He's a police officer—"

"I heard that cock and bull story before."

"—and I work for the governor."

"Governor? You mean *gauleiter*, don't you? Governor of what? Lower Saxony?"

Tom and Cass exchanged a wide-eyed look in the moonlight that said, "This guy's nuts. What do we do now?"

"What the devil are you talking about?" Tom demanded.

"I've been watching you two ever since you came out of that dump over there, the Adams."

How the hell does this guy know where we're staying? One of several ugly questions that instantly formed in Tom's mind. Another: Was he alone or did he have a cop somewhere in the shadows? A cop would search them and find all kinds of 1988 stuff he couldn't possibly understand, like plastic Visa cards and driver's licenses with expiration dates almost fifty years in the future. They'd be turned over to the FBI and locked up God knows where.

Could he take this guy if he had to? Tom figured the odds. Cagney was much smaller but looked quick and seemed to be in shape. Yeah, Tom could take him, but that would be a crazy, last-ditch thing to try. He hoped it wouldn't come to that.

"Tell me what you're up to. Did they land you by sub?"

Tom laughed. "Right, a German U-boat took us through the Panama Canal, then unloaded us and our big Mercedes at the Long Beach Pier."

Cagney thought about it. "No, you're probably Americans, but your folks were born in the Fatherland. Maybe you were, too, but you came here when you were little, learned the lingo."

"Learned the lingo? What bad movie is that from?" He'd probably call a pistol a gat, Tom thought.

"Always stayed loyal. When the Fuehrer took over, you Krauts were only too ready to help out the Third Reich."

This idiot wouldn't let up. "Jesus," Tom said, "I used to respect the hell out of you. You were great in 'Yankee Doodle Dandy'—"

"Better believe it."

"—and 'Johnny Come Lately.'"

"Ha, now I've got you. We don't start filming 'Johnny Come Lately' for a couple of months. The average Joe knows nothing about it. But a spy might."

Damn, another mistake. Tom decided to take the offensive. He pulled out his badge holder and flipped it open. "Like the lady said, I'm a cop."

"Cop? Ha. The Gestapo supply you with that piece of tin?"

"It's a Sacramento PD badge, pal. We're visiting here and we're getting damn tired of this game."

"This is no game. Tell me your names. What's your mission here?"

"Oh for Christ sake," Tom barked. "Our mission here is to get some sleep. Come on, Cass." He turned and started toward the motor court.

Cagney caught up fast, then made his big mistake. He roughly grabbed Tom's arm—"Not so fast, Fritz"—and tried to spin him around.

That was it. This little clown had gone too far. Crazy, last-ditch time had arrived.

Tom's right hand became a fist. He put all his hundred and eighty pounds behind the wallop he threw at Cagney's jaw. The actor went down like a load of coal, his snap-brim hat flying.

"Tom!" Cass gasped.

Tom's hand throbbed. He leaned over the man, grabbed a handful of his shirt front, and pulled him to his feet. Cass picked up his hat and put it on Cagney's head at a cockeyed angle.

The actor wobbled. Tom steadied him and said, "We're going for a little walk."

Cagney's body shivered all over for a second as if he were cold. Then he got himself balanced and rubbed his jaw. "Y-you Nazis are r-ruthless."

"Shut up," Tom snarled. "Don't say another word."

"What are we going to do with him?" Cass asked.

"Take him back to the motel. We've got to keep this guy quiet till morning."

"Spy bastard. You'll rot in San Quentin the rest of your life for this."

"I said shut up. Not another goddamned word." Like a schoolyard bully, Tom twisted Cagney's arm behind his back.

They walked back toward the Adams Motor Court, luckily encountering no one along the way. Apparently Cagney had come alone. No cop. Cocky son of a bitch thought he'd capture some German spies all by his brave little self, be a big hero in real life, not just on the silver screen.

Cass said, "We're going to keep him there all night?"

"We've got to keep this fool out of circulation till morning. You got a better idea?"

"Well, I . . . no."

Tom clutched Cagney's left arm, the actor's right arm

swinging free as they walked. After a few steps, Cagney reached inside his jacket with his free hand. Cass suddenly yelled "No!" and lunged at him. He'd pulled a gun.

Tom pounced, threw a shoulder into Cagney, and knocked him off balance. All three of them scuffled, grunting, breathing hard. Cass had hold of his jacket. Tom clutched at Cagney's arm, still trying to get the gun. This little guy was stronger than he looked. Tom got hold of the elbow of his gun arm, but Cagney twisted loose and bumped head-on into Cass.

Tom heard a sharp click. "My God," Cass yelped.

Adrenaline pulsing, Tom finally got a solid grip on Cagney's wrist and wrenched the gun away.

Cass stepped back, breathing hard, her body shaking like a poplar leaf. "It was sticking right in my gut," she cried.

"Dumb shit still had the safety on." Tom jabbed the gun in Cagney's back.

"The safety's not on now, pal. Get moving."

"You'll burn in hell."

"Shut up and walk."

So this is why the guy didn't have any backup. Thought he and his trusty little pistol could handle anything. Thought he was in one of his tough-guy movies.

"You okay, Cass?"

"Yeah, I think so."

"Stupid of me, not patting this guy down. Should've known better."

Reaching the motel, they skirted around the office, which was closed and dark, and went straight to their cottage.

Inside, Tom had Cass cover their squirming, snarling prisoner—all stage presence gone—while he tore a pillowcase. Tom tied Cagney's hands behind his back, ripped another strip of cloth, and gagged him. Then he shoved him in the tiny closet and made him sit with his back propped against the wall. It was a tight fit. Tom used more strips to tie his feet, then forced his knees up close to his chest in order to get the door closed.

"You almost killed a wonderful woman," he growled at the fuming figure. "You should have believed us. You'll have a bad night, but then we'll be gone in the morning."

"Mmphglmph," came the muffled answer, sounding not at all like Little Johnny Jones, the jockey in "Yankee Doodle Dandy." His eyes glowed red and furious.

Tom sang, a bit off-key, ". . . you *are* that Yankee Doodle boy." And shut the door on him.

Cass plopped into a chair, looking ashen and frightened. She glanced at the closet door. "He can't see us in there, can he?"

"Nah," Tom said. "There's not even a keyhole."

"What if he has to use the bathroom?"

"His tough luck. His own damn fault."

"We're way beyond the pale now," Cass murmured.

The rest of this night would be very different from last night, Tom knew, remembering the gusto with which they'd made love amid teasing about Cass getting luckier than Ginger Rogers.

Cass had slept naked last night. Tonight, with a famous actor trussed up in the closet, she stripped only to her bra and panties, jumped in bed, and quickly pulled up the covers.

When Tom joined her, they snuggled and kissed self-consciously, but he knew that lovemaking was out and that Cass felt the same. They'd gagged Cagney's mouth, not his ears.

"Thank God his gun didn't go off," Cass muttered.

"Amen."

Cass whispered, "Got to admit, Fritz, you impressed the heck out of me, punching him out like that."

Tom laughed. "Fritz?"

"How did he ever find us down here in San Pedro?" Cass asked.

"Must've found out from Ginger Rogers."

"Ginger Rogers," Cass snarled. "The babe you trusted. The one who'd really help us out."

"Maybe I was wrong about that."

"You, the brilliant detective? Wrong?"

Tom hated being needled at this moment, but he let it pass. Neither spoke for several minutes.

Occasional kicking and bumping sounds came from the closet. Good thing this was a free-standing cottage. Neighboring lodgers wouldn't be able to hear.

Tom remembered Ginger Rogers saying she'd like to see his badge, and smiled. He rubbed his bruised right hand and lay awake a long time, trying to grasp all this. They'd traveled to a world that hadn't existed for decades, and he'd clobbered and abducted a famous and popular actor. Tomorrow, if all went well—man, it had better go well—he'd see his dad when he was still a very young man. And, oh yeah, a big deadly air raid will come sweeping over this town.

Sleep came hard. Beside him, Cass tossed and turned more than usual. At one point she whispered, "Tom? You awake?"

"Mm hmm."

"This has been awful," she said.

"I know." Just how awful tomorrow might be he didn't want to imagine.

8 - THE FORT

WHEN MORNING finally came, Tom figured they'd had no more than two hours of sleep. They dressed quickly.

He left two dollars on the dresser along with a note. "Management: We really must complain about finding a pervert hiding in our closet pretending to be a movie star."

He opened the closet door and said, "Good morning, Sunshine. Next time a cop tells you something, believe him. Now don't fret, your mommy will come and get you pretty soon."

"Mmphglmph." Bloodshot eyes stared hatred.

Tom tossed James Cagney's .38—it was a Colt Mustang—on the bed. He hoofed a few steps of a very bad buck and wing and sang out, off-key, "Give my regards to Broadway, remember me to to Herald Square . . ."

"You'll never make it on the stage," Cass said, shoving him toward the door.

Out on Pacific Avenue, Tom saw that the big Mercedes was gone. "Wonder whose that was?" he said.

Ribbons of pink and magenta streaked a brightening sky behind the hump of Signal Hill and the distant Santa Ana Mountains.

There was little traffic at this early hour. It took ten minutes to find a cab, so they were late arriving at Fort MacArthur's main gate.

"Damn, damn," Tom said, flexing and unflexing his fingers while the guard checked his clipboard and waved them in. "Stupid to show up late."

The headquarters was a two-story stucco building with a red tile roof, not quite Spanish Colonial in style. A sign above the entrance read "Los Angeles Harbor Defenses" and an insignia featured cannon barrels crossed to form an 'X'.

In the anteroom, Tom was stunned to see Dizzy Dean on his way out of Colonel Hicks' office. Wide-brimmed Western hat, embroidered denim shirt. Dean took him by the arm and pulled him aside. "You'd better git a move on, pardner."

"What are you doing here?" Tom insisted, wide-eyed.

"Settin' up a ball clinic for the GIs." Dean leaned closer and said in a hushed voice, "I don't know what's goin' on, but Alexa asked me to watch out for ya. She also said to git m'self long gone before seven. I don't know what's gonna happen, but all's I can say is, do whatever you gotta do, quick-pitch this guy, and haul ass outta here."

He turned to Cass, touched his hat brim and said, "'Day, ma'am," in a normal voice. Then he walked off, singing, ". . . *We'll carry him home to victory on the Wabash Cannonball.*"

Tom and Cass looked at each other quizzically. Tom glanced at his watch. 6:45. Fifteen minutes late. If Dizzy Dean and Jake's book were right, they had very little time. Slanting through a window, the morning sun caught the watch face. He noticed its oval reflection dancing on the wall.

A moment later they were ushered in to see Colonel Hicks. The office was spare, with a battered wooden desk, a sideboard, three hardwood chairs, and a framed photo of President Roosevelt on the wall. A cigarette butt smoldered in a tin ash tray. Hicks looked to be in his fifties, with sloping shoulders, thinning hair going from brown to gray, and an annoyed look on a pallid face.

"So there are two of you," he grumped. "Coffee?" Tom and Cass nodded, and the colonel took an enameled percolator off a hotplate and poured into heavy gray mugs.

Then he leaned against his desk. "I'll level with you. I almost called the FBI in here this morning." He made a steeple of his hands and regarded Tom with icy brown eyes. "I checked with the Sacramento police. They've never heard of you."

Tom swallowed hard, hoped it didn't show.

"On the other hand, I got a call from Ginger Rogers, the actress, who said you were a homicide officer and she'd appreciate my helping you out. This Dizzy Dean fellow said the same thing.

"Why would Miss Rogers say you're a cop while Sacramento claims they've never heard of you? I've got no time to fool around. Come clean now. Who are you? What are you up to? What do you want with recruit Cavanaugh?"

"Tom really is a policeman," Cass said, "and a damned good—"

"Your language, miss." Hicks looked shocked.

"Sorry, sir."

"Listen," Tom said, "I *am* a cop, and it's vitally important that we see Private Cavanaugh."

"He's a dogface recruit, not a private. He won't get a stripe till he goes through basic."

"Right. Whatever he is, sir, I have to question him." Tom jumped into his story and told it just as they'd rehearsed.

When he finished, Hicks drank some coffee and said, "But that's a lot of malarkey. Sacramento never heard of you."

"Sir, I *am* a cop there." Tom reached for his badge holder. "Detective sergeant. I'm just not on the duty roster right now."

"Prove it to me," Hicks said.

Tom handed over his badge. Hicks looked at it closely, then examined the maroon leather of the holder. They had this kind of leather in those days, didn't they? Tom wondered. His palms began to sweat.

"This badge," Hicks said at last, "looks real enough." He stared at Tom, studied his eyes. He handed the badge back. "And why aren't you on the duty roster?"

"Sir, I'm on a secret assignment down here. Working

with the FBI."

"Are you FBI?" he asked Cass.

"No, I'm with the governor's office."

Hicks turned back to Tom. "You got a business card?" Tom produced one and the colonel squinted at it. "What are all these numbers after the word Sacramento?"

"A ZIP Code."

"And that's what, exactly?"

"A post off—, it's the way we number our beats, our police beats around the city."

"Okay, okay," Hicks said, wringing his hands, "there's a war on. I've got boys to process, quotas to fill. Let's bring Cavanaugh in here and get to the bottom of this." He picked up his black phone and said, "Sergeant, get that Cavanaugh boy in here."

He put the receiver back in its Bakelite cradle, crossed his arms and said, "This is a mighty strange morning."

You ain't seen nothin' yet, Tom thought.

The door opened and a sergeant appeared with a salute, saying, "Recruit Cavanaugh is here, sir."

"Send him in," Hicks said, returning the salute carelessly.

A muscle quivered in Tom's neck. His throat turned to sand. He was about to meet his father—nine years before he, Tom, was born.

The sergeant stood aside, stiffened his shoulders and back, and made room for a skinny young man who stepped into the room, face filled with trepidation.

Tom had been preparing himself for this moment. It was still a shock. Seeing this boyish face and lean body was like an old snapshot from the family album springing to life.

The recruit snapped to attention. "Stand easy, son," Hicks said.

"Hello Cavanaugh," Tom said. "I need to take you off the base for a short while for some questioning."

"Huh uh, no dice," Hicks snarled, standing straighter

and sticking out his chest. The young man's eyes widened in puzzlement and shot from Tom to Cass to the colonel. "No one's agreed to anything like that. Do you know this man?" Hicks asked the flustered recruit, jerking his head in Tom's direction.

"Um, no sir," he said hesitantly, but his eyes didn't look so sure.

At that moment the boom of a distant explosion rattled the window. "What in blazes!" Hicks shouted. Too late! Tom thought. They'd wasted too damn much time.

The phone jangled urgently. Hicks grabbed the receiver. "What?" he shouted. "The Japs. Here? Now? Is Battery Osgood manned? And Merriam? . . . Good God, yes! Free to fire." He slammed the phone down.

"You," he snapped at Desmond Cavanaugh. "Back to your barracks on the double. You two—" he stared at Tom and Cass. "Sergeant! In here," he shouted through the open door while Tom's father did an about-face and started through it.

Another explosion sounded, and another.

Tom darted through the door after his father. "Stop!" Hicks shouted. He reached for Tom, grabbed his shoulder, but couldn't hold on.

In the outer office, Tom shoved his way past the sergeant who'd accompanied his father a moment before. Outside, an MP in an old-style inverted soupbowl helmet started to unsnap a holster. Tom ignored him and dashed after his father, out onto a large groomed parade ground surrounded by sand-colored two-story buildings under tiled roofs.

"Dad, er, Cavanaugh," he shouted. "Hold up. You, Cavanaugh, wait a second."

Tom glanced back over his shoulder and saw Cass deliver a solid kick to the MP's shin with one of her clunky antique shoes. "Ouch. Goddammit lady." The MP started hobbling on one foot. Two more explosions pulsed the air like distant thunder. Desmond Cavanaugh turned to look back. "Who are you, sir?" he called from twenty yards ahead. "Uncle Harold from Indiana? You look familiar. What the devil's going on?"

"Yeah," said Tom, thinking fast. "I'm Uncle Harold and I've gotta get you out of here. Now." Tom heard the growl of an engine being pushed flat-out, then the sharp clatter of machine gun fire.

A drab green plane whined low over one of the outer buildings, jagged flashes of white winking on its wings. Tom raced toward his father. "Get down," he shouted. Chunks of turf jumped from the lawn in a straight line. The air seemed to crack and splinter. The string of bullets raced straight toward them.

Tom leaped at his father, struck his lower back and toppled him off to the side. They tumbled to the ground. The streak of bullets surged past, inches away, spraying them with dirt and grass. A tart smell of sulfur and cordite overpowered the sweet scent of mown grass.

A shadow swept over, then a low ceiling of sound as the plane howled past. Tom looked up, saw red circles on the undersides of each wing.

Spiky columns of fire swept onto a building. Chunks flew from the wall, men screamed. The plane made a tight turning climb and pulled away from the parade ground, whining like the furies of hell.

"Holy smoke," Tom's father gasped. "Thanks for the shove. You just saved my life." They both lay there, staring at the black rips in the grass, straight as railroad tracks, and so damn close. Tom reached over and probed one of the holes with his finger.

As the sound faded, someone shouted, "You. You're under arrest." The MP had reached them, wielding a huge .45. Tom and his father got to their feet. Cass arrived then, too, out of breath, clutching her purse strap like a weapon.

"Don't be a chump, lady," the MP snarled. "You're my prisoner, too."

Tom looked down and saw his watch reflecting the

sunlight. He twisted his wrist and made a glaring disk of light flash across the MP's eyes. As he squinted, Tom chopped his right hand down on the man's wrist. The gun fell. Cass swung her purse, connecting with his head. Then, to Tom's surprise, Desmond Cavanaugh threw his body at the MP, tackling him like a linebacker.

Tom scooped up the pistol and leveled it at the MP. "Come with us," he demanded. "Back there."

Tom, Cass, Tom's father and the humiliated MP all headed toward the office. Another fighter plane appeared. They broke into a run.

The plane swung in low, wing guns flashing in another strafing attack. Twin lines of fire stitched along the grass with a sinister *whap-whap-whap*, tearing up a line of turf directly across the spot they'd just vacated. "Shee-it," Desmond Cavanaugh muttered.

The plane screamed overhead and Tom caught a glimpse of its tail number: 22. Tatsu Matsumoto, Tom recalled from his uncle's book. The squadron leader from Honshu who wrote poetry. And would die in the next few minutes.

Five or six men fell, screaming, twitching.

"My God!" Cass cried.

"Medic!" someone screamed. "Medic." Tom saw a soldier, his leg bleeding, fire at the plane with a pistol. A string of bullet holes marched up a building on the far side. Windows shattered.

As the plane began its climb-out to the west, four more Zeros appeared from the east. Just as their guns began blazing, Tom and the others reached the HQ building, gasping, throwing themselves against the wall, clinging to it for safety.

Tom pinned Cass against the wall, his father on one side of him, the MP on the other. Cass's body was shaking. The MP mumbled something, a prayer maybe.

Tom looked back over his shoulder. Twenty or thirty men were caught in the open. Those not already hit hugged the ground, most of them face down, hands covering their heads. Some curled in the fetal position.

Tom heard a fearsome clatter above his head, then shards of roof tile showered down around them.

The four Zeros howled over the base, columns of bullets spiking across the ground. Men bounced and twitched and bled. Chunks of stucco exploded from buildings, and then the planes climbed away. They joined up and headed off in a cluster. Columns of smoke rose in the east, the direction of the harbor.

Tom stepped back from Cass. "You okay, babe?" She was still trembling.

"I, I . . . ," gasping, ". . . guess so. You?"

"Think so. How about you guys?" Tom asked his father and the MP. Desmond Cavanaugh nodded shakily. "You saved my bacon, mister."

Tom saw a dark stain at the crotch of the MP's pants and pretended not to notice.

"I think the raid is over," he said. He handed the .45 to the MP. "You can arrest us or whatever you want, but we'd better go and help those poor guys out there first."

The MP took the gun. "There's a first aid kit in the HQ. I'll get it. We've got medics in the infirmary. That building there." As he pointed, they came streaming out, carrying their little black bags.

"Who are you really?" Desmond Cavanaugh said to Tom. "You're not Uncle Harold, are you?"

"Let's just say I'm a friend of the family."

"If you hadn't been here, I would've—"

"Yeah, maybe."

His father stared into Tom's face. For an instant, those eyes pulled at him, like the sun tugging at the earth.

Colonel Hicks charged out of the door, his face hot and panicky, gaping at the fallen men. Suddenly he noticed Tom and Cass. "You two are going to the guardhouse," he yelled. "Right now."

"We can help," Cass retorted.

"No. You're not medics. I don't know who the hell you are, but the FBI can decide." An ambulance careened between two buildings, sideswiped a palm tree, and raced into the open yard.

"Now," Hicks barked. "Move."

Tom turned for a last glance at his father. Hicks shouted to a rifle-toting MP, "Lock 'em up fast and get back here." Tom and Cass were led away. The MP steered them into a one-story building next door, then down a staircase and into a basement.

Three cells stood empty, their doors open. "Get in that first one," the MP said, motioning with what Tom thought was a Springfield rifle.

The iron-barred door clanged shut. The MP turned the lock, pocketed the key, and rushed off.

"Whew!" Cass gasped. Tom hugged her, an embrace as tight and close as when they'd first showed up in this strange year two days ago. Over her head, which she'd buried in his shoulder, he saw rough concrete walls, a canvas cot, a sink and an open toilet. When they finally pulled apart, they sank side by side onto the cot. Cass put a hand on his leg.

After several long moments of silence, she covered her eyes with her other hand. "I've seen dead people before," she said, "but never anything like that. I'll have nightmares forever. How many do you think died?"

"Jake's book said eighteen. We must've seen ten or eleven of them."

"Thank God your dad wasn't one of them. Whatever happens now, whatever dimension we're in, you succeeded, Tom. You saved your father's life. Well done."

"Hey, you were pretty good yourself, kicking that MP."

"I'm a tough broad, you know. And how about your dad, knocking that guy down?"

"Dad was a real cowboy out there. Men are fearless at that age."

"He knew we were on his side, knew we needed his

help."

"Did you see the way he looked at me? He sensed some kind of connection."

Cass nodded. After a long silence, Tom said, "I'd always wondered what would have happened if the Japanese had attacked California after Pearl Harbor. They could have, you know, before the Battle of Midway knocked 'em for a loop."

"Now you know. I've got a ton of questions for your Aunt Vee when we get back." Cass glanced around the tiny cell, which was about ten by ten. "It's not the Ritz Carlton. What happens now? Think they have room service?"

"Probably the next people we see will be the FBI," Tom said. "Oh oh," he blurted. "Just thought of something. Does this place even exist in the year 1988? What if it's been bulldozed and filled in? We're below ground here."

"Oh no!" Cass blurted. "When this electron stuff wears off, we'd be buried alive." She sprang to the door and started rattling the bars. "Let us out, let us out. Someone, anyone. I'm sick, I'm very sick. I need a doctor." Then she remembered what every doctor on the base was doing at that moment.

9 - 'WHO ARE YOU?'

NO ONE CAME. Muted sounds of sirens died into silence.

Tom stood there listening for a sound. A door opening. Footsteps. A radio. Anything.

He had locked up lots of people in cells. He'd never been locked in one himself. Not till now. He thought about the jailhouse sounds he was familiar with, toilets flushing, iron doors rattling, fierce shouts in bad Spanish and worse English. He heard none of that now. The quiet settled around him like a cold mist.

He looked at his watch. A couple of hours left. Maybe. Maybe less. A couple of hours left in this strange trip? Or in their whole lives?

Cass paced awhile, pushed at the barred door, then paced some more, her shoes clacking on the concrete. She stopped and glared at the open toilet. "I have to use that in full view of anyone who might pass by? What kind of degrading bullshit is this?"

Tom had rarely heard her use that word.

Finally Cass sat on the cot, but not for long. She rummaged through her purse, extracted a fingernail file, went to the bars, reached through and tried to blindly insert the file into the keyhole on the other side. "Damn it," she said. "Here, you're the cop, see what you can do."

Tom gave it a try. With his longer reach, he managed to manipulate the file into the hole. He imagined he was a safecracker with a delicate touch. When that didn't work, he tried to force it. No matter what he did, the lock refused to be sprung. He wished he had his picklocks, but those were miles, and years, away.

"You have anything else? A hairpin maybe?"

"A hairpin?" Cass shook her head, sending her short hair flying to emphasize the point.

Tom tried the top of the infamous BIC pen. That didn't work either.

He kicked the door. It rattled in defiance, just as a guard showed up, carrying a newspaper. "Give it up," he snorted. "That door's the toughest Pittsburgh iron. You're in here till the colonel says different. Get used to it. Here, read the funny papers."

Cass took the paper through the bars. The *Examiner*. Nothing on the front page about the air attack. But of course there hadn't been time for the papers to get out their extras. She sat on the cot and began to scan the paper.

Tom sat beside her, leaned against the wall and closed his eyes. Exhaustion began to sink in. The long morning had been filled with phenomenal stimuli that ate up energy, overwhelmed the senses. He grew sleepy. Minutes lengthened.

Distantly, he heard Cass laugh. That snapped him awake. Cass hadn't laughed since yesterday, or was it the day before?

"Tom, you devil," she said, "you're in the paper, sort of. Me too." The paper was open to the movie section. She was reading Louella Parsons' gossip column. She pointed to this item:

> Who was that lanky dreamboat Ginger Rogers was making eyes at the other day at Musso & Frank on the Boulevard? A Joel McCrea look-alike. With Lew "I Won't Fight" Ayres out of the Dancing Diva's life, could this mystery man be next in line to do the Rogers Rhumba? . . . But not so fast there, Ginny girl. Three's a crowd, they say, and who was that third party at the table? Another strawberry blonde, just as leggy as La Rogers, my

snoops tell me, only taller, and with a
face Paulette Goddard could've modeled for
...Stay tuned for more on this Tantalizing
Triangle.

That's great," Tom said.

"Paulette Goddard. What did she look like?"

"Gorgeous."

Cass smiled victoriously.

"Put that in your purse," Tom said. "We'll take it back.
What a souvenir that'll make."

"*If* we get back," Cass said.

"We will. Alexa said this has always worked; no one's
ever been stranded in time."

"I wonder what happened to that darned Cagney,"
Cass said.

"I'd love to have seen his face when the maid found
him," Tom answered. "Big time humiliation."

A minute later, they heard a rattling at the door. It was
Tom's father! With a key. Was Tom still dozing? He wasn't
sure he trusted his eyes.

His father unlocked the door. "I don't know who you
are, but you saved my life out there. I'm gonna get you out
of here. Hicks thinks you're spies. Somehow, I know you're
not."

Desmond Cavanaugh stared at Tom, eyes flickering
with curiosity. "Who are you, really?" A pause. "No, forget
it. Don't tell me. Just get yourselves out of here fast while
Hicks has his hands full outside."

He didn't look a minute over nineteen. Although in fact
he was twenty-two, he sounded much older and wiser. "I've
got to get outta here, too. That guard I knocked on the
head won't be out very long."

"Right," Tom said. "Hope he didn't get a good look at
you."

"He didn't. Hit him from behind."

"Good . . . Say, if years from now you have a son and

he tries to become a cop, tell him to be a history teacher, okay?" Desmond Cavanaugh's brow scrunched in perplexity. "And if he bangs up a fender while you're teaching him to drive . . . well, never mind."

Cass shook her head and grinned knowingly. Desmond Cavanaugh forced an I-don't-get-it grin. "Now move, get yourselves outta here," he said with a last look. "So long and good luck." He bounded up the stairs.

"Buy IBM," Cass called, but he was gone.

Tom was reaching for Cass's hand when his body shuddered with a charged flash of shock. He blinked. Couldn't see. Grew dizzy. Panic set in.

Several bad seconds passed before his vision returned. He put a hand against one of the bars to steady himself. The cell door still stood open, but at a much wider angle. The walls that had been bare concrete were now painted mint green.

Cass wasn't there.

10 - ESCAPE

"DAMN," CASS MUTTERED, her body trembling. That was twice now she'd seen Tom vanish like that. She liked it even less than before.

Well, old lover, you've gone and done it again. I hope you're safe and sound in 1988. Tell you what, I'm not hanging around down here to find out.

She bolted through the open doorway and raced for the stairs. She started bounding up them—and stopped. A soldier blocked her path. He sat there, groaning and rubbing his head. He was the same MP she'd kicked out on the parade ground, the one who'd locked them in the cell. And obviously had just been knocked loopy by Tom's father.

His eyes taking focus, he blurted, "Where the hell you going, lady? Get back downstairs." He put his hands on a step to push himself to his feet.

"Oh no," Cass shouted, and stomped on one of those hands with her clunky shoe. The MP yelped and grabbed her leg with his other hand. Cass fell back against the wall of the stairwell. She tried to shake his grip. She couldn't. But then the guy started to stand and had to let go of her calf as he got to his feet.

Almost crazed with adrenaline, Cass kicked his shin and dashed past, scaling stairs like a puma. She heard his footsteps in pursuit, echoing loud and harsh in the stair-well like gunshots.

She reached the landing—and grew dizzy. Sparks flared in her eyes. Her body shivered with shock. She thought she heard the MP mutter "What the hell!" as she fell into blind darkness.

*   *   *

Tom jerked every which way, scanning the whole room. "Cass? Cass!"

The canvas army cot was gone, replaced by a metal affair, topped by a small beige mattress. He was completely alone. He paced back and forth, looked at his watch. Had he bounced back from 1942? He was tempted to leave the cell and run upstairs, but decided no, if he'd slid safely back to the present, Cass should reappear right here. If everything worked right. And if she hadn't wandered up the stairs or something while still in 1942.

But wait, going upstairs would have been smart, to avoid the possibility of getting crushed down here.

He looked at his watch again and noticed that the small scab where he'd scraped his hand was gone, completely gone without a trace.

He was about to run upstairs when the clatter of footsteps echoed in the stairwell. He heard Cass saying, "I think he's down here."

"I'm not sure I follow you, ma'am." A man's voice. "What do you mean?"

Then Cass was there, alongside a young man in Air Force blue with sergeant's chevrons on his arm. Hmm, the Air Force, crossed Tom's mind. They have this place now?

Cass leaped off the last step, jumped into his arms and hugged him like a million dollars.

"Thank God," she murmured. "You're here. God, I was blind again for a moment." Tom squeezed her tightly.

"What are you doing here, sir?" the sergeant said.

"We were getting a tour," Tom said, pulling away from Cass and showing his badge, "but somehow I got separated from your CO."

"The CO? Colonel Parker?"

"Right. If you'll just show us to the door, we'll get on back to his office."

11 - HOME

THREE HOURS LATER, at the retirement home in the San Fernando Valley, Tom and Cass sat at a shaded picnic table with Great Aunt Vee and Alexa Kadinsky, whose resemblance to each other was uncanny.

Three of the coffee mugs in front of them contained zinfandel from Ravenswood Vintners, which Tom had snuck in. Alexa's mug, though, held Stolichnaya vodka.

"We're on our way home," Tom said. "Our flight leaves in four hours, but we couldn't go without seeing you again." A horseshoe clanged against iron in the background.

"This has all been too astounding," Cass said, taking a sip from her mug. "Stupefying."

"I take it you wouldn't care to go on another trip," Alexa said.

"No way." Cass shook her head decisively. "It scared me to death. Shook me to the very core."

"You had some kicks back there," Tom said.

"Funny." Cass offered a thin smile. "I mean it, seeing your dad when he was barely more than a boy was spooky enough, but then that horrible attack on the base . . . " She shivered and clutched herself. "Those planes shooting up the place, those men getting cut apart. I'll have nightmares forever."

"Remember," Vee said, "I saw men get cut up, too."

"I know." Cass nodded. "But you got to help them. You were magnificent. I just got thrown in jail."

"Wasn't your fault," Vee said, reaching over and touching Cass's shoulder. "I hope you won't have nightmares, but you accomplished what you set out to do, saving Tom's father's young life. Extraordinary achievement."

"That was Tom's doing. But you're right, I'll try to dwell on the positive. I'll admit, it was all very fascinating. James Cagney turned out to be a misguided fool, and I sure didn't trust that Ginger Rogers."

"Hey, she was a big help," Tom interjected.

"Yeah, for one reason only. She had the hots for you."

The older women laughed, and then Vee asked what she meant about Cagney.

So Cass told how the great James Cagney tried to make a citizen's arrest and ended up spending the night tied up in a little closet.

"Oh my, he must have been furious," Vee said, laughing.

"It's not funny," Cass said. "He almost shot me. Maybe some day it'll be funny, but not now."

"Of course," Vee said, touching her hand.

"We made out pretty well at the coin shop," Tom said, "selling back old bills, plus some Liberty quarters and buffalo nickels we'd gotten as change. Kept a couple for ourselves, though. But let me tell you, I was sure glad to get out of those embarrassing old clothes."

He picked up his copy of Jake's book, THE DAY THEY BOMBED L.A., which had been sitting on the table next to Vee's faded wirephoto of a P-38 shooting down a Japanese plane in Long Beach. He flipped pages and found the old napkin with the note, "T.Cav. Hicks. Ft.Mac," and showed it to the women.

"We saw him write this, in the Continental, the day before the attack. But why did he stick it in this book, which he wrote several years later?"

"He didn't," Alexa said. "I put it there. Vee and I were going through his file of research for the book, his notes, clippings and so on. This was long after he was killed. We found that note and I placed it in this copy of the book."

"Why?"

"I thought it would mean something to someone some day," Alexa said with a mysterious smile.

"Meaning you," Cass said, staring at Tom.

"Well . . ." He didn't finish the thought. "Anyway, this will take a place of honor on our bookshelves." He looked at Alexa and said, "You know, Cass bought into this before I did. I was skeptical, but she said, 'There could be something to this electron spin business, keep an open mind.' Now, about the two time tracks merging again. As we came up here by cab on the Harbor Freeway the damndest thing happened. South of downtown, I glanced off to the east and I swear I saw Wrigley Field, the Angels' old ballpark. But I know it was torn down years ago. I reached over to touch Cass's arm and show her. When I looked back, it was gone. For a moment, though, I swear I saw it."

"Maybe you did," Alexa said. "The merging phenomenon is now quite well advanced. Dr. Hastings at UCLA calculates that it's almost complete. It is good that you acted on your father when you did."

She picked up Jake's book. "Let's have a look here." She thumbed to the Appendices, found Military Casualties, and began searching under Killed. "Ballard," she read. "Cartwright. Casey. Dixon. Dixon? See, we've gone past it. It's not there. No Cavanaugh."

"I know," said Tom, smiling broadly. "I checked that out first thing. Now, please tell me about Dizzy Dean. Did you really send him to Fort MacArthur to warn us to hurry up? Did you bring him to the present and talk to him?"

"Yes, I put a bug in his ear, but I didn't bring him here. I went there. You see, I met Mr. Dean on one of my time reversal excursions and we, well . . ." Alexa began to blush. "My Sergei had passed away, after all."

Cass's mouth dropped open.

"We've all had our Corky Helds," Vee said with a laugh. She winked at Alexa, who was taking a swig of her vodka.

Alexa put her mug down. For a moment her long

fingers played idly over the book's maroon cover.

Cass picked up the old wirephoto from the air raid and looked at it intently.

Vee pushed up the sleeve of her blouse. She and Tom gazed at the jagged scar on her forearm.

"Say, I've been meaning to ask," Tom said. "What about the other *you*? In fact, both other *yous*." He looked at each woman in turn. "Your counterparts in the other dimension. What happened to them?"

"That's right," Cass said. "You had to exist in both dimensions."

"You don't really want to go into that," Alexa said.

"Sure we do," Tom said.

Alexa and Vee stared at each other.

"What about it?" Tom urged.

Finally, with a hand on her chin, Vee said, "You're family. I guess you have a right to know. Okay then, my father was an agronomist at the University of Illinois. In 1924, he went on a League of Nations mission to Estonia, where they were having problems with their wheat. My mom and I went along. I was nine that summer. It was to be a great family adventure. Our ship was just off Tallinn, the capital, when a sudden Baltic storm roared up out of nowhere. Our little ship was blown several miles off course, and finally took refuge at St. Petersburg, or Leningrad, as it had just been named. Those were the turbulent early days of the Soviet Union. Stalin versus Trotsky, civil war with the White Russians and all that.

"The port authorities put us up for the night in a second-rate pension, thirty or forty of us jammed in the same room, barracks style. All kinds of strange people in there. Dad stuck his wallet and our passports in his underwear."

"Say, 1924," Tom said, "that's when the big solar storm hit, wasn't it?"

"Exactly. And it was that very night that the earth's time sphere divided." Vee's eyes searched Alexa's face. At length, she said, "I think you'd better take it from here, dear."

"If you like," Alexa said. "Well, that night she was kidnapped. Hauled right out of bed before she was wide awake. At first I thought it must be father rushing me out of there."

Rushing *you*? Tom thought. The old girl's getting mixed up.

"Pretty soon I was bundled off and driven away in a horse-drawn wagon."

"*You* were bundled off? Are you saying—"

"That I was Valerie Jean? Yes, Tom, until 1924, I was."

"My God," Cass gasped.

Tom shook his head. "Oh, come on now."

"It's all true," Vee interjected. "Remember, you wanted to hear about the other me." She nodded to Alexa. "Go on, dear."

Alexa took a drink of her vodka, then said, "In her time track, Valerie Jean spent the night safely and reboarded the ship in the morning with our parents. I, however, had been nabbed by a childless couple desperate for a girl of their own. I tried to run away from them several times, but never succeeded. Where could I go in that strange land? I was miserable the next two or three years, but during that time I picked up the Russian language. I finally resigned myself to my fate; what choice did I have? There was no American embassy or legation—the U.S. hadn't recognized the Soviet Union yet.

"I started doing well in school after those first bad years, even grew to like the name they gave me. In Russia, you see, Valeriy is a boy's name. My new parents were kind to me, although I never forgave them. I missed my real father and mother for years. Then, when I was seventeen, I met my Sergei. From then on, life was good, although I never forgot my American beginnings."

"Amazing," Cass said. "No wonder you look so much alike."

"Somewhat. Russian winters weren't so very kind to this old flesh of mine."

"Hey, wait a minute," Tom said, "if the time tracks are merging—"

"Yes, one of us will disappear soon. We're quite resigned to that." Alexa reached out and took Vee's hand.

Vee smiled wistfully. "We're both grateful," she said, "for our long and varied lives. Wonderful experiences. Whichever one of us survives will have only a short time left anyway." They looked at each other, their identical cerulean eyes full of peace.

"You're extraordinary people, both of you," Cass said. "It's a privilege to know you." She got up and hugged them, pulling them close, an arm around each one.

At last, Alexa said, "You mustn't worry about us, that won't do. We're absolutely fine. Now then"—her eyes twinkling—"would you like to go back to Roosevelt Field in New York and watch Lindbergh take off for Paris?"

"No thanks!" Cass exclaimed. "One of those trips was enough."

"Hold on, babe, why don't we go to Paris and watch him *land*?" Cass punched Tom's arm, then smiled and rested her head on his shoulder.

"Or," Tom said, "maybe I should go back to 1965 and punch my freshman algebra teacher in the mouth."

Cass looked up and shook her head.

Late that afternoon, they were walking down a long concourse toward their gate at Los Angeles International. Tom said, "You know, this used to be Mines Field. Became L.A.'s main airport after the war."

"So that Okada guy dropped his bombs right about here?" Cass asked.

"A few blocks east, on North American. But he flew right over this spot."

Just then two old, well-dressed Asian men approached

from the opposite direction. One had hair the color of steel, the other no hair at all. One of them toted a carry-on bag, the other an expensive camera. Looked to Tom like a Nikon. That triggered the memory. These were the guys who'd asked him to take their picture four days ago. No, five. It seemed like years.

"Excuse me. I met you gentlemen downtown the other day. What are you doing here at LAX?"

"Finishing up a week of reminiscing," said the bald one. "Two old cousins, reliving the past."

Tom remembered how they'd turned into young men for an instant, one of them in an old-fashioned flight suit, when he looked through the viewfinder. Shocked the hell out of him.

Cass looked puzzled.

"You're welcome to it," Tom said. "I've had enough of the past. More than enough."

The men smiled and walked on.

Tom called back over his shoulder, "Have a nice day, Kaz and Mori."

Cass's brows arched. She swung around and gawked.

The gray-haired man raised a hand and twirled it in acknowledgment without looking back.

■

AUTHOR'S NOTE

After their crushing attack on Pearl Harbor on December 7, 1941, Japanese forces had the capability of launching devastating attacks on U.S. Pacific Coast ports. This remained a viable threat until the critical U.S. victory in the Battle of Midway in June 1942.

The Imperial Japanese Navy began to harass the West Coast of the mainland almost immediately after Pearl Harbor. Nine submarines from its Sixth Fleet were moved into attack positions off California and Oregon. Seven of them carried small float planes with removable wings. On December 20, one of the subs attacked and destroyed the American tanker *Emidio* off Crescent City in northern California. Three days later another sub sank the tanker *Montebello* near William Randolph Hearst's castle at San Simeon. Several other U.S. ships were attacked at the same time but not sunk.

Californians became so war-jittery that the Rose Bowl game of January 1, 1942, was moved to Durham, N.C. The big stadium in Pasadena was considered too inviting a target for enemy bombers.

On February 23, 1942, the submarine I-17 surfaced north of Santa Barbara and fired twenty-five shells at storage tanks in the Elwood oil field. They missed.

The next night panicky anti-aircraft gunners in Los Angeles fired more than 1,400 rounds into the sky at phantom Japanese planes in the embarrassing "Battle of Los Angeles."

A Japanese sub attacked a Canadian telegraph station near Vancouver on June 20, 1942, and the next day another sub shelled Fort Stevens, Oregon.

On September 9, 1942, a pilot named Nobuo Fujita flew a float plane from the submarine I-25 over the forests fifty miles east of Cape Blanco, Oregon and dropped bombs. He repeated this attack on September 29. Both raids started small forest fires but didn't amount to much thanks to rainy conditions.

In November 1944, after Japanese scientists had discovered the jet stream, the Japanese military began launching hot-air balloon bombs into the North Pacific winds with the aim of creating huge forest fires in the U.S. and Canada. Nine thousand balloon bombs were sent aloft, 290 of which actually reached America, most of them landing in the Pacific Northwest. One was found as far east as Michigan and another landed in Mexico. The balloon bombs did no strategic damage although six people, five of them children, were killed on May 5, 1945, at a church picnic near Bly, Oregon.

The Kawanishi H8K, a four-engine seaplane, could carry four tons of bombs and had a range of 4,500 miles. The Japanese planned to have six of these set down off the California coast, be refueled by submarines, and bomb Los Angeles. If this worked, the next step was to have thirty H8K's go to a point off Baja California, refuel, then fly east to raid oil fields in Texas. The scheme was never carried out, probably because of the crippling losses at Midway.

Actually, no major multi-plane air raid was ever mounted against targets in California during World War II . . . *well, at least not in the time dimension in which you and I dwell. But be warned, the next big sun storm will occur in 2012.*